LETTERS OF TRAVEL

THE DOMINIONS EDITION
LETTERS OF TRAVEL
(1892-1913)

BY RUDYARD KIPLING

MACMILLAN AND CO., LIMITED
ST. MARTIN'S STREET, LONDON

1920

This book has been published by:

Contact: sales@nuvisionpublications.com

URL: http://www.nuvisionpublications.com

Publishing Date: 2008

ISBN# 1-59547-614-8

Please see our website for several books created for education, research and entertainment.

Specializing in rare, out-of-print books still in demand.

NuVision Publications, LLC is dedicated to bringing new life to rare, historic, and formerly out-of-print books. Most re-print publishers simply photocopy, or scan and print the pages from the original book, which can make the book hard to read as most re-print books are 100+ years old. It is our policy to take the time to convert the original faded, sometimes blotched text into crisp, clear digital text. All of our printed books have been completely reformatted to be easy to read and enjoy.

Please note that we do not correct out-of-date facts or grammar-type errors that were in the original book. We do our best to retain the original composition of the text, the way the author intended it.

NuVision Publications, LLC
Sioux Falls, SD USA

CONTENTS

FROM TIDEWAY TO TIDEWAY
IN SIGHT OF MONADNOCK 7
ACROSS A CONTINENT 15
THE EDGE OF THE EAST 23
OUR OVERSEAS MEN 31
SOME EARTHQUAKES 37
HALF-A-DOZEN PICTURES 43
'CAPTAINS COURAGEOUS' 49
ON ONE SIDE ONLY 55
LEAVES FROM A WINTER NOTE-BOOK 61

LETTERS TO THE FAMILY
THE ROAD TO QUEBEC 69
A PEOPLE AT HOME 75
CITIES AND SPACES 81
NEWSPAPERS AND DEMOCRACY 87
LABOUR 93
THE FORTUNATE TOWNS 101
MOUNTAINS AND THE PACIFIC 109
A CONCLUSION 117

EGYPT OF THE MAGICIANS
I. SEA TRAVEL 123
II. A RETURN TO THE EAST 131
III. A SERPENT OF OLD NILE 137
IV. UP THE RIVER 143
V. DEAD KINGS 151
VI. THE FACE OF THE DESERT 157
VII. THE RIDDLE OF EMPIRE 163

FROM TIDEWAY TO TIDEWAY

1892-95

IN SIGHT OF MONADNOCK

After the gloom of gray Atlantic weather, our ship came to America in a flood of winter sunshine that made unaccustomed eyelids blink, and the New Yorker, who is nothing if not modest, said, 'This isn't a sample of our really fine days. Wait until such and such times come, or go to such and a such a quarter of the city.' We were content, and more than content, to drift aimlessly up and down the brilliant streets, wondering a little why the finest light should be wasted on the worst pavements in the world; to walk round and round Madison Square, because that was full of beautifully dressed babies playing counting-out games, or to gaze reverently at the broad-shouldered, pug-nosed Irish New York policemen. Wherever we went there was the sun, lavish and unstinted, working nine hours a day, with the colour and the clean-cut lines of perspective that he makes. That any one should dare to call this climate muggy, yea, even 'subtropical,' was a shock. There came such a man, and he said, 'Go north if you want weather—weather that *is* weather. Go to New England.' So New York passed away upon a sunny afternoon, with her roar and rattle, her complex smells, her triply over-heated rooms, and much too energetic inhabitants, while the train went north to the lands where the snow lay. It came in one sweep—almost, it seemed, in one turn of the wheels—covering the winter-killed grass and turning the frozen ponds that looked so white under the shadow of lean trees into pools of ink.

As the light closed in, a little wooden town, white, cloaked, and dumb, slid past the windows, and the strong light of the car lamps fell upon a sleigh (the driver furred and muffled to his nose) turning the corner of a street. Now the sleigh of a picture-book, however well one knows it, is altogether different from the thing in real life, a means of conveyance at a journey's end; but it is well not to be over-curious in the matter, for the same American who has been telling you at length how he once followed a kilted Scots soldier from Chelsea to the Tower, out of pure wonder and curiosity at his bare knees and sporran, will laugh at your interest in 'just a cutter.'

The staff of the train—surely the great American nation would be lost if deprived of the ennobling society of brakeman, conductor, Pullman-car conductor, negro porter, and newsboy—told pleasant tales, as they spread themselves at ease in the smoking compartments, of snowings up the line to Montreal, of desperate attacks—four engines together and a snow-plough in front—on drifts thirty feet high, and the pleasures of walking along the tops of goods wagons to brake a train, with the thermometer thirty below freezing. 'It comes cheaper to kill men that way than to put air-brakes on freight-cars,' said the brakeman.

Thirty below freezing! It was inconceivable till one stepped out into it at midnight, and the first shock of that clear, still air took away the breath as does a plunge into sea-water. A walrus sitting on a woolpack was our host in his sleigh, and he wrapped us in hairy goatskin coats, caps that came down over the ears, buffalo robes and blankets, and yet more buffalo-robes till we, too, looked like walruses and moved almost as gracefully. The night was as keen as the edge of a newly-ground sword; breath froze on the coat-lapels in snow; the nose became without sensation, and the eyes wept bitterly because the horses were in a hurry to get home; and whirling through air at zero brings tears. But for the jingle of the sleigh-bells the ride might have taken place in a dream, for there was no sound of hoofs upon the snow, the runners sighed a little now and again as they glided over an inequality, and all the sheeted hills round about were as dumb as death. Only the Connecticut River kept up its heart and a lane of black water through the packed ice; we could hear the stream worrying round the heels of its small bergs. Elsewhere there was nothing but snow under the moon—snow drifted to the level of the stone fences or curling over their tops in a lip of frosted silver; snow banked high on either side of the road, or lying heavy on the pines and the hemlocks in the woods, where the air seemed, by comparison, as warm as a conservatory. It was beautiful beyond expression, Nature's boldest sketch in black and white, done with a Japanese disregard of perspective, and daringly altered from time to time by the restless pencils of the moon.

In the morning the other side of the picture was revealed in the colours of the sunlight. There was never a cloud in the sky that rested on the snow-line of the horizon as a sapphire on white velvet. Hills of pure white, or speckled and furred with woods, rose up above the solid white levels of the fields, and the sun rioted over their embroideries till the eyes ached. Here and there on the exposed slopes the day's warmth—the thermometer was nearly forty degrees—and the night's cold had made a bald and shining crust upon the snow; but the most part was soft powdered stuff, ready to catch the light on a thousand crystals and multiply it sevenfold. Through this magnificence, and thinking nothing of it, a wood-sledge drawn by two shaggy red steers, the unbarked logs diamond-dusted with snow, shouldered down the road in a cloud of frosty breath. It is the mark of inexperience in this section of the country to confound a sleigh which you use for riding with the sledge that is devoted to heavy work; and it is, I believe, a still greater sign of worthlessness to think that oxen are driven, as they are in most places, by scientific twisting of the tail. The driver with red mittens on his hands, felt overstockings that come up to his knees, and, perhaps, a silvery-gray coon-skin coat on his back, walks beside, crying, 'Gee, haw!' even as is written in American stories. And the speech of the driver explains many things in regard to the dialect story, which at its best is an infliction to many. Now that I have heard the long, unhurried drawl of Vermont, my wonder is, not that the New England tales should be printed in what, for the sake of argument, we will call English and its type, but rather that they should not have appeared in Swedish or Russian. Our alphabet is too limited. This part of the country belongs by laws unknown to the United States, but which obtain all the world over, to the New England story and the ladies who write it. You feel this in the air as soon as you see the white-painted wooden houses left out in the snow, the austere schoolhouse, and the people—the men of the farms, the women who work as hard as they with, it may be, less enjoyment of life—the other houses, well painted and quaintly roofed, that belong to Judge This, Lawyer That, and Banker Such an one; all powers in the metropolis of six thousand folk over by the railway station. More acutely still, do you realise the atmosphere when you read in the local paper announcements of 'chicken suppers' and 'church sociables' to be given by such and such a denomination, sandwiched between paragraphs of genial and friendly interest, showing that the countryside live (and without slaying each other) on terms of terrifying intimacy.

The folk of the old rock, the dwellers in the older houses, born and raised hereabouts, would not live out of the town for any consideration, and there are insane people from the South—men and women from Boston and the like—who actually build houses out in the open country, two, and even three miles from Main Street which is nearly 400 yards long, and the centre of life and population. With the strangers, more particularly if they do not buy their groceries 'in the street,' which means, and is, the town, the town has little to do; but it knows everything, and much more also, that goes on among them. Their dresses, their cattle, their views, the manners of their children, their manner towards their servants, and every other conceivable thing, is reported, digested, discussed, and rediscussed up and down Main Street. Now, the wisdom of Vermont, not being at all times equal to grasping all the problems of everybody else's life with delicacy, sometimes makes pathetic mistakes, and the town is set by the ears. You will see, therefore, that towns of a certain size do not differ materially all the world over. The talk of the men of the farms is of their farms—purchase, mortgage, and sale, recorded rights, boundary lines, and road tax. It was in the middle of New Zealand, on the edge of the Wild horse plains, that I heard this talk last, when a man and his wife, twenty miles from the nearest neighbour, sat up half the night discussing just the same things that the men talked of in Main Street, Vermont, U.S.A.

There is one man in the State who is much exercised over this place. He is a farm-hand, raised in a hamlet fifteen or twenty miles from the nearest railway, and, greatly daring, he has wandered here. The bustle and turmoil of Main Street, the new glare of the electric lights and the five-storeyed brick business block, frighten and distress him much. He has taken service on a farm well away from these delirious delights, and, says he, 'I've been offered $25 a month to work in a bakery at New York. But you don't get me to no New York, I've seen this place an' it just scares me,' His strength is in the drawing of hay and the feeding of cattle. Winter life on a farm does not mean the comparative idleness that is so much written of. Each hour seems to have its sixty minutes of work; for the cattle are housed and eat eternally; the colts must be turned out for their drink, and the ice broken for them if necessary; then ice must be stored for the summer use, and then the real work of hauling logs for firewood begins. New England depends for its fuel on the woods. The trees are 'blazed' in the autumn just before the fall of the leaf, felled later, cut into four-foot lengths, and, as soon as the friendly snow makes sledging possible, drawn down to the woodhouse. Afterwards the needs of the farm can be attended to, and a farm, like an arch, is never at rest. A little later will come maple-sugar time, when the stately maples are tapped as the sap begins to stir, and be-ringed with absurd little buckets (a cow being milked into a thimble gives some idea of the disproportion), which are emptied into cauldrons. Afterwards (this is the time of the 'sugaring-off parties') you pour the boiled syrup into tins full of fresh snow, where it hardens, and you pretend to help and become very sticky and make love, boys and girls together. Even the introduction of patent sugar evaporators has not spoiled the love-making.

There is a certain scarcity of men to make love with; not so much in towns which have their own manufactories and lie within a lover's Sabbath-day journey of New York, but in the farms and villages. The men have gone away—the young men are fighting fortune further West, and the women remain—remain for ever as women must. On the farms, when the children depart, the old man and the old woman strive to hold things together without help, and the woman's portion is work and monotony. Sometimes she goes mad to an extent which appreciably affects statistics and is put down in census reports. More often, let us hope, she dies. In the villages where the necessity for heavy work is not so urgent the women find consolation in the formation of literary clubs and circles, and so gather to themselves a great deal of wisdom in their own way. That way is not altogether lovely. They desire facts and the knowledge that they are at a certain page in a German or an Italian book before a certain time, or that they have read the proper books in a proper way. At any rate, they have something to do that seems as if they were doing something. It has been said that the New England stories are cramped and narrow. Even a far-off view of the iron-bound life whence they are drawn justifies the author. You can carve a nut in a thousand different ways by reason of the hardness of the shell.

Twenty or thirty miles across the hills, on the way to the Green Mountains, lie some finished chapters of pitiful stories—a few score abandoned farms, started in a lean land, held fiercely so long as there was any one to work them, and then left on the hill-sides. Beyond this desolation are woods where the bear and the deer still find peace, and sometimes even the beaver forgets that he is persecuted and dares to build his lodge. These things were told me by a man who loved the woods for their own sake and not for the sake of slaughter—a quiet, slow-spoken man of the West, who came across the drifts on show-shoes and refrained from laughing when I borrowed his foot-gear and tried to walk. The gigantic lawn-tennis bats strung with hide are not easy to manoeuvre. If you forget to keep the long heels down and trailing in the snow you turn over and become as a man who fails into deep water with a life-belt tied to his ankles. If you lose your balance, do not attempt to recover it, but drop, half-sitting and half-kneeling, over as large an area as possible. When you have mastered the wolf-step, can slide one shoe above the other deftly, that is to say, the sensation of paddling over a ten-foot-deep drift and taking short cuts by buried fences is worth the ankle-ache. The man from the West interpreted to me the signs on the snow, showed how a fox (this section of the country is full of foxes, and men shoot them because riding is impossible) leaves one kind of spoor, walking with circumspection as becomes a thief, and a dog, who has nothing to be ashamed of, but widens his four legs and plunges, another; how coons go to sleep for the winter and squirrels too, and how the deer on the Canada border trample down deep paths that are called yards and are caught there by inquisitive men with cameras, who hold them by their tails when the deer have blundered into deep snow, and so photograph their frightened dignity. He told me of people also—the manners and customs of New Englanders here, and how they blossom and develop in the Far West on the newer railway lines, when matters come very nearly to civil war between rival companies racing for the same cañon; how there is a country not very far away called Caledonia, populated by the Scotch, who can give points to a New Englander in a bargain, and how these same Scotch-Americans by birth, name their townships still after the cities of their thrifty race. It was all as new and delightful as the steady 'scrunch' of the snow-shoes and the dazzling silence of the hills.

Beyond the very furthest range, where the pines turn to a faint blue haze against the one solitary peak—a real mountain and not a hill—showed like a gigantic thumbnail pointing heavenward.

'And that's Monadnock,' said the man from the West; 'all the hills have Indian names. You left Wantastiquet on your right coming out of town,'

You know how it often happens that a word shuttles in and out of many years, waking all sorts of incongruous associations. I had met

Monadnock on paper in a shameless parody of Emerson's style, before ever style or verse had interest for me. But the word stuck because of a rhyme, in which one was

> ... crowned coeval With Monadnock's crest,
> And my wings extended
> Touch the East and West.

Later the same word, pursued on the same principle as that blessed one Mesopotamia, led me to and through Emerson, up to his poem on the peak itself—the wise old giant 'busy with his sky affairs,' who makes us sane and sober and free from little things if we trust him. So Monadnock came to mean everything that was helpful, healing, and full of quiet, and when I saw him half across New Hampshire he did not fail. In that utter stillness a hemlock bough, overweighted with snow, came down a foot or two with a tired little sigh; the snow slid off and the little branch flew nodding back to its fellows.

For the honour of Monadnock there was made that afternoon an image of snow of Gautama Buddha, something too squat and not altogether equal on both sides, but with an imperial and reposeful waist. He faced towards the mountain, and presently some men in a wood-sledge came up the road and faced him. Now, the amazed comments of two Vermont farmers on the nature and properties of a swag-bellied god are worth hearing. They were not troubled about his race, for he was aggressively white; but rounded waists seem to be out of fashion in Vermont. At least, they said so, with rare and curious oaths.

Next day all the idleness and trifling were drowned in a snowstorm that filled the hollows of the hills with whirling blue mist, bowed the branches of the woods till you ducked, but were powdered all the same when you drove through, and wiped out the sleighing tracks. Mother Nature is beautifully tidy if you leave her alone. She rounded off every angle, broke down every scarp, and tucked the white bedclothes, till not a wrinkle remained, up to the chine of the spruces and the hemlocks that would not go to sleep.

'Now,' said the man of the West, as we were driving to the station, and alas! to New York, 'all my snow-tracks are gone; but when that snow melts, a week hence or a month hence, they'll all come up again and show where I've been.'

Curious idea, is it not? Imagine a murder committed in the lonely woods, a snowstorm that covers the tracks of the flying man before the avenger of blood has buried the body, and then, a week later, the withdrawal of the traitorous snow, revealing step by step the path Cain took—the six-inch dee-trail of his snow-shoes—each step a dark disk on the white till the very end.

There is so much, so very much to write, if it were worth while, about that queer little town by the railway station, with its life running, to all outward seeming, as smoothly as the hack-coupés on their sleigh mounting, and within disturbed by the hatreds and troubles and jealousies that vex the minds of all but the gods. For instance—no, it is better to remember the lesson Monadnock, and Emerson has said, 'Zeus hates busy-bodies and people who do too much.'

That there are such folk, a long nasal drawl across Main Street attests. A farmer is unhitching his horses from a post opposite a store. He stands with the tie-rope in his hand and gives his opinion to his neighbour and the world generally—'But them there Andersons, they ain't got no notion of etikwette!'

ACROSS A CONTINENT

It is not easy to escape from a big city. An entire continent was waiting to be traversed, and, for that reason, we lingered in New York till the city felt so homelike that it seemed wrong to leave it. And further, the more one studied it, the more grotesquely bad it grew—bad in its paving, bad in its streets, bad in its street-police, and but for the kindness of the tides would be worse than bad in its sanitary arrangements. No one as yet has approached the management of New York in a proper spirit; that is to say, regarding it as the shiftless outcome of squalid barbarism and reckless extravagance. No one is likely to do so, because reflections on the long, narrow pig-trough are construed as malevolent attacks against the spirit and majesty of the great American people, and lead to angry comparisons. Yet, if all the streets of London were permanently up and all the lamps permanently down, this would not prevent the New York streets taken in a lump from being first cousins to a Zanzibar foreshore, or kin to the approaches of a Zulu kraal. Gullies, holes, ruts, cobbles-stones awry, kerbstones rising from two to six inches above the level of the slatternly pavement; tram-lines from two to three inches above street level; building materials scattered half across the street; lime, boards, cut stone, and ash-barrels generally and generously everywhere; wheeled traffic taking its chances, dray *versus* brougham, at cross roads; sway-backed poles whittled and unpainted; drunken lamp-posts with twisted irons; and, lastly, a generous scatter of filth and more mixed stinks than the winter wind can carry away, are matters which can be considered quite apart from the 'Spirit of Democracy' or 'the future of this great and growing country.' In any other land, they would be held to represent slovenliness, sordidness, and want of capacity. Here it is explained, not once but many times, that they show the speed at which the city has grown and the enviable indifference of her citizens to matters of detail. One of these days, you are told, everything will be taken in hand and put straight. The unvirtuous rulers of the city will be swept away by a cyclone, or a tornado, or something big and booming, of popular indignation; everybody will unanimously elect the right men, who will justly earn the enormous salaries that are at present being paid to inadequate aliens for road sweepings, and all will be well. At the same time the lawlessness ingrained by governors among the governed during the last thirty, forty, or it may be fifty years; the brutal levity of the public conscience in regard to public duty; the toughening and suppling of public morals, and the reckless disregard for human life, bred by impotent laws and fostered by familiarity with needless accidents and criminal neglect, will miraculously disappear. If the laws of cause and effect that control even the freest people in the world say otherwise, so much the worse for the laws. America makes her own. Behind her stands the ghost of the most bloody war of the century caused in a peaceful land by long temporising with lawlessness, by letting things slide, by shiftlessness and blind disregard for all save the material need of the hour, till the hour long conceived and let alone stood up full-armed, and men said, 'Here is an unforeseen crisis,' and killed each other in the name of God for four years.

In a heathen land the three things that are supposed to be the pillars of moderately decent government are regard for human life, justice, criminal and civil, as far as it lies in man to do justice, and good roads. In this Christian city they think lightly of the first—their own papers, their own speech, and their own actions prove it; buy and sell the second at a price openly and without shame; and are, apparently, content to do without the third. One would almost expect racial sense of humour would stay them from expecting only praise—slab, lavish, and slavish—from the stranger within their gates. But they do not. If he holds his peace, they forge tributes to their own excellence which they put into his mouth, thereby treating their own land which they profess to honour as a quack treats his pills. If he speaks—but you shall see for yourselves what happens then. And they cannot see that by untruth and invective it is themselves alone that they injure.

The blame of their city evils is not altogether with the gentlemen, chiefly of foreign extraction, who control the city. These find a people made to their hand—a lawless breed ready to wink at one evasion of the law if they themselves may profit by another, and in their rare leisure hours content to smile over the details of a clever fraud. Then, says the cultured American, 'Give us time. Give us time, and we shall arrive.' The otherwise American, who is aggressive, straightway proceeds to thrust a piece of half-hanged municipal botch-work under the nose of the alien as a sample of perfected effort. There is nothing more delightful than to sit for a strictly limited time with a child who tells you what he means to do when he is a man; but when that same child, loud-voiced, insistent, unblushingly eager for praise, but thin-skinned as the most morbid of hobbledehoys, stands about all your ways telling you the same story in the same voice, you begin to yearn for something made and finished—say Egypt and a completely dead mummy. It is neither seemly nor safe to hint that the government of the largest city in the States is a despotism of the alien by the alien for the alien, tempered with occasional insurrections of the decent folk. Only the Chinaman washes the dirty linen of other lands.

St. Paul, Minnesota.

Yes, it is very good to get away once more and pick up the old and ever fresh business of the vagrant, loafing through new towns, learned in the manners of dogs, babies, and perambulators half the world over, and tracking the seasons by the up-growth of flowers in stranger-people's gardens. St. Paul, standing at the barn-door of the Dakota and Minnesota granaries, is all things to all men except to Minneapolis, eleven miles away, whom she hates and by whom she is patronised. She calls herself the capital of the North-West, the new North-West, and her citizens wear, not only the tall silk hat of trade, but the soft slouch of the West. She talks in another tongue than the New Yorker, and—sure sign that we are far across the continent—her papers argue with the San Francisco ones over rate wars and the competition of railway companies. St. Paul has been established many years, and if one were reckless enough to go down to the business quarters one would hear all about her and more also. But the residential parts of the town are the crown of it. In common with scores of other cities, broad-crowned suburbs—using the word in the English sense—that make the stranger jealous. You get here what you do not get in the city—well-paved or asphalted roads, planted with trees, and trim side-walks, studded with houses of individuality, not boorishly fenced off from each other, but standing each on its plot of well-kept turf running down to the pavement. It is always Sunday in these streets of a morning. The cable-car has taken the men down town to business, the children are at school, and the big dogs, three and a third to each absent child, lie nosing the winter-killed grass and wondering when the shoots will make it possible for a gentleman to take his spring medicine. In the afternoon, the children on tricycles stagger up and down the asphalt with due proportion of big dogs at each wheel; the cable-cars coming up hill begin to drop the men each at his own door—the door of the house that he built for himself (though the architect incited him to that vile little attic tower and useless loggia), and, naturally enough, twilight brings the lovers walking two by two along the very quiet ways. You can tell from the houses almost the exact period at which they were built, whether in the jig-saw days, when if behoved respectability to use unlovely turned rails and pierced gable-ends, or during the Colonial craze, which means white paint and fluted pillars, or in the latest domestic era, a most pleasant mixture, that is, of stained shingles, hooded dormer-windows, cunning verandas, and recessed doors. Seeing these things, one begins to understand why the Americans visiting England are impressed with the old and not with the new. He is not much more than a hundred years ahead of the English in design, comfort, and economy, and (this is most important) labour-saving appliances in his house. From Newport to San Diego you will find the same thing to-day.

Last tribute of respect and admiration. One little brown house at the end of an avenue is shuttered down, and a doctor's buggy stands before it. On the door a large blue and white label says—' Scarlet Fever.' Oh, most excellent municipality of St. Paul. It is because of these little things, and not by rowdying and racketing in public places, that a nation becomes great and free and honoured. In the cars to-night they will be talking wheat, girding at Minneapolis, and sneering at Duluth's demand for twenty feet of water from Duluth to the Atlantic—matters of no great moment compared with those streets and that label.

A day later .

'Five days ago there wasn't a foot of earth to see. It was just naturally covered with snow,' says the conductor standing in the rear car of the Great Northern train. He speaks as though the snow had hidden something priceless. Here is the view: One railway track and a line of staggering telegraph poles ending in a dot and a blur on the horizon. To the left and right, a sweep as it were of the sea, one huge plain of corn land waiting for the spring, dotted at rare intervals with wooden farmhouses, patent self-reapers and binders almost as big as the houses, ricks left over from last year's abundant harvest, and mottled here and there with black patches to show that the early ploughing had begun. The snow lies in a last few streaks and whirls by the track; from sky-line to sky-line is black loam and prairie grass so dead that it seems as though no one year's sun would waken it. This is the granary of the land where the farmer who bears the burdens of the State—and who, therefore, ascribes last year's bumper crop to the direct action of the McKinley Bill—has, also, to bear the ghastly monotony of earth and sky. He keeps his head, having many things to attend to, but his wife sometimes goes mad as the women do in Vermont. There is little variety in Nature's big wheat-field. They say that when the corn is in the ear, the wind, chasing shadows across it for miles on miles, breeds as it were a vertigo in those who must look and cannot turn their eyes away. And they tell a nightmare story of a woman who lived with her husband for fourteen years at an Army post in just such a land as this. Then they were transferred to West Point, among the hills over the Hudson, and she came to New York, but the terror of the tall houses grew upon her and grew till she went down with brain fever, and the dread of her delirium was that the terrible things would topple down and crush her. That is a true story.

They work for harvest with steam-ploughs here. How could mere horses face the endless furrows? And they attack the earth with toothed, cogged, and spiked engines that would be monstrous in the shops, but here are only speckles on the yellow grass. Even the locomotive is cowed. A train of freight cars is passing along a line that comes out of the blue and goes on till it meets the blue again. Elsewhere the train would move off with a joyous, vibrant roar. Here it steals away down the vista of the telegraph poles with an awed whisper—steals away and sinks into the soil.

Then comes a town deep in black mud—a straggly, inch-thick plank town, with dull red grain elevators. The open country refuses to be subdued even for a few score rods. Each street ends in the illimitable open, and it is as though the whole houseless, outside earth were racing through it. Towards evening, under a gray sky, flies by an unframed picture of desolation. In the foreground a farm wagon almost axle deep in mud, the mire dripping from the slow-turning wheels as the man flogs the horses. Behind him on a knoll of sodden soggy grass, fenced off by raw rails from the landscape at large, are a knot of utterly uninterested citizens who have flogged horses and raised wheat in their time, but to-day lie under chipped and weather-worn wooden headstones. Surely burial here must be more awful to the newly-made ghost than burial at sea.

There is more snow as we go north, and Nature is hard at work breaking up the ground for the spring. The thaw has filled every depression with a sullen gray-black spate, and out on the levels the water lies six inches deep, in stretch upon stretch, as far as the eye can reach. Every culvert is full, and the broken ice clicks against the wooden pier-guards of the bridges. Somewhere in this flatness there is a refreshing jingle of spurs along the cars, and a man of the Canadian Mounted Police swaggers through with his black fur cap and the yellow tab aside, his well-fitting overalls and his better set-up back. One wants to shake hands with him because he is clean and does not slouch nor spit, trims his hair, and walks as a man should. Then a custom-house officer wants to know too much about cigars, whisky, and Florida water. Her Majesty the Queen of England and Empress of India has us in her keeping. Nothing has happened to the landscape, and Winnipeg, which is, as it were, a centre of distribution for emigrants, stands up to her knees in the water of the thaw. The year has turned in earnest, and somebody is talking about the 'first ice-shove' at Montreal, 1300 or 1400 miles east.

They will not run trains on Sunday at Montreal, and this is Wednesday. Therefore, the Canadian Pacific makes up a train for Vancouver at Winnipeg. This is worth remembering, because few people travel in that train, and you escape any rush of tourists running westward to catch the Yokohama boat. The car is your own, and with it the service of the porter. Our porter, seeing things were slack, beguiled himself with a guitar, which gave a triumphal and festive touch to the journey, ridiculously out of keeping with the view. For eight-and-twenty long hours did the bored locomotive trail us through a flat and hairy land, powdered, ribbed, and speckled with snow, small snow that drives like dust-shot in the wind—the land of Assiniboia. Now and again, for no obvious reason to the outside mind, there was a town. Then the towns gave place to 'section so and so'; then there were trails of the buffalo, where he once walked in his pride; then there was a mound of white bones, supposed to belong to the said buffalo, and then the wilderness took up the tale. Some of it was good ground, but most of it seemed to have fallen by the wayside, and the tedium of it was eternal.

At twilight—an unearthly sort of twilight—there came another curious picture. Thus—a wooden town shut in among low, treeless, rolling ground, a calling river that ran unseen between scarped banks; barracks of a detachment of mounted police, a little cemetery where ex-troopers rested, a painfully formal public garden with pebble paths and foot-high fir trees, a few lines of railway buildings, white women walking up and down in the bitter cold with their bonnets off, some Indians in red blanketing with buffalo horns for sale trailing along the platform, and, not ten yards from the track, a cinnamon bear and a young grizzly standing up with extended arms in their pens and begging for food. It was strange beyond anything that this bald telling can suggest—opening a door into a new world. The only commonplace thing about the spot was its name—Medicine Hat, which struck me instantly as the only possible name such a town could carry. This is that place which later became a town; but I had seen it three years before when it was even smaller and was reached by me in a freight-car, ticket unpaid for.

That next morning brought us the Canadian Pacific Railway as one reads about it. No pen of man could do justice to the scenery there. The guide-books struggle desperately with descriptions, adapted for summer reading, of rushing cascades, lichened rocks, waving pines, and snow-capped mountains; but in April these things are not there. The place is locked up—dead as a frozen corpse. The mountain torrent is a boss of palest emerald ice against the dazzle of the snow; the pine-stumps are capped and hooded with gigantic mushrooms of snow; the rocks are overlaid five feet deep; the rocks, the fallen trees, and the lichens together, and the dumb white lips curl up to the track cut in the side of the mountain, and grin there fanged with gigantic icicles. You may listen in vain when the train stops for the least sign of breath or power among the hills. The snow has smothered the rivers, and the great looping trestles run over what might be a lather of suds in a huge wash-tub. The old snow near by is blackened and smirched with the smoke of locomotives, and its dulness is grateful to aching eyes. But the men who live upon the line have no consideration for these things. At a halting-place in a gigantic gorge walled in by the snows, one of them reels from a tiny saloon into the middle of the track where half-a-dozen dogs are chasing a pig off the metals. He is beautifully and eloquently drunk. He sings, waves his hands, and collapses behind a shunting engine, while four of the loveliest peaks that the Almighty ever moulded look down upon him. The landslide that should have wiped that saloon into kindlings has missed its mark and has struck a few miles down the line. One of the hillsides moved a little in dreaming of the spring and caught a passing freight train. Our cars grind cautiously by, for the wrecking engine has only just come through. The deceased engine is standing on its head in soft earth thirty or forty feet down the slide, and two long cars loaded with shingles are dropped carelessly atop of it. It looks so marvellously like a toy train flung aside by a child, that one cannot realise what it means till a voice cries, 'Any one killed?' The answer comes back, 'No; all jumped'; and you perceive with a sense of personal insult that this slovenliness of the mountain is an affair which may touch your own sacred self. In which case.... But the train is out on a trestle, into a tunnel, and out on a trestle again. It was here that every one began to despair of the line when it was under construction, because there seemed to be no outlet. But a man came, as a man always will, and put a descent thus and a curve in this manner, and a trestle so; and behold, the line went on. It is in this place that we heard the story of the Canadian Pacific Railway told as men tell a many-times-repeated tale, with exaggerations and omissions, but an imposing tale, none the less. In the beginning, when they would federate the Dominion of Canada, it was British Columbia who saw objections to coming in, and the Prime Minister of those days promised it for a bribe, an iron band between tidewater and tidewater that should not break. Then everybody laughed, which seems necessary to the health of most big enterprises, and while they were laughing, things were being done. The Canadian Pacific Railway was given a bit of a line here and a bit of a line there and almost as much land as it wanted, and the laughter was still going on when the last spike was driven between east and west, at the very place where the drunken man sprawled behind the engine, and the iron band ran from tideway to tideway as the Premier said, and people in England said 'How interesting,' and proceeded to talk about the 'bloated Army estimates.' Incidentally, the man who told us—he had nothing to do with the Canadian Pacific Railway—explained how it paid the line to encourage immigration, and told of the arrival at Winnipeg of a train-load of Scotch crofters on a Sunday. They wanted to stop then and there for the Sabbath—they and all the little stock they had brought with them. It was the Winnipeg agent who had to go among them arguing (he was Scotch too, and they could not quite understand it) on the impropriety of dislocating the company's traffic. So their own minister held a service in the station, and the agent gave them a good dinner, cheering them in Gaelic, at which they wept, and they went on to settle at Moosomin, where they lived happily ever afterwards. Of the manager, the head of the line from Montreal to Vancouver, our companion spoke with reverence that was almost awe. That manager lived in a palace at Montreal, but from time to time he would sally forth in his special car and whirl over his 3000 miles at 50 miles an hour. The regulation pace is twenty-two, but he sells his neck with his head. Few drivers cared for the honour of taking him over the road. A mysterious man he was, who 'carried the profile of the line in his head,' and, more than that, knew intimately the possibilities of back country which he had never seen nor travelled over. There is always one such man on every line. You can hear similar tales from drivers on the Great Western in England or Eurasian stationmasters on the big North-Western in India. Then a fellow-traveller spoke, as many others had done, on the possibilities of Canadian union with the United States; and his language was not the language of Mr. Goldwin Smith. It was brutal in places. Summarised it came to a pronounced objection to having anything to do with a land rotten before it was ripe, a land with seven million negroes as yet unwelded into the population, their race-type unevolved, and rather more than crude notions on murder, marriage, and honesty. 'We've picked up their ways of politics,' he said mournfully. 'That comes of living next door to them; but I don't think we're anxious to mix up with their other messes. They say they don't want us. They keep on saying it. There's a nigger on the fence somewhere, or they wouldn't lie about it.'

'But does it follow that they are lying?'

'Sure. I've lived among 'em. They can't go straight. There's some dam' fraud at the back of it.'

From this belief he would not be shaken. He had lived among them—perhaps had been bested in trade. Let them keep themselves and their manners and customs to their own side of the line, he said.

This is very sad and chilling. It seemed quite otherwise in New York, where Canada was represented as a ripe plum ready to fell into Uncle Sam's mouth when he should open it. The Canadian has no special love for England—the Mother of Colonies has a wonderful gift for alienating the affections of her own household by neglect—but, perhaps, he loves his own country. We ran out of the snow through mile upon mile of snow-sheds, braced with twelve-inch beams, and planked with two-inch planking. In one place a snow slide had caught just the edge of a shed and scooped it away as a knife scoops cheese. High up the hills men had built diverting barriers to turn the drifts, but the drifts had swept over everything, and lay five deep on the top of the sheds. When we woke it was on the banks of the muddy Fraser River and the spring was hurrying to meet us. The snow had gone; the pink blossoms of the wild currant were open, the budding alders stood misty green against the blue black of the pines, the brambles on the burnt stumps were in tenderest leaf, and every moss on every stone was this year's work, fresh from the hand of the Maker. The land opened into clearings of soft black earth. At one station a hen had laid an egg and was telling the world about it. The world answered with a breath of real spring—spring that flooded the stuffy car and drove us out on the platform to snuff and sing and rejoice and pluck squashy green marsh-flags and throw them at the colts, and shout at the wild duck that rose from a jewel-green lakelet. God be thanked that in travel one can follow the year! This, my spring, I lost last November in New Zealand. Now I shall hold her fast through Japan and the summer into New Zealand again.

Here are the waters of the Pacific, and Vancouver (completely destitute of any decent defences) grown out of all knowledge in the last three years. At the railway wharf, with never a gun to protect her, lies the *Empress of India* —the Japan boat—and what more auspicious name could you wish to find at the end of one of the strong chains of empire?

THE EDGE OF THE EAST

The mist was clearing off Yokohama harbour and a hundred junks had their sails hoisted for the morning breeze, and the veiled horizon was stippled with square blurs of silver. An English man-of-war showed blue-white on then haze, so new was the daylight, and all the water lay out as smooth as the inside of an oyster shell. Two children in blue and white, their tanned limbs pink in the fresh air, sculled a marvellous boat of lemon-hued wood, and that was our fairy craft to the shore across the stillness and the mother o' pearl levels.

There are ways and ways of entering Japan. The best is to descend upon it from America and the Pacific—from the barbarians and the deep sea. Coming from the East, the blaze of India and the insolent tropical vegetation of Singapore dull the eye to half-colours and little tones. It is at Bombay that the smell of All Asia boards the ship miles off shore, and holds the passenger's nose till he is clear of Asia again. That is a violent, and aggressive smell, apt to prejudice the stranger, but kin none the less to the gentle and insinuating flavour that stole across the light airs of the daybreak when the fairy boat went to shore—a smell of very clean new wood; split bamboo, wood-smoke, damp earth, and the things that people who are not white people eat—a homelike and comforting smell. Then followed on shore the sound of an Eastern tongue, that is beautiful or not as you happen to know it. The Western races have many languages, but a crowd of Europeans heard through closed doors talk with the Western pitch and cadence. So it is with the East. A line of jinrickshaw coolies sat in the sun discoursing to each other, and it was as though they were welcoming a return in speech that the listener must know as well as English. They talked and they talked, but the ghosts of familiar words would not grow any clearer till presently the Smell came down the open streets again, saying that this was the East where nothing matters, and trifles old as the Tower of Babel mattered less than nothing, and that there were old acquaintances waiting at every corner beyond the township. Great is the Smell of the East! Railways, telegraphs, docks, and gunboats cannot banish it, and it will endure till the railways are dead. He who has not smelt that smell has never lived.

Three years ago Yokohama was sufficiently Europeanised in its shops to suit the worst and wickedest taste. To-day it is still worse if you keep to the town limits. Ten steps beyond into the fields all the civilisation stops exactly as it does in another land a few thousand miles further West. The globe-trotting, millionaires anxious to spend money, with a hose on whatever caught their libertine fancies, had explained to us aboard-ship that they came to Japan in haste, advised by their guide-books to do so, lest the land should be suddenly civilised between steamer-sailing and steamer-sailing. When they touched land they ran away to the curio shops to buy things which are prepared for them—mauve and magenta and blue-vitriol things. By this time they have a 'Murray' under one arm and an electric-blue eagle with a copperas beak and a yellow '*E pluribus unum* ' embroidered on apple-green silk, under the other.

We, being wise, sit in a garden that is not ours, but belongs to a gentleman in slate-coloured silk, who, solely for the sake of the picture, condescends to work as a gardener, in which employ he is sweeping delicately a welt of fallen cherry blossoms from under an azalea aching to burst into bloom. Steep stone steps, of the colour that nature ripens through long winters, lead up to this garden by way of clumps of bamboo grass. You see the Smell was right when it talked of meeting old friends. Half-a-dozen blue-black pines are standing akimbo against a real sky—not a fog-blur nor a cloud-bank, nor a gray dish-clout wrapped round the sun—but a blue sky. A cherry tree on a slope below them throws up a wave of blossom that breaks all creamy white against their feet, and a clump of willows trail their palest green shoots in front of all. The sun sends for an ambassador through the azalea bushes a lordly swallow-tailed butterfly, and his squire very like the flitting 'chalk-blue' of the English downs. The warmth of the East, that goes through, not over, the lazy body, is added to the light of the East—the splendid lavish light that clears but does not bewilder the eye. Then the new leaves of the spring wink like fat emeralds and the loaded branches of cherry-bloom grow transparent and glow as a hand glows held up against flame. Little, warm sighs come up from the moist, warm earth, and the fallen petals stir on the ground, turn over, and go to sleep again. Outside, beyond the foliage, where the sunlight lies on the slate-coloured roofs, the ridged rice-fields beyond the roofs, and the hills beyond the rice-fields, is all Japan—only all Japan; and this that they call the old French Legation is the Garden of Eden that most naturally dropped down here after the Fall. For some small hint of the beauties to be shown later there is the roof of a temple, ridged and fluted with dark tiles, flung out casually beyond the corner of the bluff on which the garden stands. Any other curve of the eaves would not have consorted with the sweep of the pine branches; therefore, this curve was made, and being made, was perfect. The congregation of the globe-trotters are in the hotel, scuffling for guides, in order that they may be shown the sights of Japan, which is all one sight. They must go to Tokio, they must go to Nikko; they must surely see all that is to be seen and then write home to their barbarian families that they are getting used to the sight of bare, brown legs. Before this day is ended, they will all, thank goodness, have splitting headaches and burnt-out eyes. It is better to lie still and hear the grass grow—to soak in the heat and the smell and the sounds and the sights that come unasked.

Our garden overhangs the harbour, and by pushing aside one branch we look down upon a heavy-sterned fishing-boat, the straw-gold mats of the deck-house pushed back to show the perfect order and propriety of the housekeeping that is going forward. The father-fisher, sitting frog-fashion, is poking at a tiny box full of charcoal, and the light, white ash is blown back into the face of a largish Japanese doll, price two shillings and threepence in Bayswater. The doll wakes, turns into a Japanese baby something more valuable than money could buy—a baby with a shaven head and aimless legs. It crawls to the thing in the polished brown box, is picked up just as it is ready to eat live coals, and is set down behind a thwart, where it drums upon a bucket, addressing the firebox from afar. Half-a-dozen cherry blossoms slide off a bough, and waver down to the water close to the Japanese doll, who in another minute will be overside in pursuit of these miracles. The father-fisher has it by the pink hind leg, and this time it is tucked away, all but the top-knot, out of sight among umber nets and sepia cordage. Being an Oriental it makes no protest, and the boat scuds out to join the little fleet in the offing.

Then two sailors of a man-of-war come along the sea face, lean over the canal below the garden, spit, and roll away. The sailor in port is the only superior man. To him all matters rare and curious are either 'them things' or 'them other things.' He does not hurry himself, he does not seek Adjectives other than those which custom puts into his mouth for all occasions; but the beauty of life penetrates his being insensibly till he gets drunk, falls foul of the local policeman, smites him into the nearest canal, and disposes of the question of treaty revision with a hiccup. All the same, Jack says that he has a grievance against the policeman, who is paid a dollar for every strayed seaman he brings up to the Consular Courts for overstaying his leave, and so forth. Jack says that the little fellows deliberately hinder him from getting back to his ship, and then with devilish art and craft of wrestling tricks—'there are about a hundred of 'em, and they can throw you with every qualified one'—carry him to justice. Now when Jack is softened with drink he does not tell lies. This is his grievance, and he says that them blanketed consuls ought to know. 'They plays into each other's hands, and stops you at the Hatoba'—the policemen do. The visitor who is neither a seaman nor drunk, cannot swear to the truth of this, or indeed anything else. He moves not only among fascinating scenes and a lovely people but, as he is sure to find out before he has been a day ashore, between stormy questions. Three years ago there were no questions that were not going to be settled off-hand in a blaze of paper lanterns. The Constitution was new. It has a gray, pale cover with a chrysanthemum at the back, and a Japanese told me then, 'Now we have Constitution same as other countries, and *so* it is all right. Now we are quite civilised because of Constitution.'

[A perfectly irrelevant story comes to mind here. Do you know that in Madeira once they had a revolution which lasted just long enough for the national poet to compose a national anthem, and then was put down? All that is left of the revolt now is the song that you hear on the twangling *nachettes* , the baby-banjoes, of a moonlight night under the banana fronds at the back of Funchal. And the high-pitched nasal refrain of it is 'Consti-tuci- *oun* !']

Since that auspicious date it seems that the questions have impertinently come up, and the first and the last of them is that of Treaty Revision. Says the Japanese Government, 'Only obey our laws, our new laws that we have carefully compiled from all the wisdom of the West, and you shall go up country as you please and trade where you will, instead of living cooped up in concessions and being judged by consuls. Treat us as you would treat France or Germany, and we will treat you as our own subjects.'

Here, as you know, the matter rests between the two thousand foreigners and the forty million Japanese—a God-send to all editors of Tokio and Yokohama, and the despair of the newly arrived in whose nose, remember, is the smell of the East, One and Indivisible, Immemorial, Eternal, and, above all, Instructive.

Indeed, it is only by walking out at least half a mile that you escape from the aggressive evidences of civilisation, and come out into the rice-fields at the back of the town. Here men with twists of blue and white cloth round their heads are working knee deep in the thick black mud. The largest field may be something less than two tablecloths, while the smallest is, say, a speck of undercliff, on to which it were hard to back a 'rickshaw, wrested from the beach and growing its clump of barley within spray-shot of the waves. The field paths are the trodden tops of the irrigating cuts, and the main roads as wide as two perambulators abreast. From the uplands—the beautiful uplands planted in exactly the proper places with pine and maple—the ground comes down in terraced pocket on pocket of rich earth to the levels again, and it would seem that every heavily-thatched farmhouse was chosen with special regard to the view. If you look closely when the people go to work you will see that a household spreads itself over plots, maybe, a quarter of a mile apart. A revenue map of a village shows that this scatteration is apparently designed, but the reason is not given. One thing at least is certain. The assessment of these patches can be no light piece of work—just the thing, in fact, that would give employment to a large number of small and variegated Government officials, any one of whom, assuming that he was of an Oriental cast of mind, might make the cultivator's life interesting. I remember now—a second-time-seen place brings back things that were altogether buried—seeing three years ago the pile of Government papers required in the case of one farm. They were many and systematic, but the interesting thing about them was the amount of work that they must have furnished to those who were neither cultivators nor Treasury officials.

If one knew Japanese, one could collogue with that gentleman in the straw-hat and the blue loincloth who is chopping within a sixteenth of an inch of his naked toes with the father and mother of all weed-spuds. His version of local taxation might be inaccurate, but it would sure to be picturesque. Failing his evidence, be pleased to accept two or three things that may or may not be facts of general application. They differ in a measure from statements in the books. The present land-tax is nominally 2-1/2 per cent, payable in cash on a three, or as some say a five, yearly settlement. But, according to certain officials, there has been no settlement since 1875. Land lying fallow for a season pays the same tax as land in cultivation, unless it is unproductive through flood or calamity (read earthquake here). The Government tax is calculated on the capital value of the land, taking a measure of about 11,000 square feet or a quarter of an acre as the unit.

Now, one of the ways of getting at the capital value of the land is to see what the railways have paid for it. The very best rice land, taking the Japanese dollar at three shillings, is about £65:10s per acre. Unirrigated land for vegetable growing is something over £9:12s., and forest £2:11s. As these are railway rates, they may be fairly held to cover large areas. In private sales the prices may reasonably be higher.

It is to be remembered that some of the very best rice land will bear two crops of rice in the year. Most soil will bear two crops, the first being millet, rape, vegetables, and so on, sown on dry soil and ripening at the end of May. Then the ground is at once prepared for the wet crop, to be harvested in October or thereabouts. Land-tax is payable in two instalments. Rice land pays between the 1st November and the middle of December and the 1st January and the last of February. Other land pays between July and August and September and December. Let us see what the average yield is. The gentleman in the sun-hat and the loin-cloth would shriek at the figures, but they are approximately accurate. Rice naturally fluctuates a good deal, but it may be taken in the rough at five Japanese dollars (fifteen shillings) per *koku* of 330 lbs. Wheat and maize of the first spring crop is worth about eleven shillings per *koku* . The first crop gives nearly 1-3/4 *koku* per *tau* (the quarter acre unit of measurement aforesaid), or eighteen shillings per quarter acre, or £3:12s. per acre. The rice crop at two *koku* or £1:10s. the quarter acre gives £6 an acre. Total £9:12s. This is not altogether bad if you reflect that the land in question is not the very best rice land, but ordinary No. 1, at £25:16s. per acre, capital value.

A son has the right to inherit his father's land on the father's assessment, so long as its term runs, or, when the term has expired, has a prior claim as against any one else. Part of the taxes, it is said, lies by in the local prefecture's office as a reserve fund against inundations. Yet, and this seems a little confusing, there are between five and seven other local, provincial, and municipal taxes which can reasonably be applied to the same ends. No one of these taxes exceeds a half of the land-tax, unless it be the local prefecture tax of 2-1/2 per cent.

In the old days the people were taxed, or perhaps squeezed would be the better word, to about one-half of the produce of the land. There are those who may say that the present system is not so advantageous as it looks. Beforetime, the farmers, it is true, paid heavily, but only, on their nominal holdings. They could, and often did, hold more land than they were assessed on. Today a rigid bureaucracy surveys every foot of their farms, and upon every foot they have to pay. Somewhat similar complaints are made still by the simple peasantry of India, for if there is one thing that the Oriental detests more than another, it is the damnable Western vice of accuracy. That leads to doing things by rule. Still, by the look of those terraced fields, where the water is led so cunningly from level to level, the Japanese cultivator must enjoy at least one excitement. If the villages up the valley tamper with the water supply, there must surely be excitement down the valley—argument, protest, and the breaking of heads.

The days of romance, therefore, are not all dead.

This that follows happened on the coast twenty miles through the fields from Yokohama, at Kamakura, that is to say, where the great bronze Buddha sits facing the sea to hear the centuries go by. He has been described again and again—his majesty, his aloofness, and every one of his dimensions, the smoky little shrine within him, and the plumed hill that makes the background to his throne. For that reason he remains, as he remained from the beginning, beyond all hope of description—as it might be, a visible god sitting in the garden of a world made new. They sell photographs of him with tourists standing on his thumb nail, and, apparently, any brute of any gender can scrawl his or its ignoble name over the inside of the massive bronze plates that build him up. Think for a moment of the indignity and the insult! Imagine the ancient, orderly gardens with their clipped trees, shorn turf, and silent ponds smoking in the mist that the hot sun soaks up after rain, and the green-bronze image of the Teacher of the Law wavering there as it half seems through incense clouds. The earth is all one censer, and myriads of frogs are making the haze ring. It is too warm to do more than to sit on a stone and watch the eyes that, having seen all things, see no more—the down-dropped eyes, the forward droop of the head, and the colossal simplicity of the folds of the robe over arm and knee. Thus, and in no other fashion, did Buddha sit in the-old days when Ananda asked questions and the dreamer began to dream of the lives that lay behind him ere the lips moved, and as the Chronicles say: 'He told a tale.' This would be the way he began, for dreamers in the East tell something the same sort of tales to-day: 'Long ago when Devadatta was King of Benares, there lived a virtuous elephant, a reprobate ox, and a King without understanding.' And the tale would end, after the moral had been drawn for Ananda's benefit: 'Now, the reprobate ox was such an one, and the King was such another, but the virtuous elephant was I, myself, Ananda.' Thus, then, he told the tales in the bamboo grove, and the bamboo grove is there to-day. Little blue and gray and slate robed figures pass under its shadow, buy two or three joss-sticks, disappear into the shrine, that is, the body of the god, come out smiling, and drift away through the shrubberies. A fat carp in a pond sucks at a fallen leaf with just the sound of a wicked little worldly kiss. Then the earth steams, and steams in silence, and a gorgeous butterfly, full six inches from wing to wing, cuts through the steam in a zigzag of colour and flickers up to the forehead of the god. And Buddha said that a man must look on everything as illusion—even light and colour—the time-worn bronze of metal against blue-green of pine and pale emerald of bamboo—the lemon sash of the girl in the cinnamon dress, with coral pins in her hair, leaning against a block of weather-bleached stone—and, last, the spray of blood-red azalea that stands on the pale gold mats of the tea-house beneath the honey-coloured thatch. To overcome desire and covetousness of mere gold, which is often very vilely designed, that is conceivable; but why must a man give up the delight of the eye, colour that rejoices, light that cheers, and line that satisfies the innermost deeps of the heart? Ah, if the Bodhisat had only seen his own image!

OUR OVERSEAS MEN

All things considered, there are only two kinds of men in the world—those that stay at home and those that do not. The second are the most interesting. Some day a man will bethink himself and write a book about the breed in a book called 'The Book of the Overseas Club,' for it is at the clubhouses all the way from Aden to Yokohama that the life of the Outside Men is best seen and their talk is best heard. A strong family likeness runs through both buildings and members, and a large and careless hospitality is the note. There is always the same open-doored, high-ceiled house, with matting on the floors; the same come and go of dark-skinned servants, and the same assembly of men talking horse or business, in raiment that would fatally scandalise a London committee, among files of newspapers from a fortnight to five weeks old. The life of the Outside Men includes plenty of sunshine, and as much air as may be stirring. At the Cape, where the Dutch housewives distil and sell the very potent Vanderhum, and the absurd home-made hansom cabs waddle up and down the yellow dust of Adderley Street, are the members of the big import and export firms, the shipping and insurance offices, inventors of mines, and exploiters of new territories with now and then an officer strayed from India to buy mules for the Government, a Government House aide-de-camp, a sprinkling of the officers of the garrison, tanned skippers of the Union and Castle Lines, and naval men from the squadron at Simon's Town. Here they talk of the sins of Cecil Rhodes, the insolence of Natal, the beauties or otherwise of the solid Boer vote, and the dates of the steamers. The *argot* is Dutch and Kaffir, and every one can hum the national anthem that begins 'Pack your kit and trek, Johnny Bowlegs.' In the stately Hongkong Clubhouse, which is to the further what the Bengal Club is to the nearer East, you meet much the same gathering, *minus* the mining speculators and *plus* men whose talk is of tea, silk, shortings, and Shanghai ponies. The speech of the Outside Men at this point becomes fearfully mixed with pidgin-English and local Chinese terms, rounded with corrupt Portuguese. At Melbourne, in a long verandah giving on a grass plot, where laughing-jackasses laugh very horribly, sit wool-kings, premiers, and breeders of horses after their kind. The older men talk of the days of the Eureka Stockade and the younger of 'shearing wars' in North Queensland, while the traveller moves timidly among them wondering what under the world every third word means. At Wellington, overlooking the harbour (all right-minded clubs should command the sea), another, and yet a like, sort of men speak of sheep, the rabbits, the land-courts, and the ancient heresies of Sir Julius Vogel; and their more expressive sentences borrow from the Maori. And elsewhere, and elsewhere, and elsewhere among the Outside Men it is the same—the same mixture of every trade, calling, and profession under the sun; the same clash of conflicting interests touching the uttermost parts of the earth; the same intimate, and sometimes appalling knowledge of your neighbour's business and shortcomings; the same large-palmed hospitality, and the same interest on the part of the, younger men in the legs of a horse. Decidedly, it is at the Overseas Club all the world over that you get to know some little of the life of the community. London is egoistical, and the world for her ends with the four-mile cab radius. There is no provincialism like the provincialism of London. That big slack-water coated with the drift and rubbish of a thousand men's thoughts esteems itself the open sea because the waves of all the oceans break on her borders. To those in her midst she is terribly imposing, but they forget that there is more than one kind of imposition. Look back upon her from ten thousand miles, when the mail is just in at the Overseas Club, and she is wondrous tiny. Nine-tenths of her news—so vital, so epoch-making over there—loses its significance, and the rest is as the scuffling of ghosts in a back-attic.

Here in Yokohama the Overseas Club has two mails and four sets of papers—English, French, German, and American, as suits the variety of its constitution—and the verandah by the sea, where the big telescope stands, is a perpetual feast of the Pentecost. The population of the club changes with each steamer in harbour, for the sea-captains swing in, are met with 'Hello! where did you come from?' and mix at the bar and billiard-tables for their appointed time and go to sea again. The white-painted warships supply their contingent of members also, and there are wonderful men, mines of most fascinating adventure, who have an interest in sealing-brigs that go to the Kurile Islands, and somehow get into trouble with the Russian authorities. Consuls and judges of the Consular Courts meet men over on leave from the China ports, or it may be Manila, and they all talk tea, silk, banking, and exchange with its fixed residents. Everything is always as bad as it can possibly be, and everybody is on the verge of ruin. That is why, when they have decided that life is no longer worth living, they go down to the skittle-alley—to commit suicide. From the outside, when a cool wind blows among the papers and there is a sound of smashing ice in an inner apartment, and every third man is talking about the approaching races, the life seems to be a desirable one. 'What more could a man need to make him happy?' says the passer-by. A perfect climate, a lovely country, plenty of pleasant society, and the politest people on earth to deal with. The resident smiles and invites the passer-by to stay through July and August. Further, he presses him to do business with the politest people on earth, and to continue so doing for a term of years. Thus the traveller perceives beyond doubt that the resident is prejudiced by the very fact of his residence, and gives it as his matured opinion that Japan is a faultless land, marred only by the presence of the foreign community. And yet, let us consider. It is the foreign community that has made it possible for the traveller to come and go from hotel to hotel, to get his passport for inland travel, to telegraph his safe arrival to anxious friends, and generally enjoy himself much more than he would have been able to do in his own country. Government and gunboats may open a land, but it is the men of the Overseas Club that keep it open. Their reward (not alone in Japan) is the bland patronage or the scarcely-veiled contempt of those who profit by their labours. It is hopeless to explain to a traveller who has been 'ohayoed' into half-a-dozen shops and 'sayonaraed' out of half-a-dozen more and politely cheated in each one, that the Japanese is an Oriental, and, therefore, embarrassingly economical of the truth. 'That's his politeness,' says the traveller. 'He does not wish to hurt your feelings. Love him and treat him like a brother, and he'll change.' To treat one of the most secretive of races on a brotherly basis is not very easy, and the natural politeness that enters into a signed and sealed contract and undulates out of it so soon as it does not sufficiently pay is more than embarrassing. It is almost annoying. The want of fixity or commercial honour may be due to some natural infirmity of the artistic temperament, or to the manner in which the climate has affected, and his ruler has ruled, the man himself for untold centuries.

Those who know the East know, where the system of 'squeeze,' which is commission, runs through every transaction of life, from the sale of a groom's place upward, where the woman walks behind the man in the streets, and where the peasant gives you for the distance to the next town as many or as few miles as he thinks you will like, that these things must be so. Those who do not know will not be persuaded till they have lived there. The Overseas Club puts up its collective nose scornfully when it hears of the New and Regenerate Japan sprung to life since the 'seventies. It grins, with shame be it written, at an Imperial Diet modelled on the German plan and a Code Napoléon à la Japonaise. It is so far behind the New Era as to doubt that an Oriental country, ridden by etiquette of the sternest, and social distinctions almost as hard as those of caste, can be turned out to Western gauge in the compass of a very young man's fife. And it *must* be prejudiced, because it is daily and hourly in contact with the Japanese, except when it can do business with the Chinaman whom it prefers. Was there ever so disgraceful a club!

Just at present, a crisis, full blown as a chrysanthemum, has developed in the Imperial Diet. Both Houses accuse the Government of improper interference—this Japanese for 'plenty stick and some bank-note'—at the recent elections. They then did what was equivalent to passing a vote of censure on the Ministry and refusing to vote government measures. So far the wildest advocate of representative government could have desired nothing better. Afterwards, things took a distinctly Oriental turn. The Ministry refused to resign, and the Mikado prorogued the Diet for a week to think things over. The Japanese papers are now at issue over the event. Some say that representative government implies party government, and others swear at large. The Overseas Club says for the most part—'Skittles!'

It is a picturesque situation—one that suggests romances and extravaganzas. Thus, imagine a dreaming Court intrenched behind a triple line of moats where the lotus blooms in summer—a Court whose outer fringe is aggressively European, but whose heart is Japan of long ago, where a dreaming King sits among some wives or other things, amused from time to time with magic-lantern shows and performing fleas—a holy King whose sanctity is used to conjure with, and who twice a year gives garden-parties where every one must come in top-hat and frock coat. Round this Court, wavering between the splendours of the sleeping and the variety shows of the Crystal Palace, place in furious but carefully-veiled antagonism the fragments of newly shattered castes, their natural Oriental eccentricities overlaid with borrowed Western notions. Imagine now, a large and hungry bureaucracy, French in its fretful insistence on detail where detail is of no earthly moment, Oriental in its stress on etiquette and punctillo, recruited from a military caste accustomed for ages past to despise alike farmer and trader. This caste, we will suppose, is more or less imperfectly controlled by a syndicate of three clans, which supply their own nominees to the Ministry. These are adroit, versatile, and unscrupulous men, hampered by no western prejudice in favour of carrying any plan to completion. Through and at the bidding of these men, the holy Monarch acts; and the acts are wonderful. To criticise these acts exists a wild-cat Press, liable to suppression at any moment, as morbidly sensitive to outside criticism as the American, and almost as childishly untruthful, fungoid in the swiftness of its growth, and pitiable in its unseasoned rashness. Backers of this press in its wilder moments, lawless, ignorant, sensitive and vain, are the student class, educated in the main at Government expense, and a thorn in the side of the State. Judges without training handle laws without precedents, and new measures are passed and abandoned with almost inconceivable levity. Out of the welter of classes and interests that are not those of the common folk is evolved the thing called Japanese policy that has the proportion and the perspective of a Japanese picture.

Finality and stability are absent from its councils. To-day, for reasons none can explain, it is pro-foreign to the verge of servility. To-morrow, for reasons equally obscure, the pendulum swings back, and—the students are heaving mud at the foreigners in the streets. Vexatious, irresponsible, incoherent, and, above all, cheaply mysterious, is the rule of the land—stultified by intrigue and counter-intrigue, chequered with futile reforms begun on European lines and light-heartedly thrown aside; studded, as a bower-bird's run is studded with shells and shining pebbles, with plagiarisms from half the world—an operetta of administration, wherein the shadow of the King among his wives, Samurai policemen, doctors who have studied under Pasteur, kid-gloved cavalry officers from St. Cyr, judges with University degrees, harlots with fiddles, newspaper correspondents, masters of the ancient ceremonies of the land, paid members of the Diet, secret societies that borrow the knife and the dynamite of the Irish, sons of dispossessed Daimios returned from Europe and waiting for what may turn up, with ministers of the syndicate who have wrenched Japan from her repose of twenty years ago, circle, flicker, shift, and reform, in bewildering rings, round the foreign resident. Is the extravaganza complete?

Somewhere in the background of the stage are the people of the land—of whom a very limited proportion enjoy the privileges of representative government. Whether in the past few years they have learned what the thing means, or, learning, have the least intention of making any use of it, is not clear. Meantime, the game of government goes forward as merrily as a game of puss-in-the-corner, with the additional joy that not more than half-a-dozen men know who is controlling it or what in the wide world it intends to do. In Tokio live the steadily-diminishing staff of Europeans employed by the Emperor as engineers, railway experts, professors in the colleges and so forth. Before many years they will all be dispensed with, and the country will set forth among the nations alone and on its own responsibility.

In fifty years then, from the time that the intrusive American first broke her peace, Japan will experience her new birth and, reorganised from sandal to top-knot, play the *samisen* in the march of modern progress. This is the great advantage of being born into the New Era, when individual and community alike can get something for nothing— pay without work, education without effort, religion' without thought, and free government without slow and bitter toil.

The Overseas Club, as has been said, is behind the spirit of the age. It has to work for what it gets, and it does not always get what it works for. Nor can its members take ship and go home when they please. Imagine for a little, the contented frame of mind that is bred in a man by the perpetual contemplation of a harbour full of steamers as a Piccadilly cab-rank of hansoms. The weather is hot, we will suppose; something has gone wrong with his work that day, or his children are not looking so well as might be. Pretty tiled bungalows, bowered in roses and wistaria, do not console him, and the voices of the politest people on earth jar sorely. He knows every soul in the club, has thoroughly talked out every subject of interest, and would give half a year's—oh, five years'—pay for one lung-filling breath of air that has life in it, one sniff of the haying grass, or half a mile of muddy London street where the muffin bell tinkles in the four o'clock fog. Then the big liner moves out across the staring blue of the bay. So-and-so and such-an-one, both friends, are going home in her, and some one else goes next week by the French mail. He, and he alone, it seems to him, must stay on; and it is so maddeningly easy to go—for every one save himself. The boat's smoke dies out along the horizon, and he is left alone with the warm wind and the white dust of the Bund. Now Japan is a good place, a place that men swear by and live in for thirty years at a stretch.

There are China ports a week's sail to the westward where life is really hard, and where the sight of the restless shipping hurts very much indeed. Tourists and you who travel the world over, be very gentle to the men of the Overseas Clubs. Remember that, unlike yourselves, they have not come here for the good of their health, and that the return ticket in your wallet may possibly colour your views of their land. Perhaps it would not be altogether wise on the strength of much kindness from Japanese officials to recommend that these your countrymen be handed over lock, stock, and barrel to a people that are beginning to experiment with fresh-drafted half-grafted codes which do not include juries, to a system that does not contemplate a free Press, to a suspicious absolutism from which there is no appeal. Truly, it might be interesting, but as surely it would begin in farce and end in tragedy, that would leave the politest people on earth in no case to play at civilised government for a long time to come. In his concession, where he is an apologetic and much sat-upon importation, the foreign resident does no harm. He does not always sue for money due to him on the part of a Japanese. Once outside those limits, free to move into the heart of the country, it would only be a question of time as to where and when the trouble would begin. And in the long run it would not be the foreign resident that would suffer. The imaginative eye can see the most unpleasant possibilities, from a general overrunning of Japan by the Chinaman, who is far the most important foreign resident, to the shelling of Tokio by a joyous and bounding Democracy, anxious to vindicate her national honour and to learn how her newly-made navy works.

But there are scores of arguments that would confute and overwhelm this somewhat gloomy view. The statistics of Japan, for instance, are as beautiful and fit as neatly as the woodwork of her houses. By these it would be possible to prove anything.

SOME EARTHQUAKES

A Radical Member of Parliament at Tokio has just got into trouble with his constituents, and they have sent him a priceless letter of reproof. Among other things they point out that a politician should not be 'a waterweed which wobbles hither and thither according to the motion of the stream.' Nor should he 'like a ghost without legs drift along before the wind.' 'Your conduct,' they say, 'has been both of a waterweed and a ghost, and we purpose in a little time to give you proof of our true Japanese spirit.' That member will very likely be mobbed in his 'rickshaw and prodded to inconvenience with sword-sticks; for the constituencies are most enlightened. But how in the world can a man under these sides behave except as a waterweed and a ghost? It is in the air—the wobble and the legless drift An energetic tourist would have gone to Hakodate, seen Ainos at Sapporo, ridden across the northern island under the gigantic thistles, caught salmon, looked in at Vladivostock, and done half a hundred things in the time that one lazy loafer has wasted watching the barley turn from green to gold, the azaleas blossom and burn out, and the spring give way to the warm rains of summer. Now the iris has taken up the blazonry of the year, and the tide of the tourists ebbs westward.

The permanent residents are beginning to talk of hill places to go to for the hot weather, and all the available houses in the resort are let. In a little while the men from China will be coming over for their holidays, but just at present we are in the thick of the tea season, and there is no time to waste on frivolities. 'Packing' is a valid excuse for anything, from forgetting a dinner to declining a tennis party, and the tempers of husbands are judged leniently. All along the sea face is an inspiring smell of the finest new-mown hay, and canals are full of boats loaded up with the boxes jostling down to the harbour. At the club men say rude things about the arrivals of the mail. There never was a post-office yet that did not rejoice in knocking a man's Sabbath into flinders. A fair office day's work may begin at eight and end at six, or, if the mail comes in, at midnight. There is no overtime or eight-hours' baby-talk in tea. Yonder are the ships; here is the stuff, and behind all is the American market. The rest is your own affair.

The narrow streets are blocked with the wains bringing down, in boxes of every shape and size, the up-country rough leaf. Some one must take delivery of these things, find room for them in the packed warehouse, and sample them before they are blended and go to the firing.

More than half the elaborate processes are 'lost work' so far as the quality of the stuff goes; but the markets insist on a good-looking leaf, with polish, face and curl to it, and in this, as in other businesses, the call of the markets is the law. The factory floors are made slippery with the tread of bare-footed coolies, who shout as the tea whirls through its transformations. The over-note to the clamour—an uncanny thing too—is the soft rustle-down of the tea itself—stacked in heaps, carried in baskets, dumped through chutes, rising and falling in the long troughs where it is polished, and disappearing at last into the heart of the firing-machine—always this insistent whisper of moving dead leaves. Steam-sieves sift it into grades, with jarrings and thumpings that make the floor quiver, and the thunder of steam-gear is always at its heels; but it continues to mutter unabashed till it is riddled down into the big, foil-lined boxes and lies at peace.

A few days ago the industry suffered a check which, lasting not more than two minutes, lost several hundred pounds of hand-fired tea. It was something after this way. Into the stillness of a hot, stuffy morning came an unpleasant noise as of batteries of artillery charging up all the roads together, and at least one bewildered sleeper waking saw his empty boots where they 'sat and played toccatas stately at the clavicord.' It was the washstand really but the effect was awful. Then a clock fell and a wall cracked, and heavy hands caught the house by the roof-pole and shook it furiously. To preserve an equal mind when things are hard is good, but he who has not fumbled desperately at bolted jalousies that will not open while a whole room is being tossed in a blanket does not know how hard it is to find any sort of mind at all. The end of the terror was inadequate—a rush into the still, heavy outside air, only to find the' servants in the garden giggling (the Japanese would giggle through the Day of Judgment) and to learn that the earthquake was over. Then came the news, swift borne from the business quarters below the hill, that the coolies of certain factories had fled shrieking at the first shock, and that all the tea in the pans was burned to a crisp. That, certainly, was some consolation for undignified panic; and there remained the hope that a few tall chimneys up the line at Tokio would have collapsed. They stood firm, however, and the local papers, used to this kind of thing, merely spoke of the shock as 'severe.' Earthquakes are demoralising; but they bring out all the weaknesses of human nature. First is downright dread; the stage of—'only let me get into the open and I'll reform,' then the impulse to send news of the most terrible shock of modern times flying east and west among the cables. (Did not your own hair stand straight on end, and, therefore, must not everybody else's have done likewise?) Last, as fallen humanity picks itself together, comes the cry of the mean little soul: 'What! Was *that* all? I wasn't frightened from the beginning.'

It is wholesome and tonic to realise the powerlessness of man in the face of these little accidents. The heir of all the ages, the annihilator of time and space, who politely doubts the existence of his Maker, hears the roof-beams crack and strain above him, and scuttles about like a rabbit in a stoppered warren. If the shock endures for twenty minutes, the annihilator of time and space must camp out under the blue and hunt for his dead among the rubbish. Given a violent convulsion (only just such a slipping of strata as carelessly piled volumes will accomplish in a book-case) and behold, the heir of all the ages is stark, raving mad—a brute among the dishevelled hills. Set a hundred of the world's greatest spirits, men of fixed principles, high aims, resolute endeavour, enormous experience, and the modesty that these attributes bring—set them to live through such a catastrophe as that which wiped out Nagoya last October, and at the end of three days there would remain few whose souls might be called their own.

So much for yesterday's shock. To-day there has come another; and a most comprehensive affair it is. It has broken nothing, unless maybe an old heart or two cracks later on; and the wise people in the settlement are saying that they predicted it from the first. None the less as an earthquake it deserves recording.

It was a very rainy afternoon; all the streets were full of gruelly mud, and all the business men were at work in their offices when it began. A knot of Chinamen were studying a closed door from whose further side came a most unpleasant sound of bolting and locking up. The notice on the door was interesting. With deep regret did the manager of the New Oriental Banking Corporation, Limited (most decidedly limited), announce that on telegraphic orders from home he had suspended payment. Said one Chinaman to another in pidgin-Japanese: 'It is shut,' and went away. The noise of barring up continued, the rain fell, and the notice stared down the wet street. That was all. There must have been two or three men passing by to whom the announcement meant the loss of every penny of their savings—comforting knowledge to digest after tiffin. In London, of course, the failure would not mean so much; there are many banks in the City, and people would have had warning. Here banks are few, people are dependent on them, and this news came out of the sea unheralded, an evil born with all its teeth.

After the crash of a bursting shell every one who can picks himself up, brushes the dirt off his uniform, and tries to make a joke of it. Then some one whips a handkerchief round his hand—a splinter has torn it—and another finds warm streaks running down his forehead. Then a man, overlooked till now and past help, groans to the death. Everybody perceives with a start that this is no time for laughter, and the dead and wounded are attended to.

Even so at the Overseas Club when the men got out of office. The brokers had told them the news. In filed the English, and Americans, and Germans, and French, and 'Here's a pretty mess!' they said one and all. Many of them were hit, but, like good men, they did not say how severely.

'Ah!' said a little P. and O. official, wagging his head sagaciously (he had lost a thousand dollars since noon), 'it's all right *now* . They're trying to make the best of it. In three or four days we shall hear more about it. I meant to draw my money just before I went down coast, but——' Curiously enough, it was the same story throughout the Club. Everybody had intended to withdraw, and nearly everybody had—not done so. The manager of a bank which had *not* failed was explaining how, in his opinion, the crash had come about. This was also very human. It helped none. Entered a lean American, throwing back his waterproof all dripping with the rain; his face was calm and peaceful. 'Boy, whisky and soda,' he said.

'How much haf you losd?' said a Teuton bluntly. 'Eight-fifty,' replied the son of George Washington sweetly. 'Don't see how that prevents me having a drink. My glass, sirr.' He continued an interrupted whistling of 'I owe ten dollars to O'Grady' (which he very probably did), and his countenance departed not from its serenity. If there is anything that one loves an American for it is the way he stands certain kinds of punishment. An Englishman and a heavy loser was being chaffed by a Scotchman whose account at the Japan end of the line had been a trifle overdrawn. True, he would lose in England, but the thought of the few dollars saved here cheered him.

More men entered, sat down by tables, stood in groups, or remained apart by themselves, thinking with knit brows. One must think quickly when one's bills are falling due. The murmur of voices thickened, and there was no rumbling in the skittle alley to interrupt it. Everybody knows everybody else at the Overseas Club, and everybody sympathises. A man passed stiffly and some one of a group turned to ask lightly, 'Hit, old man?' 'Like hell,' he said, and went on biting his unlit cigar. Another man was telling, slowly and somewhat bitterly, how he had expected one of his children to join him out here, and how the passage had been paid with a draft on the O.B.C. But now ... *There* , ladies and gentlemen, is where it hurts, this little suspension out here. It destroys plans, pretty ones hoped for and prayed over, maybe for years; it knocks pleasant domestic arrangements galleywest over and above all the mere ruin that it causes. The curious thing in the talk was that there was no abuse of the bank. The men were in the Eastern trade themselves and they knew. It was the Yokohama manager and the clerks thrown out of employment (connection with a broken bank, by the way, goes far to ruin a young man's prospects) for whom they were sorry. 'We're doing ourselves well this year,' said a wit grimly. 'One free-shooting case, one thundering libel case, and a bank smash. Showing off pretty before the globe-trotters, aren't we?'

'Gad, think of the chaps at sea with letters of credit. Eh? They'll land and get the best rooms at the hotels and find they're penniless,' said another.

'Never mind the globe-trotters,' said a third. 'Look nearer home. This does for so-and-so, and so-and-so, and so-and-so, all old men; and every penny of theirs goes.' Poor devils!'

'That reminds me of some one else,' said yet another voice, ' *His* wife's at home, too. Whew!' and he whistled drearily. So did the tide of voices run on till men got to talking over the chances of a dividend, 'They went to the Bank of England,' drawled an American, 'and the Bank of England let them down; said their securities weren't good enough.'

'Great Scott!'—a hand came down on a table to emphasise the remark—'I sailed half way up the Mediterranean once with a Bank of England director; wish I'd tipped him over the rail and lowered him a boat on his own security—if it was good enough.'

'Baring's goes. The O.B.C. don't,' replied the American, blowing smoke through his nose. 'This business looks de-ci-ded-ly prob-le-mat-i-cal. What-at?'

'Oh, they'll pay the depositors in full. Don't you fret,' said a man who had lost nothing and was anxious to console.

'I'm a shareholder,' said the American, and smoked on.

The rain continued to fall, and the umbrellas dripped in the racks, and the wet men came and went, circling round the central fact that it was a bad business, till the day, as was most fit, shut down in drizzling darkness. There was a refreshing sense of brotherhood in misfortunes in the little community that had just been electrocuted and did not want any more shocks. All the pain that in England would be taken home to be borne in silence and alone was here bulked, as it were, and faced in line of company. Surely the Christians of old must have fought much better when they met the lions by fifties at a time.

At last the men departed; the bachelors to cast up accounts by themselves (there should be some good ponies for sale shortly) and the married men to take counsel. May heaven help him whose wife does not stand by him now! But the women of the Overseas settlements are as thorough as the men. There will be tears for plans forgone, the changing of the little ones' schools and elder children's careers, unpleasant letters to be written home, and more unpleasant ones to be received from relatives who 'told you so from the first.' There will be pinchings too, and straits of which the outside world will know nothing, but the women will pull it through smiling.

Beautiful indeed are the operations of modern finance—especially when anything goes wrong with the machine. To-night there will be trouble in India among the Ceylon planters, the Calcutta jute and the Bombay cotton-brokers, besides the little households of small banked savings. In Hongkong, Singapore, and Shanghai there will be trouble too, and goodness only knows what wreck at Cheltenham, Bath, St. Leonards, Torquay, and the other camps of the retired Army officers. They are lucky in England who know what happens when it happens, but here the people are at the wrong end of the cables, and the situation is not good. Only one thing seems certain. There is a notice on a shut door, in the wet, and by virtue of that notice all the money that was theirs yesterday is gone away, and it may never come back again. So all the work that won the money must be done over again; but some of the people are old, and more are tired, and all are disheartened. It is a very sorrowful little community that goes to bed to-night, and there must be as sad ones the world over. Let it be written, however, that of the sections under fire here (and some are cruelly hit) no man whined, or whimpered, or broke down. There was no chance of fighting. It was bitter defeat, but they took it standing.

HALF-A-DOZEN PICTURES

'Some men when they grow rich, store pictures in a gallery,' Living, their friends envy them, and after death the genuineness of the collection is disputed under the dispersing hammer.

A better way is to spread your picture over all earth; visiting them as Fate allows. Then none can steal or deface, nor any reverse of fortune force a sale; sunshine and tempest warm and ventilate the gallery for nothing, and—in spite of all that has been said of her crudeness—Nature is not altogether a bad frame-maker. The knowledge that you may never live to see an especial treasure twice teaches the eyes to see quickly while the light lasts; and the possession of such a gallery breeds a very fine contempt for painted shows and the smeary things that are called pictures.

In the North Pacific, to the right hand as you go westward, hangs a small study of no particular value as compared with some others. The mist is down on an oily stretch of washed-out sea; through the mist the bats-wings of a sealing schooner are just indicated. In the foreground, all but leaping out of the frame, an open rowboat, painted the rawest blue and white, rides up over the shoulder of a swell. A man in blood-red jersey and long boots, all shining with moisture, stands at the bows holding up the carcase of a silver-bellied sea-otter from whose pelt the wet drips in moonstones. Now the artist who could paint the silver wash of the mist, the wriggling treacly reflection of the boat, and the raw red wrists of the man would be something of a workman.

But my gallery is in no danger of being copied at present. Three years since, I met an artist in the stony bed of a brook, between a line of 300 graven, lichened godlings and a flaming bank of azaleas, swearing horribly. He had been trying to paint one of my pictures—nothing more than a big water-worn rock tufted with flowers and a snow-capped hill for background. Most naturally he failed, because there happened to be absolutely no perspective in the thing, and he was pulling the lines about to make some for home consumption. No man can put the contents of a gallon jar into a pint mug. The protests of all uncomfortably-crowded mugs since the world began have settled that long ago, and have given us the working theories, devised by imperfect instruments for imperfect instruments, which are called Rules of Art.

Luckily, those who painted my gallery were born before man. Therefore, my pictures, instead of being boxed up by lumbering bars of gold, are disposed generously between latitudes, equinoxes, monsoons, and the like, and, making all allowance for an owner's partiality, they are really not so bad.

'Down in the South where the ships never go'—between the heel of New Zealand and the South Pole, there is a sea-piece showing a steamer trying to come round in the trough of a big beam sea. The wet light of the day's end comes more from the water than the sky, and the waves are colourless through the haze of the rain, all but two or three blind sea-horses swinging out of the mist on the ship's dripping weather side. A lamp is lighted in the wheel-house; so one patch of yellow light falls on the green-painted pistons of the steering gear as they snatch up the rudder-chains. A big sea has got home. Her stern flies up in the lather of a freed screw, and her deck from poop to the break of the foc's'le goes under in gray-green water level as a mill-race except where it spouts up above the donkey-engine and the stored derrick-booms. Forward there is nothing but this glare; aft, the interrupted wake drives far to leeward, a cut kite-string dropped across the seas. The sole thing that has any rest in the turmoil is the jewelled, unwinking eye of an albatross, who is beating across wind leisurely and unconcerned, almost within hand's touch. It is the monstrous egotism of that eye that makes the picture. By all the rules of art there should be a lighthouse or a harbour pier in the background to show that everything will end happily. But there is not, and the red eye does not care whether the thing beneath its still wings stays or staves.

The sister-panel hangs in the Indian Ocean and tells a story, but is none the worse for that. Here you have hot tropical sunlight and a foreshore clothed in stately palms running out into a still and steamy sea burnished steel blue. Along the foreshore, questing as a wounded beast quests for lair, hurries a loaded steamer never built for speed. Consequently, she tears and threshes the water to pieces, and piles it under her nose and cannot put it under her cleanly. Coir-coloured cargo bales are stacked round both masts, and her decks are crammed and double-crammed with dark-skinned passengers—from the foc's'le where they interfere with the crew to the stern where they hamper the wheel.

The funnel is painted blue on yellow, giving her a holiday air, a little out of keeping with the yellow and black cholera flag at her main. She dare not stop; she must not communicate with any one. There are leprous streaks of lime-wash trickling down her plates for a sign of this. So she threshes on down the glorious coast, she and her swarming passengers, with the sickness that destroyeth in the noonday eating out her heart.

Yet another, the pick of all the East rooms, before we have done with blue water. Most of the nations of the earth are at issue under a stretch of white awning above a crowded deck. The cause of the dispute, a deep copper bowl foil of rice and fried onions, is upset in the foreground. Malays, Lascars, Hindus, Chinese, Japanese, Burmans—the whole gamut of racetints, from saffron to tar-black—are twisting and writhing round it, while their vermilion, cobalt, amber, and emerald turbans and head-cloths are lying underfoot. Pressed against the yellow ochre of the iron bulwarks to left and right are frightened women and children in turquoise and isabella-coloured clothes. They are half protected by mounds of upset bedding, straw mats, red lacquer boxes, and plaited bamboo trunks, mixed up with tin plates, brass and copper *hukas* , silver opium pipes, Chinese playing cards, and properties enough to drive half-a-dozen artists wild. In the centre of the crowd of furious half-naked men, the fat bare back of a Burman, tattooed from collar-bone to waist-cloth with writhing patterns of red and blue devils, holds the eye first. It is a wicked back. Beyond it is the flicker of a Malay *kris* . A blue, red, and yellow macaw chained to a stanchion spreads his wings against the sun in an ecstasy of terror. Half-a-dozen red-gold pines and bananas have been knocked down from their ripening-places, and are lying between the feet of the fighters. One pine has rolled against the long brown fur of a muzzled bear. His owner, a bushy-bearded Hindu, kneels over the animal, his body-cloth thrown clear of a hard brown arm, his fingers ready to loose the muzzle-strap. The ship's cook, in blood-stained white, watches from the butcher's shop, and a black Zanzibari stoker grins through the bars of the engine-room-hatch, one ray of sun shining straight into his pink mouth. The officer of the watch, a red-whiskered man, is kneeling down on the bridge to peer through the railings, and is shifting a long, thin black revolver from his left hand to his right. The faithful sunlight that puts everything into place, gives his whiskers and the hair on the back of his tanned wrist just the colour of the copper pot, the bear's fur and the trampled pines. For the rest, there is the blue sea beyond the awnings.

Three years' hard work, beside the special knowledge of a lifetime, would be needed to copy—even to copy—this picture. Mr. So-and-so, R.A., could undoubtedly draw the bird; Mr. Such-another (equally R.A.) the bear; and scores of gentlemen the still life; but who would be the man to pull the whole thing together and make it the riotous, tossing cataract of colour and life that it is? And when it was done, some middle-aged person from the provinces, who had never seen a pineapple out of a plate, or a *kris* out of the South Kensington, would say that it did not remind him of something that it ought to remind him of, and therefore that it was bad. If the gallery could be bequeathed to the nation, something might, perhaps, be gained, but the nation would complain of the draughts and the absence of chairs. But no matter. In another world we shall see certain gentlemen set to tickle the backs of Circe's swine through all eternity. Also, they will have to tickle with their bare hands.

The Japanese rooms, visited and set in order for the second time, hold more pictures than could be described in a month; but most of them are small and, excepting always the light, within human compass. One, however, might be difficult. It was an unexpected gift, picked up in a Tokio bye-street after dark. Half the town was out for a walk, and all the people's clothes were indigo, and so were the shadows, and most of the paper-lanterns were drops of blood red. By the light of smoking oil-lamps people were selling flowers and shrubs—wicked little dwarf pines, stunted peach and plum trees, wisteria bushes clipped and twisted out of all likeness to wholesome plants, leaning and leering out of green-glaze pots. In the flickering of the yellow flames, these forced cripples and the yellow faces above them reeled to and fro fantastically all together. As the light steadied they would return to the pretence of being green things till a puff of the warm night wind among the flares set the whole line off again in a crazy dance of dwergs, their shadows capering on the house fronts behind them.

At a corner of a street, some rich men had got together and left unguarded all the gold, diamonds, and rubies of the East; but when you came near you saw that this treasure was only a gathering of goldfish in glass globes—yellow, white, and red fish, with from three to five forked tails apiece and eyes that bulged far beyond their heads. There were wooden pans full of tiny ruby fish, and little children with nets dabbled and shrieked in chase of some special beauty, and the frightened fish kicked up showers of little pearls with their tails. The children carried lanterns in the shape of small red paper fish bobbing at the end of slivers of bamboo, and these drifted through the crowd like a strayed constellation of baby stars. When the children stood at the edge of a canal and called down to unseen friends in boats the pink lights were all reflected orderly below. The light of the thousand small lights in the street went straight up into the darkness among the interlacing telegraph wires, and just at the edge of the shining haze, on a sort of pigeon-trap, forty feet above ground, sat a Japanese fireman, wrapped up in his cloak, keeping watch against fires. He looked unpleasantly like a Bulgarian atrocity or a Burmese 'deviation from the laws of humanity,' being very still and all huddled up in his roost. That was a superb picture and it arranged itself to admiration. Now, disregarding these things and others—wonders and miracles all—men are content to sit in studios and, by light that is not light, to fake subjects from pots and pans and rags and bricks that are called 'pieces of colour.' Their collection of rubbish costs in the end quite as much as a ticket, a first-class one, to new worlds where the 'props' are given away with the sunshine. To do anything because it is, or may not be, new on the market is wickedness that carries its own punishment; but surely there must be things in this world paintable other and beyond those that lie between the North Cape, say, and Algiers. For the sake of the pictures, putting aside the dear delight of the gamble, it might be worth while to venture out a little beyond the regular circle of subjects and—see what happens. If a man can draw one thing, it has been said, he can draw anything. At the most he can but fail, and there are several matters in the world worse than failure. Betting on a certainty, for instance, or playing with nicked cards is immoral, and secures expulsion from clubs. Keeping deliberately to one set line of work because you know you can do it and are certain to get money by so doing is, on the other hand, counted a virtue, and secures admission to clubs. There must be a middle way somewhere, as there must be somewhere an unmarried man with no position, reputation, or other vanity to lose, who most keenly wants to find out what his palette is set for in this life. He will pack his steamer-trunk and get into the open to wrestle with effects that he can never reproduce. All the same his will be a superb failure,

'CAPTAINS COURAGEOUS'

From Yokohama to Montreal is a long day's journey, and the forepart is uninviting. In three voyages out of five, the North Pacific, too big to lie altogether idle, too idle to get hands about the business of a storm, sulks and smokes like a chimney; the passengers fresh from Japan heat wither in the chill, and a clammy dew distils from the rigging. That gray monotony of sea is not at all homelike, being as yet new and not used to the procession of keels. It holds a very few pictures and the best of its stories—those relating to seal-poaching among the Kuriles and the Russian rookeries—are not exactly fit for publication. There is a man in Yokohama who in a previous life burned galleons with Drake. He is a gentleman adventurer of the largest and most resourceful—by instinct a carver of kingdoms, a ruler of men on the high seas, and an inveterate gambler against Death. Because he supplies nothing more than sealskins to the wholesale dealers at home, the fame of his deeds, his brilliant fights, his more brilliant escapes, and his most brilliant strategy will be lost among sixty-ton schooners, or told only in the mouths of drunken seamen whom none believe. Now there sits a great spirit under the palm trees of the Navigator Group, a thousand leagues to the south, and he, crowned with roses and laurels, strings together the pearls of those parts. When he has done with this down there perhaps he will turn to the Smoky Seas and the Wonderful Adventures of Captain—. Then there will be a tale to listen to.

But the first touch of dry land makes the sea and all upon it unreal. Five minutes after the traveller is on the C.P.R, train at Vancouver there is no romance of blue water, but another kind—the life of the train into which he comes to grow as into life aboard ship. A week on wheels turns a man into a part of the machine. He knows when the train will stop to water, wait for news of the trestle ahead, drop the dining-car, slip into a siding to let the West-bound mail go by, or yell through the thick night for an engine to help push up the bank. The snort, the snap and whine of the air-brakes have a meaning for him, and he learns to distinguish between noises—between the rattle of a loose lamp and the ugly rattle of small stones on a scarped embankment—between the 'Hoot! toot!' that scares wandering cows from the line, and the dry roar of the engine at the distance-signal. In England the railway came late into a settled country fenced round with the terrors of the law, and it has remained ever since just a little outside daily life—a thing to be respected. Here it strolls along, with its hands in its pockets and a straw in its mouth, on the heels of the rough-hewn trail or log road—a platformless, regulationless necessity; and it is treated even by sick persons and young children with a familiarity that sometimes affects the death-rate. There was a small maiden aged seven, who honoured our smoking compartment with her presence when other excitements failed, and it was she that said to the conductor, 'When do we change crews? I want to pick water-lilies—yellow ones.' A mere halt she knew would not suffice for her needs; but the regular fifteen-minute stop, when the red-painted tool-chest was taken off the rear car and a new gang came aboard. The big man bent down to little Impudence—'Want to pick lilies, eh? What would you do if the cars went on and took mama away, Sis?' 'Take the, next train,' she replied, 'and tell the conductor to send me to Brooklyn. I live there.' 'But s'pose he wouldn't?' 'He'd have to,' said Young America. 'I'd be a lost child.'

Now, from the province of Alberta to Brooklyn, U.S.A., may be three thousand miles. A great stretch of that distance is as new as the day before yesterday, and strewn with townships in every stage of growth from the city of one round house, two log huts, and a Chinese camp somewhere in the foot-hills of the Selkirks, to Winnipeg with her league-long main street and her warring newspapers. Just at present there is an epidemic of politics in Manitoba, and brass bands and notices of committee meetings are splashed about the towns. By reason of their closeness to the Stages they have caught the contagion of foul-mouthedness, and accusations of bribery, corruption, and evil-living are many. It is sweet to find a little baby-city, with only three men in it who can handle type, cursing and swearing across the illimitable levels for all the world as though it were a grown-up Christian centre.

All the new towns have their own wants to consider, and the first of these is a railway. If the town is on a line already, then a new line to tap the back country; but at all costs a line. For this it will sell its corrupted soul, and then be very indignant because the railway before which it has grovelled rides rough-shod over the place.

Each new town believes itself to be a possible Winnipeg until the glamour of the thing is a little worn off, and the local paper, sliding down the pole of Pride with the hind legs of despair, says defiantly: 'At least, a veterinary surgeon and a drug store would meet with encouragement in our midst, and it is a fact that five new buildings have been erected in our midst since the spring.' From a distance nothing is easier than to smile at this sort of thing, but he must have a cool head who can keep his pulse level when just such a wildcat town—ten houses, two churches, and a line of rails—gets 'on the boom,' The reader at home says, 'Yes, but it's all a lie.' It may be, but—did men lie about Denver, Leadville, Ballarat, Broken Hill, Portland, or Winnipeg twenty years ago—or Adelaide when town lots went begging within the memory of middle-aged men? Did they lie about Vancouver six years since, or Creede not twenty months gone? Hardly; and it is just this knowledge that leads the passer-by to give ear to the wildest statements of the wildest towns. Anything is possible, especially among the Rockies where the minerals lie over and above the mining towns, the centres of ranching country, and the supply towns to the farming districts. There are literally scores upon scores of lakelets in the hills, buried in woods now, that before twenty years are run will be crowded summer resorts. You in England have no idea of what 'summering' means in the States, and less of the amount of money that is spent on the yearly holiday. People have no more than just begun to discover the place called the Banff Hot Springs, two days west of Winnipeg. In a little time they will know half-a-dozen spots not a day's ride from Montreal, and it is along that line that money will be made. In those days, too, wheat will be grown for the English market four hundred miles north of the present fields on the west side; and British Columbia, perhaps the loveliest land in the world next to New Zealand, will have her own line of six thousand ton steamers to Australia, and the British investor will no longer throw away his money on hellicat South American republics, or give it as a hostage to the States. He will keep it in the family as a wise man should. Then the towns that are to-day the only names in the wilderness, yes, and some of those places marked on the map as Hudson Bay Ports, will be cities, because—but it is hopeless to make people understand that actually and indeed, we *do* possess an Empire of which Canada is only one portion—an Empire which is not bounded by election-returns on the North and Eastbourne riots on the South—an Empire that has not yet been scratched.

Let us return to the new towns. Three times within one year did fortune come knocking to the door of a man I know. Once at Seattle, when that town was a gray blur after a fire; once at Tacoma, in the days when the steam-tram ran off the rails twice a week; and once at Spokane Falls. But in the roar of the land-boom he did not hear her, and she went away leaving him only a tenderness akin to weakness for all new towns, and a desire, mercifully limited by lack of money, to gamble in every one of them. Of all the excitements that life offers there are few to be compared with the whirl of a red-hot boom; also it is strictly moral, because you *do* fairly earn your 'unearned increment' by labour and perspiration and sitting up far into the night—by working like a fiend, as all pioneers must do. And consider all that is in it! The headlong stampede to the new place; the money dashed down like counters for merest daily bread; the arrival of the piled cars whence the raw material of a city—men, lumber, and shingle—are shot on to the not yet nailed platform; the slashing out and pegging down of roads across the blank face of the wilderness; the heaving up amid shouts and yells of the city's one electric light—a raw sizzling arc atop of an unbarked pine pole; the sweating, jostling mob at the sale of town-lots; the roar of 'Let the woman have it!' that stops all bidding when the one other woman in the place puts her price on a plot; the packed real-estate offices; the real-estate agents themselves, lost novelists of prodigious imagination; the gorgeous pink and blue map of the town, hung up in the bar-room, with every railroad from Portland to Portland meeting in its heart; the misspelled curse against 'this dam hole in the ground' scrawled on the flank of a strayed freight-car by some man who had lost his money and gone away; the conferences at street corners of syndicates six hours established by men not twenty-five years old; the outspoken contempt for the next town, also 'on the boom,' and, therefore, utterly vile; the unceasing tramp of heavy feet on the board pavement, where stranger sometimes turns on stranger in an agony of conviction, and, shaking him by the shoulder, shouts in his ear, 'By G—d! Isn't it grand? Isn't it glorious? 'and last, the sleep of utterly worn-out men, three in each room of the shanty hotel: 'All meals two dollars. All drinks thirty-five cents. No washing done here. The manager not responsible for anything.' Does the bald catalogue of these recitals leave you cold? It is possible; but it is also possible after three days in a new town to set the full half of a truck-load of archbishops fighting for corner lots as they never fought for mitre or crozier. There is a contagion in a boom as irresistible as that of a panic in a theatre.

After a while things settle down, and then the carpenter, who is also an architect, can lay his bare arms across the bar and sell them to the highest bidder, for the houses are coming up like toadstools after rain. The men who do not build cheer those who do, in that building means backing your belief in your town—yours to you and peculiarly. Confound all other towns whatsoever. Behind the crowd of business men the weekly town paper plays as a stockwhip plays on a mob of cattle. There is honour, heaped, extravagant, imperial for the good—the employer of labour, the builder of stores, the spender of money; there is abuse, savage and outrageous, for the bad, the man who 'buys out of the town,' the man who intends to go, the sitter on the fence; with persuasion and invitation in prose, verse, and zincograph for all that outside world which prefers to live in cities other than Ours.

Now the editor, as often as not, begins as a mercenary and ends as a patriot. This, too, is all of a piece with human nature. A few years later, if Providence is good, comes the return for judicious investment. Perhaps the town has stood the test of boom, and that which was clapboard is now Milwaukee brick or dressed stone, vile in design but permanent. The shanty hotel is the Something House, with accommodation for two hundred guests. The manager who served you in his shirt-sleeves as his own hotel clerk, is gorgeous in broadcloth, and needs to be reminded of the first meeting. Suburban villas more or less adorn the flats, from which the liveliest fancy (and fancy was free in the early days) hung back. Horse-cars jingle where the prairie schooner used to stick fast in the mud-hole, scooped to that end, opposite the saloon; and there is a Belt Electric Service paying fabulous dividends. Then, do you, feeling older than Methuselah and twice as important, go forth and patronise things in general, while the manager tells you exactly what sort of millionaire you would have been if you had 'stayed by the town.'

Or else—the bottom has tumbled out of the boom, and the town new made is dead—dead as a young man's corpse laid out in the morning.

Success was not justified by success. Of ten thousand not three hundred remain, and these live in huts on the outskirts of the brick streets. The hotel, with its suites of musty rooms, is a big tomb; the factory chimneys are cold; the villas have no glass in them, and the fire-weed glows in the centre of the driveways, mocking the arrogant advertisements in the empty shops. There is nothing to do except to catch trout in the stream that was to have been defiled by the city sewage. A two-pounder lies fanning himself just in the cool of the main culvert, where the alders have crept up to the city wall. You pay your money and, more or less, you take your choice.

By the time that man has seen these things and a few others that go with a boom he may say that he has lived, and talk with his enemies in the gate. He has heard the Arabian Nights retold and knows the inward kernel of that romance, which some? little folk say is vanished. Here they lie in their false teeth, for Cortes is not dead, nor Drake, and Sir Philip Sidney dies every few months if you know where to look. The adventurers and captains courageous of old have only changed their dress a little and altered their employment to suit the world in which they move. Clive came down from Lobengula's country a few months ago protesting that there was an empire there, and finding very few that believed. Hastings studied a map of South Africa in a corrugated iron hut at Johannesburg ten years ago. Since then he has altered the map considerably to the advantage of the Empire, but the heart of the Empire is set on ballot-boxes and small lies. The illustrious Don Quixote to-day lives on the north coast of Australia where he has found the treasure of a sunken Spanish galleon. Now and again he destroys black fellows who hide under his bed to spear him. Young Hawkins, with a still younger Boscawen for his second, was till last year chasing slave-dhows round Tajurrah; they have sent him now to the Zanzibar coast to be grilled into an admiral; and the valorous Sandoval has been holding the 'Republic' of Mexico by the throat any time these fourteen years gone. The others, big men all and not very much afraid of responsibility, are selling horses, breaking trails, drinking sangaree, running railways beyond the timberline, swimming rivers, blowing up tree-stumps, and making cities where no cities were, in all the five quarters of the world. Only people will not believe this when you tell them. They are too near things and a great deal too well fed. So they say of the most cold-blooded realism: 'This is romance. How interesting!' And of over-handled, thumb-marked realism: 'This is indeed romance!' It is the next century that, looking over its own, will see the heroes of our time clearly.

Meantime this earth of ours—we hold a fair slice of it so far—is full of wonders and miracles and mysteries and marvels, and, in default, it is good to go up and down seeing and hearing tell of them all.

ON ONE SIDE ONLY

NEW OXFORD, U.S.A., *June-July* 1892.

'The truth is,' said the man in the train, 'that we live in a tropical country for three months of the year, only we won't recognise. Look at this.' He handed over a long list of deaths from heat that enlivened the newspapers. All the cities where men live at breaking-strain were sending in their butcher-bills, and the papers of the cities, themselves apostles of the Gospel of Rush, were beseeching their readers to keep cool and not to overwork themselves while the hot wave was upon them. The rivers were patched and barred with sun-dried pebbles; the logs and loggers were drought-bound somewhere up the Connecticut; and the grass at the side of the track was burned in a hundred places by the sparks from locomotives. Men—hatless, coatless, and gasping—lay in the shade of that station where only a few months ago the glass stood at 30 below zero. Now the readings were 98 degrees in the shade. Main Street—do you remember Main Street of a little village locked up in the snow this spring?[1]—had given up the business of life, and an American flag with some politician's name printed across the bottom hung down across the street as stiff as a board. There were men with fans and alpaca coats curled up in splint chairs in the verandah of the one hotel—among them an ex-President of the United States. He completed the impression that the furniture of the entire country had been turned out of doors for summer cleaning in the absence of all the inhabitants. Nothing looks so hopelessly 'ex' as a President 'returned to stores,' The stars and stripes signified that the Presidential Campaign had opened in Main Street—opened and shut up again. Politics evaporate at summer heat when all hands are busy with the last of the hay, and, as the formers put it, 'Vermont's bound to go Republican.' The custom of the land is to drag the scuffle and dust of an election over several months—to the improvement of business and manners; but the noise of that war comes faintly up the valley of the Connecticut and is lost among the fiddling of the locusts. Their music puts, as it were, a knife edge upon the heat of the day. In truth, it is a tropical country for the time being. Thunder-storms prowl and growl round the belted hills,

---

[1] See 'In Sight of Monadnock.'

spit themselves away in a few drops of rain, and leave the air more dead than before. In the woods, where even the faithful springs are beginning to run low, the pines and balsams have thrown out all their fragrance upon the heat and wait for the wind to bring news of the rain. The clematis, wild carrot, and all the gipsy-flowers camped by sufferance between fence line and road net are masked in white dust, and the golden-rod of the pastures that are burned to flax-colour burns too like burnished brass. A pillar of dust on the long hog-back of the road across the hills shows where a team is lathering between farms, and the roofs of the wooden houses flicker in the haze of their own heat. Overhead the chicken-hawk is the only creature at work, and his shrill kite-like call sends the gaping chickens from the dust-bath in haste to their mothers. The red squirrel as usual feigns business of importance among the butternuts, but this is pure priggishness. When the passer-by is gone he ceases chattering and climbs back to where the little breezes can stir his tail-plumes. From somewhere under the lazy fold of a meadow comes the drone of a mowing-machine among the hay—its *whurr-oo* and the grunt of the tired horses.

Houses are only meant to eat and sleep in. The rest of life is lived at full length in the verandah. When traffic is brisk three whole teams will pass that verandah in one day, and it is necessary to exchange news about the weather and the prospects for oats. When oats are in there will be slack time on the farm, and the farmers will seriously think of doing the hundred things that they have let slide during the summer. They will undertake this and that, 'when they get around to it.' The phrase translated is the exact equivalent to the *mañana* of the Spaniard, the *kul hojaiga* of Upper India, the *yuroshii* of the Japanese, and the long drawled *taihod* of the Maori. The only person who 'gets around' in this weather is the summer boarder—the refugee from the burning cities of the Plain, and she is generally a woman. She walks, and botanizes, and kodaks, and strips the bark off the white birch to make blue-ribboned waste-paper baskets, and the farmer regards her with wonder. More does he wonder still at the city clerk in a blazer, who has two weeks' holiday in the year and, apparently, unlimited money, which he earns in the easiest possible way by 'sitting at a desk and writing,' The farmer's wife sees the fashions of the summer boarder, and between them man and woman get a notion of the beauties of city life for which their children may live to blame them. The blazer and the town-made gown are innocent recruiting sergeants for the city brigades; and since one man's profession is ever a mystery to his fellow, blazer and gown believe that the farmer must be happy and content. A summer resort is one of the thousand windows whence to watch the thousand aspects of life in the Atlantic States. Remember that between June and September it is the desire of all who can to get away from the big cities—not on account of wantonness, as people leave London—but because of actual heat. So they get away in their millions with their millions—the wives of the rich men for five clear months, the others for as long as they can; and, like drawing like, they make communities set by set, breed by breed, division by division, over the length and breadth of the land—

from Maine and the upper reaches of the Saguenay, through the mountains and hot springs of half-a-dozen interior States, out and away to Sitka in steamers. Then they spend money on hotel bills, among ten thousand farms, on private companies who lease and stock land for sporting purposes, on yachts and canoes, bicycles, rods, châlets, cottages, reading circles, camps, tents, and all the luxuries they know. But the luxury of rest most of them do not know; and the telephone and telegraph are faithfully dragged after them, lest their men-folk should for a moment forget the ball and chain at foot.

For sadness with laughter at bottom there are few things to compare with the sight of a coat-less, muddy-booted, millionaire, his hat adorned with trout-flies, and a string of small fish in his hand, clawing wildly at the telephone of some back-of-beyond 'health resort.' Thus:

'Hello! Hello! Yes. Who's there? Oh, all right. Go ahead. Yes, it's me! Hey, what? Repeat. Sold for *how* much? Forty-four and a half? Repeat. No! I *told* you to hold on. What? What? *Who* bought at that? Say, hold a minute. Cable the other side. No. Hold on. I'll come down. (*Business with watch* .) Tell Schaefer I'll see him to-morrow.' (*Over his shoulder to his wife, who wears half-hoop diamond rings at* 10 A.M.) 'Lizzie, where's my grip? I've got to go down.'

And he goes down to eat in a hotel and sleep in his shut-up house. Men are as scarce at most of the summer places as they are in Indian hill-stations in late April. The women tell you that they can't get away, and if they did they would only be miserable to get back. Now whether this wholesale abandonment of husbands by wives is wholesome let those who know the beauties of the Anglo-Indian system settle for themselves.

That both men and women need rest very badly a glance at the crowded hotel tables makes plain—so plain, indeed, that the foreigner who has not been taught that fuss and worry are in themselves honourable wishes sometimes he could put the whole unrestful crowd to sleep for seventeen hours a day. I have inquired of not less than five hundred men and women in various parts of the States why they broke down and looked so gash. And the men said: 'If you don't keep up with the procession in America you are left'; and the women smiled an evil smile and answered that no outsider yet had discovered the real cause of their worry and strain, or why their lives were arranged to work with the largest amount of friction in the shortest given time. Now, the men can be left to their own folly, but the cause of the women's trouble has been revealed to me. It is the thing called 'Help' which is no help. In the multitude of presents that the American man has given to the American woman (for details see daily papers) he has forgotten or is unable to give her good servants, and that sordid trouble runs equally through the household of the millionaire or the flat of the small city man. 'Yes, it's easy enough to laugh,' said one woman passionately, 'we are worn out, and our children are worn out too, and we're always worrying, I know it.

What can we do? If you stay here you'll know that this is the land of all the luxuries and none of the necessities. You'll know and then you won't laugh. You'll know why women are said to take their husbands to boarding-houses and never have homes. You'll know what an Irish Catholic means. The men won't get up and attend to these things, but *we* would. If *we* had female suffrage, we'd shut the door to *all* the Irish and throw it open to *all* the Chinese, and let the women have a little protection.' It was the cry of a soul worn thin with exasperation, but it was truth. To-day I do not laugh any more at the race that depends on inefficient helot races for its inefficient service. When next you, housekeeping in England, differ with the respectable, amiable, industrious sixteen-pound maid, who wears a cap and says 'Ma'am,' remember the pauper labour of America—the wives of the sixty million kings who have no subjects. No man could get a thorough knowledge of the problem in one lifetime, but he could guess at the size and the import of it after he has descended into the arena and wrestled with the Swede and the Dane and the German and the unspeakable Celt. Then he perceives how good for the breed it must be that a man should thresh himself to pieces in naked competition with his neighbour while his wife struggles unceasingly over primitive savagery in the kitchen. In India sometimes when a famine is at hand the life of the land starts up before your eyes in all its bareness and bitter stress. Here, in spite of the trimmings and the frillings, it refuses to be subdued and the clamour and the clatter of it are loud above all other sounds—as sometimes the thunder of disorganised engines stops conversations along the decks of a liner, and in the inquiring eyes of the passengers you read the question—'This thing is made and paid to bear us to port quietly. Why does it not do so?' Only here, the rattle of the badly-put-together machine is always in the ears, though men and women run about with labour-saving appliances and gospels of 'power through repose,' tinkering and oiling and making more noise. The machine is new. Some day it is going to be the finest machine in the world. To the ranks of the amateur artificers, therefore, are added men with notebooks tapping at every nut and bolthead, fiddling with the glands, registering revolutions, and crying out from time to time that this or that is or is not 'distinctively American.' Meantime, men and women die unnecessarily in the wheels, and they are said to have fallen 'in the battle of life.'

The God Who sees us all die knows that there is far too much of that battle, but we do not, and so continue worshipping the knife that cuts and the wheel that breaks us, as blindly as the outcast sweeper worships Lal-Beg the Glorified Broom that is the incarnation of his craft. But the sweeper has sense enough not to kill himself, and to be proud of it, with sweeping.

A foreigner can do little good by talking of these things; for the same lean dry blood that breeds the fever of unrest breeds also the savage parochial pride that squeals under a steady stare or a pointed finger. Among themselves the people of the Eastern cities admit that they and their womenfolk overwork grievously and go to pieces very readily, and that the consequences for the young stock are unpleasant indeed; but before the stranger they prefer to talk about the future of their mighty continent (which has nothing to do with the case) and to call aloud on Baal of the Dollars—to catalogue their lines, mines, telephones, banks, and cities, and all the other shells, buttons, and counters that they have made their Gods over them. Now a nation does not progress upon its brain-pan, as some books would have us believe, but upon its belly as did the Serpent of old; and in the very long run the work of the brain comes to be gathered in by a slow-footed breed that have unimaginative stomachs and the nerves that know their place.

All this is very consoling from the alien's point of view. He perceives, with great comfort, that out of strain is bred impatience in the shape of a young bundle of nerves, who is about as undisciplined an imp as the earth can show. Out of impatience, grown up, habituated to violent and ugly talk, and the impatience and recklessness of his neighbours, is begotten lawlessness, encouraged by laziness and suppressed by violence when it becomes insupportable. Out of lawlessness is bred rebellion (and that fruit has been tasted once already), and out of rebellion comes profit to those who wait. He hears of the power of the People who, through rank slovenliness, neglect to see that their laws are soberly enforced from the beginning; and these People, not once or twice in a year, but many times within a month, go out in the open streets and, with a maximum waste of power and shouting, strangle other people with ropes. They are, he is told, law-abiding citizens who have executed 'the will of the people'; which is as though a man should leave his papers unsorted for a year and then smash his desk with an axe, crying, 'Am I not orderly?' He hears lawyers, otherwise sane and matured, defend this pig-jobbing murder on the grounds that 'the People stand behind the Law'—the law that they never administered. He sees a right, at present only half—but still half—conceded to anticipate the law in one's own interests; and nervous impatience (always nerves) forejudging the suspect in gaol, the prisoner in the dock, and the award between nation and nation ere it is declared. He knows that the maxim in London, Yokohama, and Hongkong in doing business with the pure-bred American is to keep him waiting, for the reason that forced inaction frets the man to a lather, as standing in harness frets a half-broken horse. He comes across a thousand little peculiarities of speech, manner, and thought—matters of nerve and stomach developed by everlasting friction—and they are all just the least little bit in the world lawless. No more so than the restless clicking together of horns in a herd of restless cattle, but certainly no less. They are all good—good for those who wait.

On the other hand, to consider the matter more humanly, there are thousands of delightful men and women going to pieces for the pitiful reason that if they do not keep up with the procession, 'they are left.' And they are left—in clothes that have no back to them, among mounds of smilax. And young men—chance-met in the streets, talk to you about their nerves which are things no young man should know anything about; and the friends of your friends go down with nervous prostration, and the people overheard in the trains talk about their nerves and the nerves of their relatives; and the little children must needs have their nerves attended to ere their milk-teeth are shed, and the middle-aged women and the middle-aged men have got them too, and the old men lose the dignity of their age in an indecent restlessness, and the advertisements in the papers go to show that this sweeping list is no lie. Atop of the fret and the stampede, the tingling self-consciousness of a new people makes them take a sort of perverted pride in the futile racket that sends up the death-rate—a child's delight in the blaze and the dust of the March of Progress. Is it not 'distinctively American'? It is, and it is not. If the cities were all America, as they pretend, fifty years would see the March of Progress brought to a standstill, as a locomotive is stopped by heated bearings....

Down in the meadow the mowing-machine has checked, and the horses are shaking themselves. The last of the sunlight leaves the top of Monadnock, and four miles away Main Street lights her electric lamps. It is band-night in Main Street, and the folks from Putney, from Marlboro', from Guildford, and even New Fane will drive in their well-filled waggons to hear music and look at the Ex-President. Over the shoulder of the meadow two men come up very slowly, their hats off and their arms swinging loosely at their sides. They do not hurry, they have not hurried, and they never will hurry, for they are of country—bankers of the flesh and blood of the ever bankrupt cities. Their children may yet be pale summer boarders; as the boarders, city-bred weeds, may take over their farms. From the plough to the pavement goes man, but to the plough he returns at last.

'Going to supper?'

'Ye-ep,' very slowly across the wash of the uncut grass.

'Say, that corncrib wants painting.'

''Do that when we get around to it.'

They go off through the dusk, without farewell or salutation steadily as their own steers. And there are a few millions of them—unhandy men to cross in their ways, set, silent, indirect in speech, and as impenetrable as that other Eastern fanner who is the bedrock of another land. They do not appear in the city papers, they are not much heard in the streets, and they tell very little in the outsider's estimate of America.

And *they* are the American.

LEAVES FROM A WINTER NOTE-BOOK

(1895)

We had walked abreast of the year from the very beginning, and that was when the first blood-root came up between the patches of April snow, while yet the big drift at the bottom of the meadow held fast. In the shadow of the woods and under the blown pine-needles, clots of snow lay till far into May, but neither the season nor the flowers took any note of them, and, before we were well sure Winter had gone, the lackeys of my Lord Baltimore in their new liveries came to tell us that Summer was in the valley, and please might they nest at the bottom of the garden?

Followed, Summer, angry, fidgety, and nervous, with the corn and tobacco to ripen in five short months, the pastures to reclothe, and the fallen leaves to hide away under new carpets. Suddenly, in the middle of her work, on a stuffy-still July day, she called a wind out of the Northwest, a wind blown under an arch of steel-bellied clouds, a wicked bitter wind with a lacing of hail to it, a wind that came and was gone in less than ten minutes, but blocked the roads with fallen trees, toppled over a barn, and—blew potatoes out of the ground! When that was done, a white cloud shaped like a dumb-bell whirled down the valley across the evening blue, roaring and twisting and twisting and roaring all alone by itself. A West Indian hurricane could not have been quicker on its feet than our little cyclone, and when the house rose a-tiptoe, like a cockerel in act to crow, and a sixty-foot elm went by the board, and that which had been a dusty road became a roaring torrent all in three minutes, we felt that the New England summer had creole blood in her veins. She went away, red-faced and angry to the last, slamming all the doors of the hills behind her, and Autumn, who is a lady, took charge.

No pen can describe the turning of the leaves—the insurrection of the tree-people against the waning year. A little maple began it, flaming blood-red of a sudden where he stood against the dark green of a pine-belt. Next morning there was an answering signal from the swamp where the sumacs grow. Three days later, the hill-sides as far as the eye could range were afire, and the roads paved, with crimson and gold.

Then a wet wind blew, and ruined all the uniforms of that gorgeous army; and the oaks, who had held themselves in reserve, buckled on their dull and bronzed cuirasses and stood it out stiffly to the last blown leaf, till nothing remained but pencil-shading of bare boughs, and one could see into the most private heart of the woods.

Frost may be looked for till the middle of May and after the middle of September, so Summer has little time for enamel-work or leaf-embroidery. Her sisters bring the gifts—Spring, wind-flowers, Solomon's-Seal, Dutchman's-breeches, Quaker-ladies, and trailing arbutus, that smells as divinely as the true May. Autumn has golden-rod and all the tribe of asters, pink, lilac, and creamy white, by the double armful. When these go the curtain comes down, and whatever Powers shift the scenery behind, work without noise. In tropic lands you can hear the play of growth and decay at the back of the night-silences. Even in England the tides of the winter air have a set and a purpose; but here they are dumb altogether. The very last piece of bench-work this season was the trailed end of a blackberry-vine, most daringly conventionalised in hammered iron, flung down on the frosty grass an instant before people came to look. The blue bloom of the furnace was still dying along the central rib, and the side-sprays were cherry red, even as they had been lifted from the charcoal. It was a detail, evidently, of some invisible gate in the woods; but we never found that workman, though he had left the mark of his cloven foot as plainly as any strayed deer. In a week the heavy frosts with scythes and hammers had slashed and knocked down all the road-side growth and the kindly bushes that veil the drop off the unfenced track.

There the seasons stopped awhile. Autumn was gone, Winter was not. We had Time dealt out to us—mere, clear, fresh Time—grace-days to enjoy. The white wooden farm-houses were banked round two feet deep with dried leaves or earth, and the choppers went out to get ready next year's stores of wood. Now, chopping is an art, and the chopper in all respects an artist. He makes his own axe-helve, and for each man there is but one perfect piece of wood in all the world. This he never finds, but the likest substitute is trimmed and balanced and poised to that ideal. One man I know has evolved very nearly the weapon of Umslopogaas. It is almost straight, lapped at the butt with leather, amazingly springy, and carries a two-edged blade for splitting and chopping. If his Demon be with him—and what artist can answer for all his moods?—he will cause a tree to fall upon any stick or stone that you choose, uphill or down, to the right or to the left. Artist-like, however, he explains that that is nothing. Any fool can play with a tree in the open, but it needs the craftsman to bring a tree down in thick timber and do no harm. To see an eighty-foot maple, four feet in the butt, dropped, deftly as a fly is cast, in the only place where it will not outrage the feelings and swipe off the tops of fifty juniors, is a revelation. White pine, hemlock, and spruce share this country with maples, black and white birches, and beech. Maple seems to have few preferences, and the white birches straggle and shiver on the outskirts of every camp; but the pines hold together in solid regiments, sending out skirmishers to invade a neglected pasture on the first opportunity. There is no overcoat warmer than the pines in a gale when the woods for miles round are singing like cathedral organs, and the first snow of the year powders the rock-ledges.

The mosses and lichens, green, sulphur, and amber, stud the copper floor of needles, where the feathery ground-pine runs aimlessly to and fro along the ground, spelling out broken words of half-forgotten charms. There are checker-berries on the outskirts of the wood, where the partridge (he is a ruffed grouse really) dines, and by the deserted logging-roads toadstools of all colours sprout on the decayed stumps. Wherever a green or blue rock lifts from the hillside, the needles have been packed and matted round its base, till, when the sunshine catches them, stone and setting together look no meaner than turquoise in dead gold. The woods are full of colour, belts and blotches of it, the colours of the savage—red, yellow, and blue. Yet in their lodges there is very little life, for the wood-people do not readily go into the shadows. The squirrels have their business among the beeches and hickories by the road-side, where they can watch the traffic and talk. We have no gray ones hereabouts (they are good to eat and suffer for it), but five reds live in a hickory hard by, and no weather puts them to sleep. The woodchuck, a marmot and a strategist, makes his burrow in the middle of a field, where he must see you ere you see him. Now and again a dog manages to cut him off his base, and the battle is worth crossing fields to watch. But the woodchuck turned in long ago, and will not be out till April. The coon lives—well, no one seems to know particularly where Brer Coon lives, but when the Hunter's Moon is large and full he descends into the corn-lands, and men chase him with dogs for his fur, which makes the finest kind of overcoat, and his flesh, which tastes like chicken. He cries at night sorrowfully as though a child were lost.

They seem to kill, for one reason or other, everything that moves in this land. Hawks, of course; eagles for their rarity; foxes for their pelts; red-shouldered blackbirds and Baltimore orioles because they are pretty, and the other small things for sport—French fashion. You can get a rifle of a kind for twelve shillings, and if your neighbour be fool enough to post notices forbidding 'hunting' and fishing, you naturally seek his woods. So the country is very silent and unalive.

There are, however, bears within a few miles, as you will see from this notice, picked up at the local tobacconist's:

JOHNNY GET YOUR GUN! BEAR HUNT!

As bears are too numerous in the town of Peltyville Corners, Vt., the hunters of the surrounding towns are invited to participate in a grand hunt to be held on Blue Mountains in the town of Peltyville Corners, Vt., Wednesday, Nov. 8th, if pleasant. If not, first fine day. Come one, come all!

They went, but it was the bear that would not participate. The notice was printed at somebody's Electric Print Establishment. Queer mixture, isn't it?

The bear does not run large as a rule, but he has a weakness for swine and calves which brings punishment. Twelve hours' rail and a little marching take you up to the moose-country; and twenty-odd miles from here as the crow flies you come to virgin timber, where trappers live, and where there is a Lost Pond that many have found once but can never find again.

Men, who are of one blood with sheep, have followed their friends and the railway along the river valleys where the towns are. Across the hills the inhabitants are few, and, outside their State, little known. They withdraw from society in November if they live on the uplands, coming down in May as the snow gives leave. Not much more than a generation ago these farms made their own clothes, soap, and candles, and killed their own meat thrice a year, beef, veal, and pig, and sat still between-times. Now they buy shop-made clothes, patent soaps, and kerosene; and it is among their tents that the huge red and gilt Biographies of Presidents, and the twenty-pound family Bibles, with illuminated marriage-registers, mourning-cards, baptismal certificates, and hundreds of genuine steel-engravings, sell best. Here, too, off the main-travelled roads, the wandering quack—Patent Electric Pills, nerve cures, etc.—divides the field with the seed and fruit man and the seller of cattle-boluses. They dose themselves a good deal, I fancy, for it is a poor family that does not know all about nervous prostration. So the quack drives a pair of horses and a gaily-painted waggon with a hood, and sometimes takes his wife with him. Once only have I met a pedlar afoot. He was an old man, shaken with palsy, and he pushed a thing exactly like a pauper's burial-cart, selling pins, tape, scents, and flavourings. You helped yourself, for his hands had no direction, and he told a long tale in which the deeding away of a farm to one of his family was mixed up with pride at the distances he still could cover daily. As much as six miles sometimes. He was no Lear, as the gift of the farm might suggest, but sealed of the tribe of the Wandering Jew—a tremulous old giddy-gaddy. There are many such rovers, gelders of colts and the like, who work a long beat, south to Virginia almost, and north to the frontier, paying with talk and gossip for their entertainment.

Yet tramps are few, and that is well, for the American article answers almost exactly to the vagrant and criminal tribes of India, being a predatory ruffian who knows too much to work. 'Bad place to beg in after dark—on a farm—very—is Vermont. Gypsies pitch their camp by the river in the spring, and cooper horses in the manner of their tribe. They have the gypsy look and some of the old gypsy names, but say that they are largely mixed with Gentile blood.

Winter has chased all these really interesting people south, and in a few weeks, if we have anything of a snow, the back farms will be unvisited save by the doctor's hooded sleigh. It is no child's play to hold a practice here through the winter months, when the drifts are really formed, and a pair can drop in up to their saddle-pads. Four horses a day some of them use, and use up—for they are good men.

Now in the big silence of the snow is born, perhaps, not a little of that New England conscience which her children write about. There is much time to think, and thinking is a highly dangerous business. Conscience, fear, undigested reading, and, it may be, not too well cooked food, have full swing. A man, and more particularly a woman, can easily hear strange voices—the Word of the Lord rolling between the dead hills; may see visions and dream dreams; get revelations and an outpouring of the spirit, and end (such things have been) lamentably enough in those big houses by the Connecticut River which have been tenderly christened The Retreat. Hate breeds as well as religion—the deep, instriking hate between neighbours, that is born of a hundred little things added up, brooded over, and hatched by the stove when two or three talk together in the long evenings. It would be very interesting to get the statistics of revivals and murders, and find how many of them have been committed in the spring. But for undistracted people winter is one long delight of the eye. In other lands one knows the snow as a nuisance that comes and goes, and is sorely man-handled and messed at the last. Here it lies longer on the ground than any crop—from November to April sometimes—and for three months life goes to the tune of sleigh-bells, which are not, as a Southern visitor once hinted, ostentation, but safeguards. The man who drives without them is not loved. The snow is a faithful barometer, foretelling good sleighing or stark confinement to barracks. It is all the manure the stony pastures receive; it cloaks the ground and prevents the frost bursting pipes; it is the best—I had almost written the only—road-maker in the States. On the other side it can rise up in the night and bid the people sit still as the Egyptians. It can stop mails; wipe out all time-tables; extinguish the lamps of twenty towns, and kill man within sight of his own door-step or hearing of his cattle unfed. No one who has been through even so modified a blizzard as New England can produce talks lightly of the snow. Imagine eight-and-forty hours of roaring wind, the thermometer well down towards zero, scooping and gouging across a hundred miles of newly fallen snow. The air is full of stinging shot, and at ten yards the trees are invisible. The foot slides on a reef, polished and black as obsidian, where the wind has skinned an exposed corner of road down to the dirt ice of early winter. The next step ends hip-deep and over, for here an unseen wall is banking back the rush of the singing drifts. A scarped slope rises sheer across the road. The wind shifts a point or two, and all sinks down, like sand in the hour-glass, leaving a pot-hole of whirling whiteness. There is a lull, and you can see the surface of the fields settling furiously in one direction—a tide that spurts from between the tree-boles. The hollows of the pasture fill while you watch; empty, fill, and discharge anew. The rock-ledges show the bare flank of a storm-chased liner for a moment, and whitening, duck under. Irresponsible snow-devils dance by the lee of a barn where three gusts meet, or stagger out into the open till they are cut down by the main wind. At the worst of the storm there is neither Heaven nor Earth, but only a swizzle into which a man may be brewed. Distances grow to nightmare scale, and that which in the summer was no more than a minute's bare-headed run, is half an hour's gasping struggle, each foot won between the lulls. Then do the heavy-timbered barns talk like ships in a cross-sea, beam working against beam. The winter's hay is ribbed over with long lines of snow dust blown between the boards, and far below in the byre the oxen clash their horns and moan uneasily.

The next day is blue, breathless, and most utterly still. The farmers shovel a way to their beasts, bind with chains their large ploughshares to their heaviest wood-sled and take of oxen as many as Allah has given them. These they drive, and the dragging share makes a furrow in which a horse can walk, and the oxen, by force of repeatedly going in up to their bellies, presently find foothold. The finished road is a deep double gutter between three-foot walls of snow, where, by custom, the heavier vehicle has the right of way. The lighter man when he turns out must drop waist-deep and haul his unwilling beast into the drift, leaving Providence to steady the sleigh.

In the towns, where they choke and sputter and gasp, the big snow turns to horsepondine. With us it stays still: but wind, sun, and rain get to work upon it, lest the texture and colour should not change daily. Rain makes a granulated crust over all, in which white shagreen the trees are faintly reflected. Heavy mists go up and down, and create a sort of mirage, till they settle and pack round the iron-tipped hills, and then you know how the moon must look to an inhabitant of it. At twilight, again, the beaten-down ridges and laps and folds of the uplands take on the likeness of wet sand—some huge and melancholy beach at the world's end—and when day meets night it is all goblin country. To westward; the last of the spent day—rust-red and pearl, illimitable levels of shore waiting for the tide to turn again. To eastward, black night among the valleys, and on the rounded hill slopes a hard glaze that is not so much light as snail-slime from the moon. Once or twice perhaps in the winter the Northern Lights come out between the moon and the sun, so that to the two unearthly lights is added the leap and flare of the Aurora Borealis.

In January or February come the great ice-storms, when every branch, blade, and trunk is coated with frozen rain, so that you can touch nothing truly. The spikes of the pines are sunk into pear-shaped crystals, and each fence-post is miraculously hilted with diamonds. If you bend a twig, the icing cracks like varnish, and a half-inch branch snaps off at the lightest tap. If wind and sun open the day together, the eye cannot look steadily at the splendour of this jewelry. The woods are full of the clatter of arms; the ringing of bucks' horns in flight; the stampede of mailed feet up and down the glades; and a great dust of battle is puffed out into the open, till the last of the ice is beaten away and the cleared branches take up their regular chant.

Again the mercury drops twenty and more below zero, and the very trees swoon. The snow turns to French chalk, squeaking under the heel, and their breath cloaks the oxen in rime. At night a tree's heart will break in him with a groan. According to the books, the frost has split something, but it is a fearful sound, this grunt as of a man stunned.

Winter that is winter in earnest does not allow cattle and horses to play about the fields, so everything comes home; and since no share can break ground to any profit for some five months, there would seem to be very little to do. As a matter of fact, country interests at all seasons are extensive and peculiar, and the day is not long enough for them when you take out that time which a self-respecting man needs to turn himself round in. Consider! The solid undisturbed hours stand about one like ramparts. At a certain time the sun will rise. At another hour, equally certain, he will set. This much we know. Why, in the name of Reason, therefore, should we vex ourselves with vain exertions? An occasional visitor from the Cities of the Plains comes up panting to do things. He is set down to listen to the normal beat of his own heart—a sound that very few men have heard. In a few days, when the lather of impatience has dried off, he ceases to talk of 'getting there' or 'being left.' He does not desire to accomplish matters 'right away,' nor does he look at his watch from force of habit, but keeps it where it should be—in his stomach. At the last he goes back to his beleaguered city, unwillingly, partially civilised, soon to be resavaged by the clash of a thousand wars whose echo does not reach here.

The air which kills germs dries out the very newspapers. They might be of to-morrow or a hundred years ago. They have nothing to do with to-day—the long, full, sunlit to-day. Our interests are not on the same scale as theirs, perhaps, but much more complex. The movement of a foreign power—an alien sleigh on this Pontic shore—must be explained and accounted for, or this public's heart will burst with unsatisfied curiosity. If it be Buck Davis, with the white mare that he traded his colt for, and the practically new sleigh-robe that he bought at the Sewell auction, *why* does Buck Davis, who lives on the river flats, cross our hills, unless Murder Hollow be blockaded with snow, or unless he has turkeys for sale? *But* Buck Davis with turkeys would surely have stopped here, unless he were selling a large stock in town. A wail from the sacking at the back of the sleigh tells the tale. It is a winter calf, and Buck Davis is going to sell it for one dollar to the Boston Market where it will be turned into potted chicken. This leaves the mystery of his change of route unexplained. After two days' sitting on tenter-hooks it is discovered, obliquely, that Buck went to pay a door-yard call on Orson Butler, who lives on the saeter where the wind and the bald granite scaurs fight it out together. Kirk Demming had brought Orson news of a fox at the back of Black Mountain, and Orson's eldest son, going to Murder Hollow with wood for the new barn floor that the widow Amidon is laying down, told Buck that he might as well come round to talk to his father about the pig. *But* old man Butler meant fox-hunting from the first, and what he wanted to do was to borrow Buck's dog, who had been duly brought over with the calf, and left on the mountain. No old man Butler did *not* go hunting alone, but waited till Buck came back from town. Buck sold the calf for a dollar and a quarter and not for seventy-five cents as was falsely asserted by interested parties. *Then* the two went after the fox together. This much learned, everybody breathes freely, if life has not been complicated in the meantime by more strange counter-marchings.

Five or six sleighs a day we can understand, if we know why they are abroad; but any metropolitan rush of traffic disturbs and excites.

LETTERS TO THE FAMILY

1908

These letters appeared in newspapers during the spring of 1908, after a trip to Canada undertaken in the autumn of 1907. They are now reprinted without alteration.

THE ROAD TO QUEBEC

(1907)

It must be hard for those who do not live there to realise the cross between canker and blight that has settled on England for the last couple of years. The effects of it are felt throughout the Empire, but at headquarters we taste the stuff in the very air, just as one tastes iodoform in the cups and bread-and-butter of a hospital-tea. So far as one can come at things in the present fog, every form of unfitness, general or specialised, born or created, during the last generation has combined in one big trust—a majority of all the minorities—to play the game of Government. Now that the game ceases to amuse, nine-tenths of the English who set these folk in power are crying, 'If we had only known what they were going to do we should never have voted for them!'

Yet, as the rest of the Empire perceived at the time, these men were always perfectly explicit as to their emotions and intentions. They said first, and drove it home by large pictures, that no possible advantage to the Empire outweighed the cruelty and injustice of charging the British working man twopence halfpenny a week on some of his provisions. Incidentally they explained, so that all Earth except England heard it, that the Army was wicked; much of the Navy unnecessary; that half the population of one of the Colonies practised slavery, with torture, for the sake of private gain, and that the mere name of Empire wearied and sickened them. On these grounds they stood to save England; on these grounds they were elected, with what seemed like clear orders to destroy the blood-stained fetish of Empire as soon as possible. The present mellow condition of Ireland, Egypt, India, and South Africa is proof of their honesty and obedience. Over and above this, their mere presence in office produced all along our lines the same moral effect as the presence of an incompetent master in a classroom. Paper pellets, books, and ink began to fly; desks were thumped; dirty pens were jabbed into those trying to work; rats and mice were set free amid squeals of exaggerated fear; and, as usual, the least desirable characters in the forms were loudest to profess noble sentiments, and most eloquent grief at being misjudged. Still, the English are not happy, and the unrest and slackness increase.

On the other hand, which is to our advantage, the isolation of the unfit in one political party has thrown up the extremists in what the Babu called 'all their naked *cui bono* .' These last are after satisfying the two chief desires of primitive man by the very latest gadgets in scientific legislation. But how to get free food, and free—shall we say—love? within the four corners of an Act of Parliament without giving the game away too grossly, worries them a little. It is easy enough to laugh at this, but we are all so knit together nowadays that a rot at what is called 'headquarters' may spread like bubonic, with every steamer. I went across to Canada the other day, for a few weeks, mainly to escape the Blight, and also to see what our Eldest Sister was doing. Have you ever noticed that Canada has to deal in the lump with most of the problems that afflict us others severally? For example, she has the Double-Language, Double-Law, Double-Politics drawback in a worse form than South Africa, because, unlike our Dutch, her French cannot well marry outside their religion, and they take their orders from Italy—less central, sometimes, than Pretoria or Stellenbosch. She has, too, something of Australia's labour fuss, minus Australia's isolation, but plus the open and secret influence of 'Labour' entrenched, with arms, and high explosives on neighbouring soil. To complete the parallel, she keeps, tucked away behind mountains, a trifle of land called British Columbia, which resembles New Zealand; and New Zealanders who do not find much scope for young enterprise in their own country are drifting up to British Columbia already.

Canada has in her time known calamity more serious than floods, frost, drought, and fire—and has macadamized some stretches of her road toward nationhood with the broken hearts of two generations. That is why one can discuss with Canadians of the old stock matters which an Australian or New Zealander could no more understand than a wealthy child understands death. Truly we are an odd Family! Australia and New Zealand (the Maori War not counted) got everything for nothing. South Africa gave everything and got less than nothing. Canada has given and taken all along the line for nigh on three hundred years, and in some respects is the wisest, as she should be the happiest, of us all. She seems to be curiously unconscious of her position in the Empire, perhaps because she has lately been talked at, or down to, by her neighbours. You know how at any gathering of our men from all quarters it is tacitly conceded that Canada takes the lead in the Imperial game. To put it roughly, she saw the goal more than ten years ago, and has been working the ball toward it ever since. That is why her inaction at the last Imperial Conference made people who were interested in the play wonder why she, of all of us, chose to brigade herself with General Botha and to block the forward rush. I, too, asked that question of many. The answer was something like this: 'We saw that England wasn't taking anything just then. Why should we have laid ourselves open to be snubbed worse than we were? We sat still.' Quite reasonable—almost too convincing. There was really no need that Canada should have done other than she did—except that she was the Eldest Sister, and more was expected of her. She is a little too modest.

We discussed this, first of all, under the lee of a wet deck-house in mid-Atlantic; man after man cutting in and out of the talk as he sucked at his damp tobacco. The passengers were nearly all unmixed Canadian, mostly born in the Maritime Provinces, where their fathers speak of 'Canada' as Sussex speaks of 'England,' but scattered about their businesses throughout the wide Dominion. They were at ease, too, among themselves, with that pleasant intimacy that stamps every branch of Our Family and every boat that it uses on its homeward way. A Cape liner is all the sub-Continent from the Equator to Simon's Town; an Orient boat is Australasian throughout, and a C.P.R. steamer cannot be confused with anything except Canada. It is a pity one may not be born in four places at once, and then one would understand the half-tones and asides, and the allusions of all our Family life without waste of precious time. These big men, smoking in the drizzle, had hope in their eyes, belief in their tongues, and strength in their hearts. I used to think miserably of other boats at the South end of this ocean—a quarter full of people deprived of these things. A young man kindly explained to me how Canada had suffered through what he called 'the Imperial connection'; how she had been diversely bedevilled by English statesmen for political reasons. He did not know his luck, nor would he believe me when I tried to point it out; but a nice man in a plaid (who knew South Africa) lurched round the corner and fell on him with facts and imagery which astonished the patriotic young mind. The plaid finished his outburst with the uncontradicted statement that the English were mad. All our talks ended on that note.

It was an experience to move in the midst of a new contempt. One understands and accepts the bitter scorn of the Dutch, the hopeless anger of one's own race in South Africa is also part of the burden; but the Canadian's profound, sometimes humorous, often bewildered, always polite contempt of the England of to-day cuts a little. You see, that late unfashionable war[2] was very real to Canada. She sent several

---

[2] Boer 'war' of 1899-1902.

men to it, and a thinly-populated country is apt to miss her dead more than a crowded one. When, from her point of view, they have died for no conceivable advantage, moral or material, her business instincts, or it may be mere animal love of her children, cause her to remember and resent quite a long time after the thing should be decently forgotten. I was shocked at the vehemence with which some men (and women) spoke of the affair. Some of them went so far as to discuss—on the ship and elsewhere—whether England would stay in the Family or whether, as some eminent statesman was said to have asserted in private talk, she would cut the painter to save expense. One man argued, without any heat, that she would not so much break out of the Empire in one flurry, as politically vend her children one by one to the nearest Power that threatened her comfort; the sale of each case to be preceded by a steady blast of abuse of the chosen victim. He quoted—really these people have viciously long memories!—the five-year campaign of abuse against South Africans as a precedent and a warning.

Our Tobacco Parliament next set itself to consider by what means, if this happened, Canada could keep her identity unsubmerged; and that led to one of the most curious talks I have ever heard. It seemed to be decided that she might—just might—pull through by the skin of her teeth as a nation—if (but this was doubtful) England did not help others to hammer her. Now, twenty years ago one would not have heard any of this sort of thing. If it sounds a little mad, remember that the Mother Country was throughout considered as a lady in violent hysterics.

Just at the end of the talk one of our twelve or thirteen hundred steerage-passengers leaped overboard, ulstered and booted, into a confused and bitter cold sea. Every horror in the world has its fitting ritual. For the fifth time—and four times in just such weather—I heard the screw stop; saw our wake curve like a whiplash as the great township wrenched herself round; the lifeboat's crew hurry to the boat-deck; the bare-headed officer race up the shrouds and look for any sign of the poor head that had valued itself so lightly. A boat amid waves can see nothing. There was nothing to see from the first. We waited and quartered the ground back and forth for a long hour, while the rain fell and the seas slapped along our sides, and the steam fluttered drearily through the escapes. Then we went ahead.

The St. Lawrence on the last day of the voyage played up nobly. The maples along its banks had turned—blood red and splendid as the banners of lost youth. Even the oak is not more of a national tree than the maple, and the sight of its welcome made the folks aboard still more happy. A dry wind brought along all the clean smell of their Continent-mixed odours of sawn lumber, virgin earth, and wood-smoke; and they snuffed it, and their eyes softened as they, identified point after point along their own beloved River—places where they played and fished and amused themselves in holiday time. It must be pleasant to have a country of one's very own to show off. Understand, they did not in any way boast, shout, squeak, or exclaim, these even-voiced returned men and women. They were simply and unfeignedly glad to see home again, and they said: 'Isn't it lovely? Don't you think it's beautiful? We love it.'

At Quebec there is a sort of place, much infested by locomotives, like a coal-chute, whence rise the heights that Wolfe's men scaled on their way to the Plains of Abraham. Perhaps of all the tide-marks in all our lands the affair of Quebec touches the heart and the eye more nearly than any other. Everything meets there; France, the jealous partner of England's glory by land and sea for eight hundred years; England, bewildered as usual, but for a wonder not openly opposing Pitt, who knew; those other people, destined to break from England as soon as the French peril was removed; Montcalm himself, doomed and resolute; Wolfe, the inevitable trained workman appointed for the finish; and somewhere in the background one James Cook, master of H.M.S. *Mercury*, making beautiful and delicate charts of the St. Lawrence River.

For these reasons the Plains of Abraham are crowned with all sorts of beautiful things—including a jail and a factory. Montcalm's left wing is marked by the jail, and Wolfe's right by the factory. There is, happily, now a movement on foot to abolish these adornments and turn the battle-field and its surroundings into a park, which by nature and association would be one of the most beautiful in our world.

Yet, in spite of jails on the one side and convents on the other and the thin black wreck of the Quebec Railway Bridge, lying like a dumped car-load of tin cans in the river, the Eastern Gate to Canada is noble with a dignity beyond words. We saw it very early, when the under sides of the clouds turned chilly pink over a high-piled, brooding, dusky-purple city. Just at the point of dawn, what looked like the Sultan Harun-al-Raschid's own private shallop, all spangled with coloured lights, stole across the iron-grey water, and disappeared into the darkness of a slip. She came out again in three minutes, but the full day had come too; so she snapped off her masthead, steering and cabin electrics, and turned into a dingy white ferryboat, full of cold passengers. I spoke to a Canadian about her. 'Why, she's the old So-and-So, to Port Levis,' he answered, wondering as the Cockney wonders when a stranger stares at an Inner Circle train. This was *his* Inner Circle—the Zion where he was all at ease. He drew my attention to stately city and stately river with the same tranquil pride that we each feel when the visitor steps across our own threshold, whether that be Southampton Water on a grey, wavy morning; Sydney Harbour with a regatta in full swing; or Table Mountain, radiant and new-washed after the Christmas rains. He had, quite rightly, felt personally responsible for the weather, and every flaming stretch of maple since we had entered the river. (The North-wester in these parts is equivalent to the South-easter elsewhere, and may impress a guest unfavourably.)

Then the autumn sun rose, and the man smiled. Personally and politically he said he loathed the city—but it was his.

'Well,' he asked at last, 'what do you think? Not so bad?'

'Oh no. Not at all so bad,' I answered; and it wasn't till much later that I realised that we had exchanged the countersign which runs clear round the Empire.

A PEOPLE AT HOME

An up-country proverb says, 'She was bidden to the wedding and set down to grind corn.' The same fate, reversed, overtook me on my little excursion. There is a crafty network of organisations of business men called Canadian Clubs. They catch people who look interesting, assemble their members during the mid-day lunch-hour, and, tying the victim to a steak, bid him discourse on anything that he thinks he knows. The idea might be copied elsewhere, since it takes men out of themselves to listen to matters not otherwise coming under their notice and, at the same time, does not hamper their work. It is safely short, too. The whole affair cannot exceed an hour, of which the lunch fills half. The Clubs print their speeches annually, and one gets cross-sections of many interesting questions—from practical forestry to State mints—all set out by experts.

Not being an expert, the experience, to me, was very like hard work. Till then I had thought speech-making was a sort of conversational whist, that any one could cut in at it. I perceive now that it is an Art of conventions remote from anything that comes out of an inkpot, and of colours hard to control. The Canadians seem to like listening to speeches, and, though this is by no means a national vice, they make good oratory on occasion. You know the old belief that the white man on brown, red, or black lands, will throw back in manner and instinct to the type originally bred there? Thus, a speech in the taal should carry the deep roll, the direct belly-appeal, the reiterated, cunning arguments, and the few simple metaphors of the prince of commercial orators, the Bantu. A New Zealander is said to speak from his diaphragm, hands clenched at the sides, as the old Maoris used. What we know of first-class Australian oratory shows us the same alertness, swift flight, and clean delivery as a thrown boomerang. I had half expected in Canadian speeches some survival of the Redskin's elaborate appeal to Suns, Moons, and Mountains—touches of grandiosity and ceremonial invocations. But nothing that I heard was referable to any primitive stock. There was a dignity, a restraint, and, above all, a weight in it, rather curious when one thinks of the influences to which the land lies open. Red it was not; French it was not; but a thing as much by itself as the speakers.

So with the Canadian's few gestures and the bearing of his body. During the (Boer) war one watched the contingents from every point of view, and, most likely, drew wrong inferences. It struck me then that the Canadian, even when tired, slacked off less than the men from the hot countries, and while resting did not lie on his back or his belly, but rather on his side, a leg doubled under him, ready to rise in one surge.

This time while I watched assemblies seated, men in hotels and passers-by, I fancied that he kept this habit of semi-tenseness at home among his own; that it was the complement of the man's still countenance, and his even, lowered voice. Looking at their footmarks on the ground they seem to throw an almost straight track, neither splayed nor in-toed, and to set their feet down with a gentle forward pressure, rather like the Australian's stealthy footfall. Talking among themselves, or waiting for friends, they did not drum with their fingers, fiddle with their feet, or feel the hair on their faces. These things seem trivial enough, but when breeds are in the making everything is worth while. A man told me once—but I never tried the experiment—that each of our Four Races light and handle fire in their own way.

Small wonder we differ! Here is a people with no people at their backs, driving the great world-plough which wins the world's bread up and up over the shoulder of the world—a spectacle, as it might be, out of some tremendous Norse legend. North of them lies Niflheim's enduring cold, with the flick and crackle of the Aurora for Bifrost Bridge that Odin and the Aesir visited. These people also go north year by year, and drag audacious railways with them. Sometimes they burst into good wheat or timber land, sometimes into mines of treasure, and all the North is foil of voices—as South Africa was once—telling discoveries and making prophecies.

When their winter comes, over the greater part of this country outside the cities they must sit still, and eat and drink as the Aesir did. In summer they cram twelve months' work into six, because between such and such dates certain far rivers will shut, and, later, certain others, till, at last, even the Great Eastern Gate at Quebec locks, and men must go in and out by the side-doors at Halifax and St. John. These are conditions that make for extreme boldness, but not for extravagant boastings.

The maples tell when it is time to finish, and all work in hand is regulated by their warning signal. Some jobs can be put through before winter; others must be laid aside ready to jump forward without a lost minute in spring. Thus, from Quebec to Calgary a note of drive—not hustle, but drive and finish-up—hummed like the steam-threshers on the still, autumn air.

Hunters and sportsmen were coming in from the North; prospectors with them, their faces foil of mystery, their pockets full of samples, like prospectors the world over. They had already been wearing wolf and coon skin coats. In the great cities which work the year round, carriage—shops exhibited one or two seductive nickel-plated sledges, as a hint; for the sleigh is 'the chariot at hand here of Love.' In the country the farmhouses were stacking up their wood-piles within reach of the kitchen door, and taking down the fly-screens, (One leaves these on, as a rule, till the double windows are brought up from the cellar, and one has to hunt all over the house for missing screws.) Sometimes one saw a few flashing lengths of new stovepipe in a backyard, and pitied the owner. There is no humour in the old, bitter-true stovepipe jests of the comic papers.

But the railways—the wonderful railways—told the winter's tale most emphatically. The thirty-ton coal cars were moving over three thousand miles of track. They grunted and lurched against each other in the switch-yards, or thumped past statelily at midnight on their way to provident housekeepers of the prairie towns. It was not a clear way either; for the bacon, the lard, the apples, the butter, and the cheese, in beautiful whitewood barrels, were rolling eastwards toward the steamers before the wheat should descend on them. That is the fifth act of the great Year-Play for which the stage must be cleared. On scores of congested sidings lay huge girders, rolled beams, limbs, and boxes of rivets, once intended for the late Quebec Bridge—now so much mere obstruction—and the victuals had to pick their way through 'em; and behind the victuals was the lumber—clean wood out of the mountains—logs, planks, clapboards, and laths, for which we pay such sinful prices in England—all seeking the sea. There was housing, food, and fuel for millions, on wheels together, and never a grain yet shifted of the real staple which men for five hundred miles were threshing out in heaps as high as fifty-pound villas.

Add to this, that the railways were concerned for their own new developments—double-trackings, loops, cutoffs, taps, and feeder lines, and great swoops out into untouched lands soon to be filled with men. So the construction, ballast, and material trains, the grading machines, the wrecking cars with their camel-like sneering cranes—the whole plant of a new civilisation—had to find room somewhere in the general rally before Nature cried, 'Lay off!'

Does any one remember that joyful strong confidence after the war, when it seemed that, at last, South Africa was to be developed—when men laid out railways, and gave orders for engines, and fresh rolling-stock, and labour, and believed gloriously in the future? It is true the hope was murdered afterward, but—multiply that good hour by a thousand, and you will have some idea of how it feels to be in Canada—a place which even an 'Imperial' Government cannot kill. I had the luck to be shown some things from the inside—to listen to the details of works projected; the record of works done. Above all, I saw what had actually been achieved in the fifteen years since I had last come that way. One advantage of a new land is that it makes you feel older than Time. I met cities where there had been nothing—literally, absolutely nothing, except, as the fairy tales say, 'the birds crying, and the grass waving in the wind.' Villages and hamlets had grown to great towns, and the great towns themselves had trebled and quadrupled. And the railways rubbed their hands and cried, like the Afrites of old, 'Shall we make a city where no city is; or render flourishing a city that is dasolate?' They do it too, while, across the water, gentlemen, never forced to suffer one day's physical discomfort in all their lives, pipe up and say, 'How grossly materialistic!'

I wonder sometimes whether any eminent novelist, philosopher, dramatist, or divine of to-day has to exercise half the pure imagination, not to mention insight, endurance, and self-restraint, which is accepted without comment in what is called 'the material exploitation' of a new country. Take only the question of creating a new city at the junction of two lines—all three in the air. The mere drama of it, the play of the human virtues, would fill a book. And when the work is finished, when the city is, when the new lines embrace a new belt of farms, and the tide of the Wheat has rolled North another unexpected degree, the men who did it break off, without compliments, to repeat the joke elsewhere.

I had some talk with a youngish man whose business it was to train avalanches to jump clear of his section of the track. Thor went to Jotunheim only once or twice, and he had his useful hammer Miolnr with him. This Thor lived in Jotunheim among the green-ice-crowned peaks of the Selkirks—where if you disturb the giants at certain seasons of the year, by making noises, they will sit upon you and all your fine emotions. So Thor watches them glaring under the May sun, or dull and doubly dangerous beneath the spring rains. He wards off their strokes with enormous brattices of wood, wing-walls of logs bolted together, and such other contraptions as experience teaches. He bears the giants no malice; they do their work, he his. What bothers him a little is that the wind of their blows sometimes rips pines out of the opposite hillsides—explodes, as it were, a whole valley. He thinks, however, he can fix things so as to split large avalanches into little ones.

Another man, to whom I did not talk, sticks in my memory. He had for years and years inspected trains at the head of a heavyish grade in the mountains—though not half so steep as the Hex[3]—where all brakes are jammed home, and the cars slither warily for ten miles. Tire-troubles there would be inconvenient, so he, as the best man, is given the heaviest job—monotony and responsibility combined. He did me the honour of wanting to speak to me, but first he inspected his train—on all fours with a hammer. By the time he was satisfied of the integrity of the underpinnings it was time for us to go; and all that I got was a friendly wave of the hand—a master craftsman's sign, you might call it.

Canada seems full of this class of materialist.

---

[3] Hex River, South Africa.

Which reminds me that the other day I saw the Lady herself in the shape of a tall woman of twenty-five or six, waiting for her tram on a street corner. She wore her almost flaxen-gold hair waved, and parted low on the forehead, beneath a black astrachan toque, with a red enamel maple-leaf hatpin in one side of it. This was the one touch of colour except the flicker of a buckle on the shoe. The dark, tailor-made dress had no trinkets or attachments, but fitted perfectly. She stood for perhaps a minute without any movement, both hands—right bare, left gloved—hanging naturally at her sides, the very fingers still, the weight of the superb body carried evenly on both feet, and the profile, which was that of Gudrun or Aslauga, thrown out against a dark stone column. What struck me most, next to the grave, tranquil eyes, was her slow, unhurried breathing in the hurry about her. She was evidently a regular fare, for when her tram stopped she smiled at the lucky conductor; and the last I saw of her was a flash of the sun on the red maple-leaf, the full face still lighted by that smile, and her hair very pale gold against the dead black fur. But the power of the mouth, the wisdom of the brow, the human comprehension of the eyes, and the outstriking vitality of the creature remained. That is how *I* would have my country drawn, were I a Canadian—and hung in Ottawa Parliament House, for the discouragement of prevaricators.

CITIES AND SPACES

What would you do with a magic carpet if one were lent you? I ask because for a month we had a private car of our very own—a trifling affair less than seventy foot long and thirty ton weight. 'You may find her useful,' said the donor casually, 'to knock about the country. Hitch on to any train you choose and stop off where you choose.'

So she bore us over the C.P.R. from the Atlantic to the Pacific and back, and when we had no more need of her, vanished like the mango tree after the trick.

A private car, though many books have been written in it, is hardly the best place from which to study a country, unless it happen that you have kept house and seen the seasons round under normal conditions on the same continent. Then you know how the cars look from the houses; which is not in the least as the houses look from the cars. Then, the very porter's brush in its nickel clip, the long cathedral-like aisle between the well-known green seats, the toll of the bell and the deep organ-like note of the engine wake up memories; and every sight, smell, and sound outside are like old friends remembering old days together. A piano-top buggy on a muddy, board-sidewalked street, all cut up by the narrow tires; the shingling at the corner of a veranda on a new-built house; a broken snake-fence girdling an old pasture of mulleins and skull-headed boulders; a wisp of Virginia creeper dying splendidly on the edge of a patch of corn; half a dozen panels of snow-fence above a cutting, or even a shameless patent-medicine advertisement, yellow on the black of a tobacco-barn, can make the heart thump and the eyes fill if the beholder have only touched the life of which they are part. What must they mean to the native-born? There was a prairie-bred girl on the train, coming back after a year on the Continent, for whom the pine-belted hills, with real mountains behind, the solemn loops of the river, and the intimate friendly farm had nothing to tell.

'You can do these landscapes better in Italy,' she explained, and, with the indescribable gesture of plains folk stifled in broken ground, 'I want to push these hills away and get into the open again! I'm Winnipeg.'

She would have understood that Hanover Road schoolmistress, back from a visit to Cape Town, whom I once saw drive off into thirty miles of mirage almost shouting, 'Thank God, here's something like home at last.'

Other people ricochetted from side to side of the car, reviving this, rediscovering that, anticipating t'other thing, which, sure enough, slid round the next curve to meet them, caring nothing if all the world knew they were home again; and the newly arrived Englishman with his large wooden packing-cases marked 'Settlers' Effects' had no more part in the show than a new boy his first day at school. But two years in Canada and one run home will make him free of the Brotherhood in Canada as it does anywhere else. He may grumble at certain aspects of the life, lament certain richnesses only to be found in England, but as surely as he grumbles so surely he returns to the big skies, and the big chances. The failures are those who complain that the land 'does not know a gentleman when it sees him.' They are quite right. The land suspends all judgment on all men till it has seen them work. Thereafter as may be; but work they must because there is a very great deal to be done.

Unluckily the railroads which made the country are bringing in persons who are particular as to the nature and amenities of their work, and if so be they do not find precisely what they are looking for, they complain in print which makes all men seem equal.

The special joy of our trip lay in having travelled the line when it was new and, like the Canada of those days, not much believed in, when all the high and important officials, whose little fingers unhooked cars, were also small and disregarded. To-day, things, men, and cities were different, and the story of the line mixed itself up with the story of the country, the while the car-wheels clicked out, 'John Kino—John Kino! Nagasaki, Yokohama, Hakodate, Heh!' for we were following in the wake of the Imperial Limited, all full of Hongkong and Treaty Ports men. There were old, known, and wonderfully grown cities to be looked at before we could get away to the new work out west, and, 'What d'you think of this building and that suburb?' they said, imperiously. 'Come out and see what has been done in this generation.'

The impact of a Continent is rather overwhelming till you remind yourself that it is no more than your own joy and love and pride in your own patch of garden written a little large over a few more acres. Again, as always, it was the dignity of the cities that impressed—an austere Northern dignity of outline, grouping, and perspective, aloof from the rush of traffic in the streets. Montreal, of the black-frocked priests and the French notices, had it; and Ottawa, of the grey stone palaces and the St. Petersburg-like shining water-frontages; and Toronto, consumingly commercial, carried the same power in the same repose. Men are always building better than they know, and perhaps this steadfast architecture is waiting for the race when their first flurry of newly-realised expansion shall have spent itself, and the present hurrah's-nest of telephone poles in the streets shall have been abolished. There are strong objections to any non-fusible, bi-lingual community within a nation, but however much the French are made to hang back in the work of development, their withdrawn and unconcerned cathedrals, schools, and convents, and one aspect of the spirit that breathes from them, make for good. Says young Canada: 'There are millions of dollars' worth of church property in the cities which aren't allowed to be taxed.' On the other hand, the Catholic schools and universities, though they are reported to keep up the old medieval mistrust of Greek, teach the classics as lovingly, tenderly, and intimately as the old Church has always taught them. After all, it must be worth something to say your prayers in a dialect of the tongue that Virgil handled; and a certain touch of insolence, more magnificent and more ancient than the insolence of present materialism, makes a good blend in a new land.

I had the good fortune to see the cities through the eyes of an Englishman out for the first time. 'Have you been to the Bank?' he cried. 'I've never seen anything like it!' 'What's the matter with the Bank?' I asked: for the financial situation across the Border was at that moment more than usual picturesque. 'It's wonderful!' said he; 'marble pillars—acres of mosaic—steel grilles—'might be a cathedral. No one ever told me.' 'I shouldn't worry over a Bank that pays its depositors,' I replied soothingly. 'There are several like it in Ottawa and Toronto.' Next he ran across some pictures in some palaces, and was downright angry because no one had told him that there were five priceless private galleries in one city. 'Look here!' he explained. 'I've been seeing Corots, and Greuzes, and Gainsboroughs, and a Holbein, and—and hundreds of really splendid pictures!' 'Why shouldn't you?' I said. 'They've given up painting their lodges with vermilion hereabouts.' 'Yes, but what I mean is, have you seen the equipment of their schools and colleges—desks, libraries, and lavatories? It's miles ahead of anything we have and—no one ever told me.' 'What was the good of telling? You wouldn't have believed. There's a building in one of the cities, on the lines of the Sheldonian, but better, and if you go as far as Winnipeg, you'll see the finest hotel in all the world.'

'Nonsense!' he said. 'You're pulling my leg! Winnipeg's a prairie-town.'

I left him still lamenting—about a Club and a Gymnasium this time—that no one had ever told him about; and still doubting all that he had heard of Wonders to come.

If we could only manacle four hundred Members of Parliament, like the Chinese in the election cartoons, and walk them round the Empire, what an all-comprehending little Empire we should be when the survivors got home!

Certainly the Cities have good right to be proud, and I waited for them to boast; but they were so busy explaining they were only at the beginning of things that, for the honour of the Family, I had to do the boasting. In this praiseworthy game I credited Melbourne (rightly, I hope, but the pace was too good to inquire) with acres of municipal buildings and leagues of art galleries; enlarged the borders of Sydney harbour to meet a statement about Toronto's, wharfage; and recommended folk to see Cape Town Cathedral when it should be finished. But Truth will out even on a visit. Our Eldest Sister has more of beauty and strength inside her three cities alone than the rest of Us put together. Yet it would do her no harm to send a commission through the ten great cities of the Empire to see what is being done there in the way of street cleaning, water-supply, and traffic-regulation.

Here and there the people are infected with the unworthy superstition of 'hustle,' which means half-doing your appointed job and applauding your own slapdasherie for as long a time as would enable you to finish off two clean pieces of work. Little congestions of traffic, that an English rural policeman, in a country town, disentangles automatically, are allowed to develop into ten-minute blocks, where wagons and men bang, and back, and blaspheme, for no purpose except to waste time.

The assembly and dispersal of crowds, purchase of tickets, and a good deal of the small machinery of life is clogged and hampered by this unstable, southern spirit which is own brother to Panic. 'Hustle' does not sit well on the national character any more than falsetto or fidgeting becomes grown men. 'Drive,' a laudable and necessary quality, is quite different, and one meets it up the Western Road where the new country is being made.

We got clean away from the Three Cities and the close-tilled farming and orchard districts, into the Land of Little Lakes—a country of rushing streams, clear-eyed ponds, and boulders among berry-bushes; all crying 'Trout' and 'Bear.'

Not so very long ago only a few wise people kept holiday in that part of the world, and they did not give away their discoveries. Now it has become a summer playground where people hunt and camp at large. The names of its further rivers are known in England, and men, otherwise sane, slip away from London into the birches, and come out again bearded and smoke-stained, when the ice is thick enough to cut a canoe. Sometimes they go to look for game; sometimes for minerals—perhaps, even, oil. No one can prophesy. 'We are only at the beginning of things.'

Said an Afrite of the Railway as we passed in our magic carpet: 'You've no notion of the size of our tourist-traffic. It has all grown up since the early 'Nineties. The trolley car teaches people in the towns to go for little picnics. When they get more money they go for long ones. All this Continent will want playgrounds soon. We're getting them ready.'

The girl from Winnipeg saw the morning frost lie white on the long grass at the lake edges, and watched the haze of mellow golden birch leaves as they dropped. 'Now that's the way trees ought to turn,' she said. 'Don't you think our Eastern maple is a little violent in colour?' Then we passed through a country where for many hours the talk in the cars was of mines and the treatment of ores. Men told one tales—prospectors' yarns of the sort one used to hear vaguely before Klondike or Nome were public property. They did not care whether one believed or doubted. They, too, were only at the beginning of things—silver perhaps, gold perhaps, nickel perhaps. If a great city did not arise at such a place—the very name was new since my day—it would assuredly be born within a few miles of it. The silent men boarded the cars, and dropped off, and disappeared beyond thickets and hills precisely as the first widely spaced line of skirmishers fans out and vanishes along the front of the day's battle.

One old man sat before me like avenging Time itself, and talked of prophecies of evil, that had been falsified. '*They* said there wasn't nothing here excep' rocks an' snow. *They* said there never *wouldn't* be nothing here excep' the railroad. There's them that can't see *yit* ,' and he gimleted me with a fierce eye. 'An' all the while, fortunes is made—piles is made—right under our noses.'

'Have you made your pile?' I asked.

He smiled as the artist smiles—all true prospectors have that lofty smile—'Me? No. I've been a prospector most o' my time, but I haven't lost anything. I've had my fun out of the game. By God, I've had my fun out of it!

I told him how I had once come through when land and timber grants could have been picked up for half less than nothing.

'Yes,' he said placidly. 'I reckon if you'd had any kind of an education you could ha' made a quarter of a million dollars easy in those days. And it's to be made now if you could see where. How? Can you tell me what the capital of the Hudson Bay district's goin' to be? You can't. Nor I. Nor yet where the six next new cities is going to arise, I get off here, but if I have my health I'll be out next summer again—prospectin' North.'

Imagine a country where men prospect till they are seventy, with no fear of fever, fly, horse-sickness, or trouble from the natives—a country where food and water always taste good! He told me curious things about some fabled gold—the Eternal Mother-lode—out in the North, which is to humble the pride of Nome. And yet, so vast is the Empire, he had never heard the name of Johannesburg!

As the train swung round the shores of Lake Superior the talk swung over to Wheat. Oh yes, men said, there were mines in the country—they were only at the beginning of mines—but that part of the world existed to clean and grade and handle and deliver the Wheat by rail and steamer. The track was being duplicated by a few hundred miles to keep abreast of the floods of it. By and by it might be a four-track road. They were only at the beginning. Meantime here was the Wheat sprouting, tender green, a foot high, among a hundred sidings where it had spilled from the cars; there were the high-shouldered, tea-caddy grain-elevators to clean, and the hospitals to doctor the Wheat; here was new, gaily painted machinery going forward to reap and bind and thresh the Wheat, and all those car-loads of workmen had been slapping down more sidings against the year's delivery of the Wheat.

Two towns stand on the shores of the lake less than a mile apart. What Lloyd's is to shipping, or the College of Surgeons to medicine, that they are to the Wheat. Its honour and integrity are in their hands; and they hate each other with the pure, poisonous, passionate hatred which makes towns grow. If Providence wiped out one of them, the survivor would pine away and die—a mateless hate-bird. Some day they must unite, and the question of the composite name they shall then carry already vexes them. A man there told me that Lake Superior was 'a useful piece of water,' in that it lay so handy to the C.P.R. tracks. There is a quiet horror about the Great Lakes which grows as one revisits them. Fresh water has no right or call to dip over the horizon, pulling down and pushing up the hulls of big steamers; no right to tread the slow, deep-sea dance-step between wrinkled cliffs; nor to roar in on weed and sand beaches between vast headlands that run out for leagues into haze and sea-fog. Lake Superior is all the same stuff as what towns pay taxes for, but it engulfs and wrecks and drives ashore, like a fully accredited ocean—a hideous thing to find in the heart of a continent. Some people go sailing on it for pleasure, and it has produced a breed of sailors who bear the same relation to the salt-water variety as a snake-charmer does to a lion-tamer.

Yet it is undoubtedly a useful piece of water.

NEWSPAPERS AND DEMOCRACY

Let it be granted that, as the loud-voiced herald hired by the Eolithic tribe to cry the news of the coming day along the caves, preceded the chosen Tribal Bard who sang the more picturesque history of the tribe, so is Journalism senior to Literature, in that Journalism meets the first tribal need after warmth, food, and women.

In new countries it shows clear trace of its descent from the Tribal Herald. A tribe thinly occupying large spaces feels lonely. It desires to hear the roll-call of its members cried often and loudly; to comfort itself with the knowledge that there are companions just below the horizon. It employs, therefore, heralds to name and describe all who pass. That is why newspapers of new countries seem often so outrageously personal. The tribe, moreover, needs quick and sure knowledge of everything that touches on its daily life in the big spaces—earth, air, and water news which the Older Peoples have put behind them. That is why its newspapers so often seem so laboriously trivial.

For example, a red-nosed member of the tribe, Pete O'Halloran, comes in thirty miles to have his horse shod, and incidentally smashes the king-bolt of his buckboard at a bad place in the road. The Tribal Herald—a thin weekly, with a patent inside—connects the red nose and the breakdown with an innuendo which, to the outsider, is clumsy libel. But the Tribal Herald understands that two-and-seventy families of the tribe may use that road weekly. It concerns them to discover whether the accident was due to Pete being drunk or, as Pete protests, to the neglected state of the road. Fifteen men happen to know that Pete's nose is an affliction, not an indication. One of them loafs across and explains to the Tribal Herald, who, next week, cries aloud that the road ought to be mended. Meantime Pete, warmed to the marrow at having focussed the attention of his tribe for a few moments, retires thirty miles up-stage, pursued by advertisements of buckboards guaranteed not to break their king-bolts, and later (which is what the tribe were after all the time) some tribal authority or other mends the road.

This is only a big-scale diagram, but with a little attention you can see the tribal instinct of self-preservation quite logically underrunning all sorts of queer modern developments.

As the tribe grows, and men do not behold the horizon from edge to unbroken edge, their desire to know all about the next man weakens a little—but not much. Outside the cities are still the long distances, the 'vast, unoccupied areas' of the advertisements; and the men who come and go yearn to keep touch with and report themselves as of old to their lodges. A man stepping out of the dark into the circle of the fires naturally, if he be a true man, holds up his hands and says, 'I, So-and-So, am here.' You can watch the ritual in full swing at any hotel when the reporter (*pro* Tribal Herald) runs his eyes down the list of arrivals, and before he can turn from the register is met by the newcomer, who, without special desire for notoriety, explains his business and intentions. Observe, it is always at evening that the reporter concerns himself with strangers. By day he follows the activities of his own city and the doings of nearby chiefs; but when it is time to close the stockade, to laager the wagons, to draw the thorn-bush back into the gap, then in all lands he reverts to the Tribal Herald, who is also the tribal Outer Guard.

There are countries where a man is indecently pawed over by chattering heralds who bob their foul torches in his face till he is singed and smoked at once. In Canada the necessary 'Stand and deliver your sentiments' goes through with the large decency that stamps all the Dominion. A stranger's words are passed on to the tribe quite accurately; no dirt is put into his mouth, and where the heralds judge that it would be better not to translate certain remarks they courteously explain why.

It was always delightful to meet the reporters, for they were men interested in their land, with the keen, unselfish interest that one finds in young house-surgeons or civilians. Thanks to the (Boer) war, many of them had reached out to the ends of our earth, and spoke of the sister nations as it did one good to hear. Consequently the interviews—which are as dreary for the reporter as the reported—often turned into pleasant and unpublished talks. One felt at every turn of the quick sentences to be dealing with made and trained players of the game—balanced men who believed in decencies not to be disregarded, confidences not to be violated, and honour not to be mocked. (This may explain what men and women have told me—that there is very little of the brutal domestic terrorism of the Press in Canada, and not much blackmailing.) They neither spat nor wriggled; they interpolated no juicy anecdotes of murder or theft among their acquaintance; and not once between either ocean did they or any other fellow-subjects volunteer that their country was 'law-abiding.'

You know the First Sign-post on the Great Main Road? 'When a Woman advertises that she is virtuous, a Man that he is a gentleman, a Community that it is loyal, or a Country that it is law-abiding—go the other way!'

Yet, while the men's talk was so good and new, their written word seemed to be cast in conventional, not to say old-fashioned, moulds. A quarter of a century ago a sub-editor, opening his mail, could identify the Melbourne *Argus* , the Sydney *Morning Herald* , or the Cape *Times* as far as he could see them. Even unheaded clippings from them declared their origin as a piece of hide betrays the beast that wore it. But he noticed then that Canadian journals left neither spoor nor scent—might have blown in from anywhere between thirty degrees of latitude—and had to be carefully identified by hand. To-day, the spacing, the headlines, the advertising of Canadian papers, the chessboard-like look of the open page which should be a daily beautiful study in black and white, the brittle pulp-paper, the machine-set type, are all as standardised as the railway cars of the Continent. Indeed, looking through a mass of Canadian journals is like trying to find one's own sleeper in a corridor train. Newspaper offices are among the most conservative organisations in the world; but surely after twenty-five years some changes might be permitted to creep in; some original convention of expression or assembly might be developed.

I drew up to this idea cautiously among a knot of fellow-craftsmen. 'You mean,' said one straight-eyed youth, 'that we are a back-number copying back-numbers?'

It was precisely what I did mean, so I made haste to deny it. 'We know that,' he said cheerfully. 'Remember we haven't the sea all round us—and the postal rates to England have only just been lowered. It will all come right.'

Surely it will; but meantime one hates to think of these splendid people using second-class words to express first-class emotions.

And so naturally from Journalism to Democracy. Every country is entitled to her reservations, and pretences, but the more 'democratic' a land is, the more make-believes must the stranger respect. Some of the Tribal Heralds were very good to me in this matter, and, as it were, nudged me when it was time to duck in the House of Rimmon. During their office hours they professed an unflinching belief in the blessed word 'Democracy,' which means any crowd on the move—that is to say, the helpless thing which breaks through floors and falls into cellars; overturns pleasure-boats by rushing from port to starboard; stamps men into pulp because it thinks it has lost sixpence, and jams and grills in the doorways of blazing theatres. Out of office, like every one else, they relaxed. Many winked, a few were flippant, but they all agreed that the only drawback to Democracy was Demos—a jealous God of primitive tastes and despotic tendencies. I received a faithful portrait of him from a politician who had worshipped him all his life. It was practically the Epistle of Jeremy—the sixth chapter of Baruch—done into unquotable English.

But Canada is not yet an ideal Democracy. For one thing she has had to work hard among rough-edged surroundings which carry inevitable consequences. For another, the law in Canada exists and is administered, not as a surprise, a joke, a favour, a bribe, or a Wrestling Turk exhibition, but as an integral part of the national character—no more to be forgotten or talked about than one's trousers. If you kill, you hang. If you steal, you go to jail. This has worked toward peace, self-respect, and, I think, the innate dignity of the people. On the other hand—which is where the trouble will begin—railways and steamers make it possible nowadays to bring in persons who need never lose touch of hot and cold water-taps, spread tables, and crockery till they are turned out, much surprised, into the wilderness. They clean miss the long weeks of salt-water and the slow passage across the plains which pickled and tanned the early emigrants. They arrive with soft bodies and unaired souls. I had this vividly brought home to me by a man on a train among the Selkirks. He stood on the safely railed rear-platform, looked at the gigantic pine-furred shoulder round which men at their lives' risk had led every yard of the track, and chirruped: 'I say, why can't all this be nationalised?' There was nothing under heaven except the snows and the steep to prevent him from dropping off the cars and hunting a mine for himself. Instead of which he went into the dining-car. That is one type.

A man told me the old tale of a crowd of Russian immigrants who at a big fire in a city 'verted to the ancestral type, and blocked the streets yelling, 'Down with the Czar!' That is another type. A few days later I was shown a wire stating that a community of Doukhobors—Russians again—had, not for the first time, undressed themselves, and were fleeing up the track to meet the Messiah before the snow fell. Police were pursuing them with warm underclothing, and trains would please take care not to run over them.

So there you have three sort of steam-borne unfitness—soft, savage, and mad. There is a fourth brand, which may be either home-grown or imported, but democracies do not recognise it, of downright bad folk—grown, healthy men and women who honestly rejoice in doing evil. These four classes acting together might conceivably produce a rather pernicious democracy; alien hysteria, blood-craze, and the like, reinforcing local ignorance, sloth, and arrogance. For example, I read a letter in a paper sympathising with these same Doukhobors. The writer knew a community of excellent people in England (you see where the rot starts!) who lived barefoot, paid no taxes, ate nuts, and were above marriage. They were a soulful folk, living pure lives. The Doukhobors were also pure and soulful, entitled in a free country to live their own lives, and not to be oppressed, etc. etc. (Imported soft, observe, playing up to Imported mad.) Meantime, disgusted police were chasing the Doukhobors into flannels that they might live to produce children fit to consort with the sons of the man who wrote that letter and the daughters of the crowd that lost their heads at the fire.

'All of which,' men and women answered, 'we admit. But what can we do? We want people.' And they showed vast and well-equipped schools, where the children of Slav immigrants are taught English and the songs of Canada. 'When they grow up,' people said, 'you can't tell them from Canadians.' It was a wonderful work. The teacher holds up pens, reels, and so forth, giving the name in English; the children repeating Chinese fashion. Presently when they have enough words they can bridge back to the knowledge they learned in their own country, so that a boy of twelve, at, say, the end of a year, will produce a well-written English account of his journey from Russia, how much his mother paid for food by the way, and where his father got his first job. He will also lay his hand on his heart, and say, 'I—am—a—Canadian.' This gratifies the Canadian, who naturally purrs over an emigrant owing everything to the land which adopted him and set him on his feet. The Lady Bountiful of an English village takes the same interest in a child she has helped on in the world. And the child repays by his gratitude and good behaviour?

Personally, one cannot care much for those who have renounced their own country. They may have had good reason, but they have broken the rules of the game, and ought to be penalised instead of adding to their score. Nor is it true, as men pretend, that a few full meals and fine clothes obliterate all taint of alien instinct and reversion. A thousand years cannot be as yesterday for mankind; and one has only to glance at the races across the Border to realise how in outlook, manner, expression, and morale the South and South-east profoundly and fatally affects the North and North-west. That was why the sight of the beady-eyed, muddy-skinned, aproned women, with handkerchiefs on their heads and Oriental bundles in their hands, always distressed one.

'But *why* must you get this stuff?' I asked. 'You know it is not your equal, and it knows that it is not your equal; and that is bad for you both. What is the matter with the English as immigrants?'

The answers were explicit: 'Because the English do not work. Because we are sick of Remittance-men and loafers sent out here. Because the English are rotten with Socialism. Because the English don't fit with our life. They kick at our way of doing things. They are always telling us how things are done in England. They carry frills! Don't you know the story of the Englishman who lost his way and was found half-dead of thirst beside a river? When he was asked why he didn't drink, he said, "How the deuce can I without a glass?"'

'But,' I argued over three thousand miles of country, 'all these are excellent reasons for bringing in the Englishman. It is true that in his own country he is taught to shirk work, because kind, silly people fall over each other to help and debauch and amuse him. Here, General January will stiffen him up. Remittance-men are an affliction to every branch of the Family, but your manners and morals can't be so tender as to suffer from a few thousand of them among your six millions. As to the Englishman's Socialism, he is, by nature, the most unsocial animal alive. What you call Socialism is his intellectual equivalent for Diabolo and Limerick competitions. As to his criticisms, you surely wouldn't marry a woman who agreed with you in everything, and you ought to choose your immigrants on the same lines. You admit that the Canadian is too busy to kick at anything. The Englishman is a born kicker. ("Yes, he is all that," they said.) He kicks on principle, and that is what makes for civilisation. So did your Englishman's instinct about the glass. Every new country needs—vitally needs—one-half of one per cent of its population trained to die of thirst rather than drink out of their hands. You are always talking of the second generation of your Smyrniotes and Bessarabians. Think what the second generation of the English are!'

They thought—quite visibly—but they did not much seem to relish it. There was a queer stringhalt in their talk—a conversational shy across the road—when one touched on these subjects. After a while I went to a Tribal Herald whom I could trust, and demanded of him point-blank where the trouble really lay, and who was behind it.

'It is Labour,' he said. 'You had better leave it alone.'

LABOUR

One cannot leave a thing alone if it is thrust under the nose at every turn. I had not quitted the Quebec steamer three minutes when I was asked point-blank: 'What do you think of the question of Asiatic Exclusion which is Agitating our Community?'

The Second Sign-Post on the Great Main Road says: 'If a Community is agitated by a Question—inquire politely after the health of the Agitator,' This I did, without success; and had to temporise all across the Continent till I could find some one to help me to acceptable answers. The Question appears to be confined to British Columbia. There, after a while, the men who had their own reasons for not wishing to talk referred me to others who explained, and on the acutest understanding that no names were to be published (it is sweet to see engineers afraid of being hoist by their own petards) one got more or less at something like facts.

The Chinaman has always been in the habit of coming to British Columbia, where he makes, as he does elsewhere, the finest servant in the world. No one, I was assured on all hands, objects to the biddable Chinaman. He takes work which no white man in a new country will handle, and when kicked by the mean white will not grossly retaliate. He has always paid for the privilege of making his fortune on this wonderful coast, but with singular forethought and statesmanship, the popular Will, some few years ago, decided to double the head-tax on his entry. Strange as it may appear, the Chinaman now charges double for his services, and is scarce at that. This is said to be one of the reasons why overworked white women die or go off their heads; and why in new cities you can see blocks of flats being built to minimise the inconveniences of housekeeping without help. The birth-rate will fall later in exact proportion to those flats.

Since the Russo-Japanese War the Japanese have taken to coming over to British Columbia. They also do work which no white man will; such as hauling wet logs for lumber mills out of cold water at from eight to ten shillings a day. They supply the service in hotels and dining-rooms and keep small shops. The trouble with them is that they are just a little too good, and when attacked defend themselves with asperity.

A fair sprinkling of Punjabis—ex-soldiers, Sikhs, Muzbis, and Jats—are coming in on the boats. The plague at home seems to have made them restless, but I could not gather why so many of them come from Shahpur, Phillour, and Jullundur way. These men do not, of course, offer for house-service, but work in the lumber mills, and with the least little care and attention could be made most valuable. Some one ought to tell them not to bring their old men with them, and better arrangements should be made for their remitting money home to their villages. They are not understood, of course; but they are not hated.

The objection is all against the Japanese. So far—except that they are said to have captured the local fishing trade at Vancouver, precisely as the Malays control the Cape Town fish business—they have not yet competed with the whites; but I was earnestly assured by many men that there was danger of their lowering the standard of life and wages. The demand, therefore, in certain quarters is that they go—absolutely and unconditionally. (You may have noticed that Democracies are strong on the imperative mood.) An attempt was made to shift them shortly before I came to Vancouver, but it was not very successful, because the Japanese barricaded their quarters and flocked out, a broken bottle held by the neck in either hand, which they jabbed in the faces of the demonstrators. It is, perhaps, easier to haze and hammer bewildered Hindus and Tamils, as is being done across the Border, than to stampede the men of the Yalu and Liaoyang.[4]

But when one began to ask questions one got lost in a maze of hints, reservations, and orations, mostly delivered with constraint, as though the talkers were saying a piece learned by heart. Here are some samples:—

A man penned me in a corner with a single heavily capitalised sentence. 'There is a General Sentiment among Our People that the Japanese Must Go,' said he.

'Very good,' said I. 'How d'you propose to set about it?'

'That is nothing to us. There is a General Sentiment,' etc.

'Quite so. Sentiment is a beautiful thing, but what are you going to do?' He did not condescend to particulars, but kept repeating the sentiment, which, as I promised, I record.

Another man was a little more explicit. 'We desire,' he said, 'to keep the Chinaman. But the Japanese must go.'

---

[4] Battles in the Russo-Japanese War.

'Then who takes their place? Isn't this rather a new country to pitch people out of?'

'We must develop our Resources slowly, sir—with an Eye to the Interests of our Children. We must preserve the Continent for Races which will assimilate with Ours. We must not be swamped by Aliens.'

'Then bring in your own races and bring 'em in quick,' I ventured.

This is the one remark one must not make in certain quarters of the West; and I lost caste heavily while he explained (exactly as the Dutch did at the Cape years ago) how British Columbia was by no means so rich as she appeared; that she was throttled by capitalists and monopolists of all kinds; that white labour had to be laid off and fed and warmed during the winter; that living expenses were enormously high; that they were at the end of a period of prosperity, and were now entering on lean years; and that whatever steps were necessary for bringing in more white people should be taken with extreme caution. Then he added that the railway rates to British Columbia were so high that emigrants were debarred from coming on there.

'But haven't the rates been reduced?' I asked.

'Yes—yes, I believe they have, but immigrants are so much in demand that they are snapped up before they have got so far West. You must remember, too, that skilled labour is not like agricultural labour. It is dependent on so many considerations. And the Japanese must go.'

'So people have told me. But I heard stories of dairies and fruit-farms in British Columbia being thrown up because there was no labour to milk or pick the fruit. Is that true, d'you think?'

'Well, you can't expect a man with all the chances that our country offers him to milk cows in a pasture. A Chinaman can do that. We want races that will assimilate with ours,' etc., etc.

'But didn't the Salvation Army offer to bring in three or four thousand English some short time ago? What came of that idea?'

'It—er—fell through.'

'Why?'

'For political reasons, I believe. We do not want People who will lower the Standard of Living. That is why the Japanese must go.'

'Then why keep the Chinese?'

'We can get on with the Chinese. We can't get on without the Chinese. But we must have Emigration of a Type that will assimilate with Our People. I hope I have made myself clear?'

I hoped that he had, too.

Now hear a wife, a mother, and a housekeeper.

'We have to pay for this precious state of things with our health and our children's. Do you know the saying that the Frontier is hard on women and cattle? This isn't the frontier, but in some respects it's worse, because we have all the luxuries and appearances—the pretty glass and silver to put on the table. We have to dust, polish, and arrange 'em after we've done our housework. I don't suppose that means anything to you, but—try it for a month! We have no help. A Chinaman costs fifty or sixty dollars a month now. Our husbands can't always afford that. How old would you take me for? I'm not thirty. Well thank God, I stopped my sister coming out West. Oh yes, it's a fine country—for men.'

'Can't you import servants from England?'

'I can't pay a girl's passage in order to have her married in three months. Besides, she wouldn't work. They won't when they see Chinamen working.'

'Do you object to the Japanese, too?'

'Of course not. No one does. It's only politics. The wives of the men who earn six and seven dollars a day—skilled labour they call it—have Chinese and Jap servants. *We* can't afford it. *We* have to think of saving for the future, but those other people live up to every cent they earn. They know *they're* all right. They're Labour. They'll be looked after, whatever happens. You can see how the State looks after me.'

A little later I had occasion to go through a great and beautiful city between six and seven of a crisp morning. Milk and fish, vegetables, etc., were being delivered to the silent houses by Chinese and Japanese. Not a single white man was visible on that chilly job.

Later still a man came to see me, without too publicly giving his name. He was in a small way of business, and told me (others had said much the same thing) that if I gave him away his business would suffer. He talked for half an hour on end.

'Am I to understand, then,' I said, 'that what you call Labour absolutely dominates this part of the world?'

He nodded.

'That it is difficult to get skilled labour into here?'

'Difficult? My God, if I want to get an extra hand for my business—I pay Union wages, of course—I have to arrange to get him here secretly. I have to go out and meet him, accidental-like, down the line, and if the Unions find out that he is coming, they, like as not, order him back East, or turn him down across the Border.'

'Even if he has his Union ticket? Why?'

'They'll tell him that labour conditions are not good here. He knows what that means. He'll turn back quick enough. I'm in a small way of business, and I can't afford to take any chances fighting the Unions.'

'What would happen if you did?'

'D'you know what's happening across the Border? Men get blown up there—with dynamite.'

'But this isn't across the Border?'

'It's a damn-sight too near to be pleasant. And witnesses get blown up, too. You see, the Labour situation ain't run from our side the line. It's worked from down under. You may have noticed men were rather careful when they talked about it?'

'Yes, I noticed all that.'

'Well, it ain't a pleasant state of affairs. I don't say that the Unions here would do anything *to* you—and please understand I'm all for the rights of Labour myself. Labour has no better friend than me—I've been a working man, though I've got a business of my own now. Don't run away with any idea that I'm against Labour—will you?'

'Not in the least. I can see that. You merely find that Labour's a little bit—er—inconsiderate, sometimes?'

'Look what happens across the Border! I suppose they've told you that little fuss with the Japanese in Vancouver was worked from down under, haven't they? I don't think our own people 'ud have done it by themselves.'

'I've heard that several times. Is it quite sporting, do you think, to lay the blame on another country?'

'*You* don't live here. But as I was saying—if we get rid of the Japs to-day, we'll be told to get rid of some one else to-morrow. There's no limit, sir, to what Labour wants. None!'

'I thought they only want a fair day's wage for a fair day's work?'

'That may do in the Old Country, but here they mean to boss the country. They do.'

'And how does the country like it?'

'We're about sick of it. It don't matter much in flush times—employers'll do most anything sooner than stop work—but when we come to a pinch, you'll hear something. We're a rich land—in spite of everything they make out—but we're held up at every turn by Labour. Why, there's businesses on businesses which friends of mine—in a small way like myself—want to start. Businesses in every direction—if they was only allowed to start in. But they ain't.'

'That's a pity. Now, what do you think about the Japanese question?'

'I don't think. I know. Both political parties are playing up to the Labour vote—if you understand what that means.'

I tried to understand.

'And neither side'll tell the truth—that if the Asiatic goes, this side of the Continent'll drop out of sight, unless we get free white immigration. And any party that proposed white immigration on a large scale 'ud be snowed under next election. I'm telling you what politicians think. Myself, I believe if a man stood up to Labour—not that I've any feeling against Labour—and just talked sense, a lot of people would follow him—quietly, of course. I believe he could even get white immigration after a while. He'd lose the first election, of course, but in the long run.... We're about sick of Labour. I wanted you to know the truth.'

'Thank you. And you don't think any attempt to bring in white immigration would succeed?'

'Not if it didn't suit Labour. You can try it if you like, and see what happens.'

On that hint I made an experiment in another city. There were three men of position, and importance, and affluence, each keenly interested in the development of their land, each asserting that what the land needed was white immigrants. And we four talked for two hours on the matter—up and down and in circles. The one point on which those three men were unanimous was, that whatever steps were taken to bring people into British Columbia from England, by private recruiting or otherwise, should be taken secretly. Otherwise the business of the people concerned in the scheme would suffer.

At which point I dropped the Great Question of Asiatic Exclusion which is Agitating all our Community; and I leave it to you, especially in Australia and the Cape, to draw your own conclusions.

Externally, British Columbia appears to be the richest and the loveliest section of the Continent. Over and above her own resources she has a fair chance to secure an immense Asiatic trade, which she urgently desires. Her land, in many places over large areas, is peculiarly fitted for the small former and fruit-grower, who can send his truck to the cities. On every hand I heard a demand for labour of all kinds. At the same time, in no other part of the Continent did I meet so many men who insistently decried the value and possibilities of their country, or who dwelt more fluently on the hardships and privations to be endured by the white immigrant. I believe that one or two gentlemen have gone to England to explain the drawbacks *viva voce* . It is possible that they incur a great responsibility in the present, and even a terrible one for the future.

THE FORTUNATE TOWNS

After Politics, let us return to the Prairie which is the High Veldt, plus Hope, Activity, and Reward. Winnipeg is the door to it—a great city in a great plain, comparing herself, innocently enough, to other cities of her acquaintance, but quite unlike any other city.

When one meets, in her own house, a woman not seen since girlhood she is all a stranger till some remembered tone or gesture links up to the past, and one cries: 'It *is* you after all.' But, indeed, the child has gone; the woman with her influences has taken her place. I tried vainly to recover the gawky, graceless city I had known, so unformed and so insistent on her shy self. I even ventured to remind a man of it. 'I remember,' he said, smiling, 'but we were young then. This thing,' indicating an immense perspective of asphalted avenue that dipped under thirty railway tracks, 'only came up in the last ten years—practically the last five. We've had to enlarge all those warehouses yonder by adding two or three stories to 'em, and we've hardly begun to go ahead yet. We're just beginning.'

Warehouses, railway-sidings, and such are only counters in the White Man's Game, which can be swept up and re-dealt as the play varies. It was the spirit in the thin dancing air—the new spirit of the new city—which rejoiced me. Winnipeg has Things in abundance, but has learned to put them beneath her feet, not on top of her mind, and so is older than many cities. None the less the Things had to be shown—for what shopping is to the woman showing off his town is to the right-minded man. First came the suburbs—miles on miles of the dainty, clean-outlined, wooden-built houses, where one can be so happy and so warm, each unjealously divided from its neighbour by the lightest of boundaries. One could date them by their architecture, year after year, back to the Early 'Nineties, which is when civilisation began; could guess within a few score dollars at their cost and the incomes of their owners, and could ask questions about the new domestic appliances of to-day.

'Asphalt streets and concrete sidewalks came up a few years ago,' said our host as we trotted over miles of it. 'We found it the only way to fight the prairie mud. Look!' Where the daring road ended, there lay unsubdued, level with the pale asphalt, the tenacious prairie, over which civilisation fought her hub-deep way to the West. And with asphalt and concrete they fight the prairie back every building season. Next came the show-houses, built by rich men with an eye to the honour and glory of their city, which is the first obligation of wealth in a new land.

We twisted and turned among broad, clean, tree-lined, sunlit boulevards and avenues, all sluiced down with an air that forbade any thought of fatigue, and talked of city government and municipal taxation, till, in a certain silence, we were shown a suburb of uncared-for houses, shops, and banks, whose sides and corners were rubbed greasy by the shoulders of loafers. Dirt and tin cans lay about the street. Yet it was not the squalor of poverty so much as the lack of instinct to keep clean. One race prefers to inhabit there.

Next a glimpse of a cold, white cathedral, red-brick schools almost as big (thank goodness!) as some convents; hospitals, institutions, a mile or so of shops, and then a most familiar-feeling lunch at a Club which would have amazed my Englishman at Montreal, where men, not yet old, talked of Fort Garry as they remembered it, and tales of the founding of the city, of early administrative shifts and accidents, mingled with the younger men's prophecies and frivolities.

There are a few places still left where men can handle big things with a light touch, and take more for granted in five minutes than an Englishman at home could puzzle out in a year. But one would not meet many English at a lunch in a London club who took the contract for building London Wall or helped bully King John into signing Magna Charta.

I had two views of the city—one on a gray day from the roof of a monster building, whence it seemed to overflow and fill with noises the whole vast cup of the horizon; and still, all round its edge, jets of steam and the impatient cries of machinery showed it was eating out into the Prairie like a smothered fire.

The other picture was a silhouette of the city's flank, mysterious as a line of unexplored cliffs, under a sky crimson—barred from the zenith to the ground, where it lay, pale emerald behind the uneven ramparts. As our train halted in the last of the dusk, and the rails glowed dull red, I caught the deep surge of it, and seven miles across the purple levels saw the low, restless aurora of its lights. It is rather an awesome thing to listen to a vanguard of civilisation talking to itself in the night in the same tone as a thousand-year-old city.

All the country hereabouts is riddled with railways for business and pleasure undreamed of fifteen years ago, and it was a long time before we reached the clear prairie of air and space and open land. The air is different from any air that ever blew; the space is ampler than most spaces, because it runs back to the unhampered Pole, and the open land keeps the secret of its magic as closely as the sea or the desert.

People here do not stumble against each other around corners, but see largely and tranquilly from a long way off what they desire, or wish to avoid, and they shape their path accordingly across the waves, and troughs, and tongues, and dips and fans of the land.

When mere space and the stoop of the high sky begin to overwhelm, earth provides little ponds and lakes, lying in soft-flanked hollows, where people can step down out of the floods of air, and delight themselves with small and known distances. Most of the women I saw about the houses were down in the hollows, and most of the men were on the crests and the flats. Once, while we halted a woman drove straight down at us from the sky-line, along a golden path between black ploughed lands. When the horse, who managed affairs, stopped at the cars, she nodded mysteriously, and showed us a very small baby in the hollow of her arm. Doubtless she was some exiled Queen flying North to found a dynasty and establish a country. The Prairie makes everything wonderful.

They were threshing the wheat on both sides or the track as far as the eye could see. The smoke of the machines went up in orderly perspective alongside the mounds of chaff—thus: a machine, a house, a mound of chaff, a stretch of wheat in stocks—and then repeat the pattern over the next few degrees of longitude. We ran through strings of nearly touching little towns, where I remembered an occasional shack; and through big towns once represented by a name-board, a siding, and two troopers of the North-West Police. In those days men proved that Wheat would not grow north of some fool's line, or other, or, if it did, that no one would grow it. And now the Wheat was marching with us as far as the eye could reach; the railways were out, two, three hundred miles north, peopling a new wheat country; and north of that again the Grand Trunk was laying down a suburban extension of a few thousand miles across the Continent, with branches perhaps to Dawson City, certainly to Hudson Bay.

'Come north and look!' cried the Afrites of the Railway. 'You're only on the fringe of it here.' I preferred to keep the old road, and to gape at miracles accomplished since my day. The old, false-fronted, hollow-stomached Western hotels were gone; their places filled by five-storey brick or stone ones, with Post Offices to match. Occasionally some overlooked fragment of the past still cleaved to a town, and marked it for an old acquaintance, but often one had to get a mile away and look back on a place—as one holds a palimpsest up against the light—to identify the long overlaid lines of the beginnings. Each town supplied the big farming country behind it, and each town school carried the Union Jack on a flagstaff in its playground. So far as one could understand, the scholars are taught neither to hate, nor despise, nor beg from, their own country.

I whispered to a man that I was a little tired of a three days' tyranny of Wheat, besides being shocked at farmers who used clean bright straw for fuel, and made bonfires of their chaff-hills. 'You're 'way behind the times,' said he. 'There's fruit and dairying and any quantity of mixed farming going forward all around—let alone irrigation further West. Wheat's not our only king by a long sight. Wait till you strike such and such a place.' It was there I met a prophet and a preacher in the shape of a Commissioner of the Local Board of Trade (all towns have them), who firmly showed me the vegetables which his district produced. They *were* vegetables too—all neatly staged in a little kiosk near the station.

I think the pious Thomas Tusser would have loved that man. 'Providence,' said he, shedding pamphlets at every gesture, 'did not intend everlasting Wheat in this section. No, sir! Our business is to keep ahead of Providence—to meet her with mixed farming. Are you interested in mixed farming? Psha! Too bad you missed our fruit and vegetable show. It draws people together, mixed farming does. I don't say Wheat is narrowing to the outlook, but I claim there's more sociability and money in mixed farming. We've been hypnotised by Wheat and Cattle. Now—the cars won't start yet awhile—I'll just tell you my ideas.'

For fifteen glorious minutes he gave me condensed essence of mixed farming, with excursions into sugar-beet (did you know they are making sugar in Alberta?), and he talked of farmyard muck, our dark mother of all things, with proper devotion.

'What we want now,' he cried in farewell, 'is men—more men. Yes, and women.'

They need women sorely for domestic help, to meet the mad rush of work at harvest time—maids who will help in house, dairy, and chicken-run till they are married.

A steady tide sets that way already; one contented settler recruiting others from England; but if a tenth of that energy wasted on 'social reform' could be diverted to decently thought out and supervised emigration work ('Labour' does not yet object to people working on the land) we might do something worth talking about. The races which work and do not form Committees are going into the country at least as fast as ours. It makes one jealous and afraid to watch aliens taking, and taking honestly, so much of this treasure of good fortune and sane living.

There was a town down the road which I had first heard discussed nigh twenty years ago by a broken-down prospector in a box-car. 'Young feller,' said he, after he had made a professional prophecy,' you'll hear of that town if you live. She's born lucky.'

I saw the town later—it was a siding by a trestle bridge where Indians sold beadwork—and as years passed I gathered that the old tramp's prophecy had come true, and that Luck of some kind had struck the little town by the big river. So, this trip, I stopped to make sure. It was a beautiful town of six thousand people, and a railway junction, beside a high-girdered iron bridge; there was a public garden with trees at the station. A company of joyous men and women, whom that air and that light, and their own goodwill, made our brothers and sisters, came along in motors, and gave us such a day as never was.

'What about the Luck?' I asked.

'Heavens!' said one. 'Haven't you heard about our natural gas—the greatest natural gas in the world? Oh, come and see!'

I was whirled off to a roundhouse full of engines and machinery-shops, worked by natural gas which comes out of the earth, smelling slightly of fried onions, at a pressure of six hundred pounds, and by valves and taps is reduced to four pounds. There was Luck enough to make a metropolis. Imagine a city's heating and light—to say nothing of power—laid on at no greater expense than that of piping!

'Are there any limits to the possibilities of it?' I demanded.

'Who knows? We're only at the beginning. We'll show you a brick-making plant, out on the prairie, run by gas. But just now we want to show you one of our pet farms.'

Away swooped the motors, like swallows, over roads any width you please, and up on to what looked like the High Veldt itself. A Major of the Mounted Police, who had done a year at the (Boer) war, told us how the ostrich-farm fencing and the little meercats sitting up and racing about South Africa had made him homesick for the sight of the gophers by the wayside, and the endless panels of wire fencing along which we rushed. (The Prairie has nothing to learn from the Veldt about fencing, or tricky gates.)

'After all,' said the Major, 'there's no country to touch this. I've had thirty years of it—from one end to the other.'

Then they pointed out all the quarters of the horizon—say, fifty miles wherever you turned—and gave them names.

The show farmer had taken his folk to church, but we friendly slipped through his gates and reached the silent, spick-and-span house, with its trim barn, and a vast mound of copper-coloured wheat, piled in the sun between two mounds of golden chaff. Every one thumbed a sample of it and passed judgment—it must have been worth a few hundred golden sovereigns as it lay, out on the veldt—and we sat around, on the farm machinery, and, in the hush that a shut-up house always imposes, we seemed to hear the lavish earth getting ready for new harvests. There was no true wind, but a push, as it were, of the whole crystal atmosphere.

'Now for the brickfield!' they cried. It was many miles off. The road fed by a never-to-be-forgotten drop, to a river broad as the Orange at Norval's Pont, rustling between mud hills. An old Scotchman, in the very likeness of Charon, with big hip boots, controlled a pontoon, which sagged back and forth by current on a wire rope. The reckless motors bumped on to this ferry through a foot of water, and Charon, who never relaxed, bore us statelily across the dark, broad river to the further bank, where we all turned to look at the lucky little town, and discuss its possibilities.

'I think you can see it best from here,' said one.

'No, from here,' said another, and their voices softened on the very name of it.

Then for an hour we raced over true prairie, great yellow-green plains crossed by old buffalo trails, which do not improve motor springs, till a single chimney broke the horizon like a mast at sea; and thereby were more light-hearted men and women, a shed and a tent or two for workmen, the ribs and frames of the brick-making mechanism, a fifteen foot square shaft sunk, sixty foot down to the clay, and, stark and black, the pipe of a natural-gas well. The rest was Prairie—the mere curve of the earth—with little grey birds calling.

I thought it could not have been simpler, more audacious or more impressive, till I saw some women in pretty frocks go up and peer at the hissing gas-valves.

'We fancied that it might amuse you,' said all those merry people, and between laughter and digressions they talked over projects for building, first their own, and next other cities, in brick of all sorts; giving figures of output and expenses of plant that made one gasp. To the eye the affair was no more than a novel or delicious picnic. What it actually meant was a committee to change the material of civilisation for a hundred miles around. I felt as though I were assisting at the planning of Nineveh; and whatever of good comes to the little town that was born lucky I shall always claim a share.

But there is no space to tell how we fed, with a prairie appetite, in the men's quarters, on a meal prepared by an artist; how we raced home at speeds no child could ever hear of, and no grown-up should attempt; how the motors squattered at the ford, and took pot-shots at the pontoon till even Charon smiled; how great horses hauled the motors up the gravelly bank into the town; how there we met people in their Sunday best, walking and driving, and pulled ourselves together, and looked virtuous; and how the merry company suddenly and quietly evanished because they thought that their guests might be tired. I can give you no notion of the pure, irresponsible frolic of it—of the almost affectionate kindness, the gay and inventive hospitality that so delicately controlled the whole affair—any more than I can describe a certain quiet half-hour in the dusk just before we left, when the company gathered to say good-bye, while young couples walked in the street, and the glare of the never-extinguished natural-gas lamps coloured the leaves of the trees a stage green.

It was a woman, speaking out of the shadow, who said, what we all felt, 'You see, we just love our town,'

'So do we,' I said, and it slid behind us.

MOUNTAINS AND THE PACIFIC

The Prairie proper ends at Calgary, among the cattle-ranches, mills, breweries, and three million acre irrigation works. The river that floats timber to the town from the mountains does not slide nor rustle like Prairie rivers, but brawls across bars of blue pebbles, and a greenish tinge in its water hints of the snows.

What I saw of Calgary was crowded into one lively half-hour (motors were invented to run about new cities). What I heard I picked up, oddly enough, weeks later, from a young Dane in the North Sea. He was qualmish, but his Saga of triumph upheld him.

'Three years ago I come to Canada by steerage—third class. *And* I have the language to learn. Look at me! I have now my own dairy business, in Calgary, and—look at me!—my own half section, that is, three hundred and twenty acres. All my land which is mine! And now I come home, first class, for Christmas here in Denmark, and I shall take out back with me, some friends of mine which are farmers, to farm on those irrigated lands near by Calgary. Oh, I tell you there is nothing wrong with Canada for a man which works.'

'And will your friends go?' I inquired.

'You bet they will. It is all arranged already. I bet they get ready to go now already; and in three years they will come back for Christmas here in Denmark, first class like me.'

'Then you think Calgary is going ahead?'

'You bet! We are only at the beginning of things. Look at me! Chickens? I raise chickens also in Calgary,' etc., etc.

After all this pageant of unrelieved material prosperity, it was a rest to get to the stillness of the big foothills, though they, too, had been inspanned for the work of civilisation. The timber off their sides was ducking and pitch-poling down their swift streams, to be sawn into house-stuff for all the world. The woodwork of a purely English villa may come from as many Imperial sources as its owner's income.

The train crept, whistling to keep its heart up, through the winding gateways of the hills, till it presented itself, very humbly, before the true mountains, the not so Little Brothers to the Himalayas. Mountains of the pine-cloaked, snow-capped breed are unchristian things.

Men mine into the flanks of some of them, and trust to modern science to pull them through. Not long ago, a mountain kneeled on a little mining village as an angry elephant kneels; but it did not get up again, and the half of that camp was no more seen on earth. The other half still stands—uninhabited. The 'heathen in his blindness' would have made arrangements with the Genius of the Place before he ever drove a pick there. 'As a learned scholar of a little-known university once observed to an engineer officer on the Himalaya-Tibet Road—'You white men gain nothing by not noticing what you cannot see. You fall off the road, or the road falls on you, and you die, and you think it all an accident. How much wiser it was when we were allowed to sacrifice a man officially, sir, before making bridges or other public works. Then the local gods were officially recognised, sir, and did not give any more trouble, and the local workmen, sir, were much pleased with these precautions.'

There are many local gods on the road through the Rockies: old bald mountains that have parted with every shred of verdure and stand wrapped in sheets of wrinkled silver rock, over which the sight travels slowly as in delirium; mad, horned mountains, wreathed with dancing mists; low-browed and bent-shouldered faquirs of the wayside, sitting in meditation beneath a burden of glacier-ice that thickens every year; and mountains of fair aspect on one side, but on the other seamed with hollow sunless clefts, where last year's snow is blackened with this year's dirt and smoke of forest-fires. The drip from it seeps away through slopes of unstable gravel and dirt, till, at the appointed season, the whole half-mile of undermined talus slips and roars into the horrified valley.

The railway winds in and out among them with little inexplicable deviations and side-twists, much as a buck walks through a forest-glade, sidling and crossing uneasily in what appears to be a plain way. Only when the track has rounded another shoulder or two, a backward and upward glance at some menacing slope shows why the train did not take the easier-looking road on the other side of the gorge.

From time to time the mountains lean apart, and nurse between them some golden valley of slow streams, fat pastures, and park-like uplands, with a little town, and cow bells tinkling among berry bushes; and children who have never seen the sun rise or set, shouting at the trains; and real gardens round the houses.

At Calgary it was a frost, and the dahlias were dead. A day later nasturtiums bloomed untouched beside the station platforms, and the air was heavy and liquid with the breath of the Pacific. One felt the spirit of the land change with the changing outline of the hills till, on the lower levels by the Fraser, it seemed that even the Sussex Downs must be nearer at heart to the Prairie than British Columbia. The Prairie people notice the difference, and the Hill people, unwisely, I think, insist on it. Perhaps the magic may lie in the scent of strange evergreens and mosses not known outside the ranges: or it may strike from wall to wall of timeless rifts and gorges, but it seemed to me to draw out of the great sea that washes further Asia—the Asia of allied mountains, mines, and forests.

We rested one day high up in the Rockies, to visit a lake carved out of pure jade, whose property is to colour every reflection on its bosom to its own tint. A belt of brown dead timber on a gravel scar, showed, upside down, like sombre cypresses rising from green turf and the reflected snows were pale green. In summer many tourists go there, but we saw nothing except the wonderworking lake lying mute in its circle of forest, where red and orange lichens grew among grey and blue moss, and we heard nothing except the noise of its outfall hurrying through a jam of bone-white logs. The thing might have belonged to Tibet or some unexplored valley behind Kin-chinjunga. It had no concern with the West.

As we drove along the narrow hill-road a piebald pack-pony with a china-blue eye came round a bend, followed by two women, black-haired, bare-headed, wearing beadwork squaw-jackets, and riding straddle. A string of pack-ponies trotted through the pines behind them.

'Indians on the move?' said I. 'How characteristic!'

As the women jolted by, one of them very slightly turned her eyes, and they were, past any doubt, the comprehending equal eyes of the civilised white woman which moved in that berry-brown face.

'Yes,' said our driver, when the cavalcade had navigated the next curve,' that'll be Mrs. So-and-So and Miss So-and-So. They mostly camp hereabout for three months every year. I reckon they're coming in to the railroad before the snow falls.'

'And whereabout do they go?' I asked.

'Oh, all about anywheres. If you mean where they come from just now—that's the trail yonder.'

He pointed to a hair-crack across the face of a mountain, and I took his word for it that it was a safe pony-trail. The same evening, at an hotel of all the luxuries, a slight woman in a very pretty evening frock was turning over photographs, and the eyes beneath the strictly-arranged hair were the eyes of the woman in the beadwork jacket who had quirted the piebald pack-pony past our buggy.

Praised be Allah for the diversity of His creatures! But do you know any other country where two women could go out for a three months' trek and shoot in perfect comfort and safety?

These mountains are only ten days from London, and people more and more use them for pleasure-grounds. Other and most unthought-of persons buy little fruit-farms in British Columbia as an excuse for a yearly visit to the beautiful land, and they tempt yet more people from England. This is apart from the regular tide of emigration, and serves to make the land known. If you asked a State-owned railway to gamble on the chance of drawing tourists, the Commissioner of Railways would prove to you that the experiment could never succeed, and that it was wrong to risk the taxpayers' money in erecting first-class hotels. Yet South Africa could, even now, be made a tourists' place—if only the railroads and steamship lines had faith.

On thinking things over I suspect I was not intended to appreciate the merits of British Columbia too highly. Maybe I misjudged; maybe she was purposely misrepresented; but I seemed to hear more about 'problems' and 'crises' and 'situations' in her borders than anywhere else. So far as eye or ear could gather, the one urgent problem was to find enough men and women to do the work in hand.

Lumber, coal, minerals, fisheries, fit soil for fruit, dairy, and poultry farms are all there in a superb climate. The natural beauty of earth and sky match these lavish gifts; to which are added thousands of miles of safe and sheltered waterways for coastal trade; deep harbours that need no dredge; the ground-works of immense and ice-free ports—all the title-deeds to half the trade of Asia. For the people's pleasure and good disport salmon, trout, quail, and pheasant play in front of and through the suburbs of her capitals. A little axe-work and road-metalling gives a city one of the loveliest water-girt parks that we have outside the tropics. Another town is presented with a hundred islands, knolls, wooded coves, stretches of beach, and dingles, laid down as expressly for camp-life, picnics, and boating parties, beneath skies never too hot and rarely too cold. If they care to lift up their eyes from their almost subtropical gardens they can behold snowy peaks across blue bays, which must be good for the soul. Though they face a sea out of which any portent may arise, they are not forced to protect or even to police its waters. They are as ignorant of drouth, murrain, pestilence locusts, and blight, as they are of the true meaning of want and fear.

Such a land is good for an energetic man. It is also not so bad for the loafer. I was, as I have told you, instructed on its, drawbacks. I was to understand that there was no certainty in any employment; and that a man who earned immense wages for six months of the year would have to be kept by the community if he fell out of work for the other six. I was not to be deceived by golden pictures set before me by interested parties (that is to say, by almost every one I met), and I was to give due weight to the difficulties and discouragements that beset the intending immigrant. Were I an intending immigrant I would risk a good deal of discomfort to get on to the land in British Columbia; and were I rich, with no attachments outside England, I would swiftly buy me a farm or a house in that country for the mere joy of it.

I forgot those doleful and unhumorous conspirators among people who fervently believed in the place; but afterwards the memory left a bad taste in my mouth. Cities, like women, cannot be too careful what sort of men they allow to talk about them.

Time had changed Vancouver literally out of all knowledge. From the station to the suburbs, and back to the wharves, every step was strange, and where I remembered open spaces and still untouched timber, the tramcars were fleeting people out to a lacrosse game. Vancouver is an aged city, for only a few days previous to my arrival the Vancouver Baby—*i.e.* the first child born in Vancouver—had been married.

A steamer—once familiar in Table Bay—had landed a few hundred Sikhs and Punjabi Jats—to each man his bundle—and the little groups walked uneasy alone, keeping, for many of them had been soldiers, to the military step. Yes, they said they had come to this country to get work. News had reached their villages that work at great wages was to be had in this country. Their brethren who had gone before had sent them the news. Yes, and sometimes the money for the passage out. The money would be paid back from the so-great wages to come. With interest? Assuredly with interest.. Did men lend money for nothing in *any* country? They were waiting for their brethren to come and show them where to eat, and later, how to work. Meanwhile this was a new country. How could they say anything about it? No, it was not like Gurgaon or Shahpur or Jullundur. The Sickness (plague) had come to all these places. It had come into the Punjab by every road, and many—many—many had died. The crops, too, had failed in some districts. Hearing the news about these so-great wages they had taken ship for the belly's sake—for the money's sake—for the children's sake.

'Would they go back again?'

They grinned as they nudged each other. The Sahib had not quite understood. They had come over for the sake of the money—the rupees, no, the dollars. The Punjab was their home where their villages lay, where their people were waiting. Without doubt—without doubt—they would go back. Then came the brethren already working in the mills—cosmopolitans dressed in ready-made clothes, and smoking cigarettes.

'This way, O you people,' they cried. The bundles were reshouldered and the turbaned knots melted away. The last words I caught were true Sikh talk: 'But what about the money, O my brother?'

Some Punjabis have found out that money can be too dearly bought.

There was a Sikh in a sawmill, had been driver in a mountain battery at home. Himself he was from Amritsar. (Oh, pleasant as cold water in a thirsty land is the sound of a familiar name in a fair country!)

'But you had your pension. Why did you come here?'

'Heaven-born, because my sense was little. And there was also the Sickness at Amritsar.'

(The historian a hundred years hence will be able to write a book on economic changes brought about by pestilence. There is a very interesting study somewhere of the social and commercial effects of the Black Death in England.)

On a wharf, waiting for a steamer, some thirty Sikhs, many of them wearing their old uniforms (which should not be allowed) were talking at the tops of their voices, so that the shed rang like an Indian railway station. A suggestion that if they spoke lower life would be easier was instantly adopted. Then a senior officer with a British India medal asked hopefully: 'Has the Sahib any orders where we are to go?'

Alas he had none—nothing but goodwill and greetings for the sons of the Khalsa, and they tramped off in fours.

It is said that when the little riot broke out in Vancouver these 'heathen' were invited by other Asiatics to join in defending themselves against the white man. They refused on the ground that they were subjects of the King. I wonder what tales they sent back to their villages, and where, and how fully, every detail of the affair was talked over. White men forget that no part of the Empire can live or die to itself.

Here is a rather comic illustration of this on the material side. The wonderful waters between Vancouver and Victoria are full of whales, leaping and rejoicing in the strong blue all about the steamer. There is, therefore, a whalery on an island near by, and I had the luck to travel with one of the shareholders.

'Whales are beautiful beasts,' he said affectionately. 'We've a contract with a Scotch firm for every barrel of oil we can deliver for years ahead. It's reckoned the best for harness-dressing.'

He went on to tell me how a swift ship goes hunting whales with a bomb-gun and explodes shells into their insides so that they perish at once.

'All the old harpoon and boat business would take till the cows come home. We kill 'em right off.'

'And how d'you strip 'em?'

It seemed that the expeditious ship carried also a large air-pump, and pumped up the carcass to float roundly till she could attend to it. At the end of her day's kill she would return, towing sometimes as many as four inflated whales to the whalery, which is a factory full of modern appliances. The whales are hauled up inclined planes like logs to a sawmill, and as much of them as will not make oil for the Scotch leather-dresser, or cannot be dried for the Japanese market, is converted into potent manure.

'No manure can touch ours,' said the shareholder. 'It's so rich in bone, d'you see. The only thing that has beat us up to date is their hides; but we've fixed up a patent process now for turning 'em into floorcloth. Yes, they're beautiful beasts. That fellow,' he pointed to a black hump in a wreath of spray, 'would cut up a miracle.'

'If you go on like this you won't have any whales left,' I said.

'That is so. But the concern pays thirty per cent, and—a few years back, no one believed in it.'

I forgave him everything for the last sentence.

A CONCLUSION

Canada possesses two pillars of Strength and Beauty in Quebec and Victoria. The former ranks by herself among those Mother-cities of whom none can say 'This reminds me.' To realise Victoria you must take all that the eye admires most in Bournemouth, Torquay, the Isle of Wight, the Happy Valley at Hong-Kong, the Doon, Sorrento, and Camps Bay; add reminiscences of the Thousand Islands, and arrange the whole round the Bay of Naples, with some Himalayas for the background.

Real estate agents recommend it as a little piece of England—the island on which it stands is about the size of Great Britain—but no England is set in any such seas or so fully charged with the mystery of the larger ocean beyond. The high, still twilights along the beaches are out of the old East just under the curve of the world, and even in October the sun rises warm from the first. Earth, sky, and water wait outside every man's door to drag him out to play if he looks up from his work; and, though some other cities in the Dominion do not quite understand this immoral mood of Nature, men who have made their money in them go off to Victoria, and with the zeal of converts preach and preserve its beauties.

We went to look at a marine junk-store which had once been Esquimalt, a station of the British Navy. It was reached through winding roads, lovelier than English lanes, along watersides and parkways any one of which would have made the fortune of a town.

'Most cities,' a man said, suddenly, 'lay out their roads at right angles. We do in the business quarters. What d'you think?'

'I fancy some of those big cities will have to spend millions on curved roads some day for the sake of a change,' I said. 'You've got what no money can buy.'

'That's what the men tell us who come to live in Victoria. And they've had experience.'

It is pleasant to think of the Western millionaire, hot from some gridiron of rectangular civilisation, confirming good Victorians in the policy of changing vistas and restful curves.

There is a view, when the morning mists peel off the harbour where the steamers tie up, or the Houses of Parliament on one hand, and a huge hotel on the other, which as an example of cunningly-fitted-in water-fronts and facades is worth a very long journey. The hotel was just being finished. The ladies' drawing-room, perhaps a hundred feet by forty, carried an arched and superbly enriched plaster ceiling of knops and arabesques and interlacings, which somehow seemed familiar.

'We saw a photo of it in *Country Life* ,' the contractor explained. 'It seemed just what the room needed, so one of our plasterers, a Frenchman—that's him—took and copied it. It comes in all right, doesn't it?'

About the time the noble original was put up in England Drake might have been sailing somewhere off this very coast. So, you see, Victoria lawfully holds the copyright.

I tried honestly to render something of the colour, the gaiety, and the graciousness of the town and the island, but only found myself piling up unbelievable adjectives, and so let it go with a hundred other wonders and repented that I had wasted my time and yours on the anxious-eyed gentlemen who talked of 'drawbacks.' A verse cut out of a newspaper seems to sum up their attitude:

As the Land of Little Leisure Is the place where things are done, So the Land of Scanty Pleasure Is the place for lots of fun. In the Land of Plenty Trouble People laugh as people should, But there's some one always kicking In the Land of Heap Too Good!

At every step of my journey people assured me that I had seen nothing of Canada. Silent mining men from the North; fruit-farmers from the Okanagan Valley; foremen of railway gangs, not so long from English public schools; the oldest inhabitant of the town of Villeneuve, aged twenty-eight; certain English who lived on the prairie and contrived to get fun and good fellowship as well as money; the single-minded wheat-growers and cattle-men; election agents; police troopers expansive in the dusk of wayside halts; officials dependent on the popular will, who talked as delicately as they walked; and queer souls who did not speak English, and said so loudly in the dining-car—each, in his or her own way, gave me to understand this. My excursion bore the same relation to their country as a 'bus-ride down the Strand bears to London, so I knew how they felt.

The excuse is that our own flesh and blood are more interesting than anybody else, and I held by birth the same right in them and their lives as they held in any other part of the Empire. Because they had become a people within the Empire my right was admitted and no word spoken; which would not have been the case a few years ago. One may mistake many signs on the road, but there is no mistaking the spirit of sane and realised nationality, which fills the land from end to end precisely as the joyous hum of a big dynamo well settled to its load makes a background to all the other shop noises. For many reasons that Spirit came late, but since it has come after the day of little things, doubts, and open or veiled contempts, there is less danger that it will go astray among the boundless wealth and luxury that await it. The people, the schools, the churches, the Press in its degree, and, above all, the women, understand without manifestoes that their land must now as always abide under the Law in deed and in word and in thought. This is their caste-mark, the ark of their covenant, their reason for being what they are. In the big cities, with their village-like lists of police court offences; in the wide-open little Western towns where the present is as free as the lives and the future as safe as the property of their inhabitants; in the coast cities galled and humiliated at their one night's riot ('It's not our habit, Sir! It's not our habit!'); up among the mountains where the officers of the law track and carefully bring into justice the astounded malefactor; and behind the orderly prairies to the barren grounds, as far as a single white man can walk, the relentless spirit of the breed follows up, and oversees, and controls. It does not much express itself in words, but sometimes, in intimate discussion, one is privileged to catch a glimpse of the inner fires. They burn hotly.

'*We* do not mean to be de-civilised,' said the first man with whom I talked about it.

That was the answer throughout—the keynote and the explanation.

Otherwise the Canadians are as human as the rest of us to evade or deny a plain issue. The duty of developing their country is always present, but when it comes to taking thought, better thought, for her defence, they refuge behind loose words and childish anticipations of miracles—quite in the best Imperial manner. All admit that Canada is wealthy; few that she is weak; still fewer that, unsupported, she would very soon cease to exist as a nation. The anxious inquirer is told that she does her duty towards England by developing her resources; that wages are so high a paid army is out of the question; that she is really maturing splendid defence schemes, but must not be hurried or dictated to; that a little wise diplomacy is all that will ever be needed in this so civilised era; that when the evil day comes something will happen (it certainly will), the whole concluding, very often, with a fervent essay on the immorality of war, all about as much to the point as carrying a dove through the streets to allay pestilence.

The question before Canada is not what she thinks or pays, but what an enemy may think it necessary to make her pay. If she continues wealthy and remains weak she will surely be attacked under one pretext or another. Then she will go under, and her spirit will return to the dust with her flag as it slides down the halliards.

'That is absurd,' is always the quick answer. 'In her own interests England could never permit it. What you speak of presupposes the fall of England.'

Not necessarily. Nothing worse than a stumble by the way; but when England stumbles the Empire shakes. Canada's weakness is lack of men. England's weakness is an excess of voters who propose to live at the expense of the State. These loudly resent that any money should be diverted from themselves; and since money is spent on fleets and armies to protect the Empire while it is consolidating, they argue that if the Empire ceased to exist armaments would cease too, and the money so saved could be spent on their creature comforts. They pride themselves on being an avowed and organised enemy of the Empire which, as others see it, waits only to give them health, prosperity, and power beyond anything their votes could win them in England. But their leaders need their votes in England, as they need their outcries and discomforts to help them in their municipal and Parliamentary careers. No engineer lowers steam in his own boilers.

So they are told little except evil of the great heritage outside, and are kept compounded in cities under promise of free rations and amusements. If the Empire were threatened they would not, in their own interests, urge England to spend men and money on it. Consequently it might be well if the nations within the Empire were strong enough to endure a little battering unaided at the first outset—till such time, that is, as England were permitted to move to their help.

For this end an influx of good men is needed more urgently every year during which peace holds—men loyal, clean, and experienced in citizenship, with women not ignorant of sacrifice.

Here the gentlemen who propose to be kept by their neighbours are our helpful allies. They have succeeded in making uneasy the class immediately above them, which is the English working class, as yet undebauched by the temptation of State-aided idleness or State-guaranteed irresponsibility. England has millions of such silent careful folk accustomed, even yet, to provide for their own offspring, to bring them up in a resolute fear of God, and to desire no more than the reward of their own labours. A few years ago this class would not have cared to shift; now they feel the general disquiet. They live close to it. Tea-and-sugar borrowing friends have told them jocularly, or with threats, of a good time coming when things will go hard with the uncheerful giver. The prospect appeals neither to their reason nor to their Savings Bank books. They hear—they do not need to read—the speeches delivered in their streets on a Sunday morning. It is one of their pre-occupations to send their children to Sunday School by roundabout roads, lest they should pick up abominable blasphemies.

When the tills of the little shops are raided, or when the family ne'er-do-well levies on his women with more than usual brutality, they know, because they suffer, what principles are being put into practice. If these people could quietly be shown a quiet way out of it all, very many of them would call in their savings (they are richer than they look), and slip quietly away. In the English country, as well as in the towns, there is a feeling—not yet panic, but the dull edge of it—that the future will be none too rosy for such as are working, or are in the habit of working. This is all to our advantage.

Canada can best serve her own interests and those of the Empire by systematically exploiting this new recruiting-ground. Now that South Africa, with the exception of Rhodesia, has been paralysed, and Australia has not yet learned the things which belong to her peace, Canada has the chance of the century to attract good men and capital into the Dominion. But the men are much more important than the money. They may not at first be as clever with the hoe as the Bessarabian or the Bokhariot, or whatever the fashionable breed is, but they have qualities of pluck, good humour, and a certain well-wearing virtue which are not altogether bad. They will not hold aloof from the life of the land, nor pray in unknown tongues to Byzantine saints; while the very tenacity and caution which made them cleave to England this long, help them to root deeply elsewhere. They are more likely to bring their women than other classes, and those women will make sacred and individual homes. A little-regarded Crown Colony has a proverb that no district can be called settled till there are pots of musk in the house-windows—sure sign that an English family has come to stay. It is not certain how much of the present steamer-dumped foreign population has any such idea. We have seen a financial panic in one country send whole army corps of aliens kiting back to the lands whose allegiance they forswore. What would they or their likes do in time of real stress, since no instinct in their bodies or their souls would call them to stand by till the storm were over?

Surely the conclusion of the whole matter throughout the whole Empire must be men and women of our own stock, habits, language, and hopes brought in by every possible means under a well-settled policy? Time will not be allowed us to multiply to unquestionable peace, but by drawing upon England we can swiftly transfuse what we need of her strength into her veins, and by that operation bleed her into health and sanity Meantime, the only serious enemy to the Empire, within or without, is that very Democracy which depends on the Empire for its proper comforts, and in whose behalf these things are urged.

EGYPT OF THE MAGICIANS

1913

And the magicians of Egypt did so with their enchantments .— EXODUS vii. 22.

I

SEA TRAVEL

I had left Europe for no reason except to discover the Sun, and there were rumours that he was to be found in Egypt.

But I had not realised what more I should find there.

A P. & O. boat carried us out of Marseilles. A serang of lascars, with whistle, chain, shawl, and fluttering blue clothes, was at work on the baggage-hatch. Somebody bungled at the winch. The serang called him a name unlovely in itself but awakening delightful memories in the hearer.

'O Serang, is that man a fool?'

'Very foolish, sahib. He comes from Surat. He only comes for his food's sake.'

The serang grinned; the Surtee man grinned; the winch began again, and the voices that called: 'Lower away! Stop her!' were as familiar as the friendly whiff from the lascars' galley or the slap of bare feet along the deck. But for the passage of a few impertinent years, I should have gone without hesitation to share their rice. Serangs used to be very kind to little white children below the age of caste. Most familiar of all was the ship itself. It had slipped my memory, nor was there anything in the rates charged to remind me, that single-screws still lingered in the gilt-edged passenger trade.

Some North Atlantic passengers accustomed to real ships made the discovery, and were as pleased about it as American tourists at Stratford-on-Avon.

'Oh, come and see!' they cried. 'She has *one* screw—only one screw! Hear her thump! And *have* you seen their old barn of a saloon? *And* the officers' library? It's open for two half-hours a day week-days and one on Sundays. You pay a dollar and a quarter deposit on each book. We wouldn't have missed this trip for anything. It's like sailing with Columbus.'

They wandered about—voluble, amazed, and happy, for they were getting off at Port Said.

I explored, too. From the rough-ironed table-linen, the thick tooth-glasses for the drinks, the slummocky set-out of victuals at meals, to the unaccommodating regulations in the curtainless cabin, where they had not yet arrived at bunk-edge trays for morning tea, time and progress had stood still with the P. & O. To be just, there were electric-fan fittings in the cabins, but the fans were charged extra; and there was a rumour, unverified, that one could eat on deck or in one's cabin without a medical certificate from the doctor. All the rest was under the old motto: '*Quis separabit* '—'This is quite separate from other lines.'

'After all,' said an Anglo-Indian, whom I was telling about civilised ocean travel, 'they don't want you Egyptian trippers. They're sure of *us* , because——' and he gave me many strong reasons connected with leave, finance, the absence of competition, and the ownership of the Bombay foreshore.

'But it's absurd,' I insisted. 'The whole concern is out of date. There's a notice on my deck forbidding smoking and the use of naked lights, and there's a lascar messing about the hold-hatch outside my cabin with a candle in a lantern.'

Meantime, our one-screw tub thumped gingerly toward Port Said, because we had no mails aboard, and the Mediterranean, exhausted after severe February hysterics, lay out like oil.

I had some talk with a Scotch quartermaster who complained that lascars are not what they used to be, owing to their habit (but it has existed since the beginning) of signing on as a clan or family—all sorts together.

The serang said that, for *his* part, he had noticed no difference in twenty years. 'Men are always of many kinds, sahib. And that is because God makes men this and that. Not all one pattern—not by any means all one pattern.' He told me, too, that wages were rising, but the price of ghee, rice, and curry-stuffs was up, too, which was bad for wives and families at Porbandar. 'And that also is thus, and no talk makes it otherwise.' After Suez he would have blossomed into thin clothes and long talks, but the bitter spring chill nipped him, as the thought of partings just accomplished and work just ahead chilled the Anglo-Indian contingent. Little by little one came at the outlines of the old stories—a sick wife left behind here, a boy there, a daughter at school, a very small daughter trusted to friends or hirelings, certain separation for so many years and no great hope or delight in the future. It was not a nice India that the tales hinted at. Here is one that explains a great deal:

There was a Pathan, a Mohammedan, in a Hindu village, employed by the village moneylender as a debt-collector, which is not a popular trade. He lived alone among Hindus, and—so ran the charge in the lower court—he wilfully broke the caste of a Hindu villager by forcing on him forbidden Mussulman food, and when that pious villager would have taken him before the headman to make reparation, the godless one drew his Afghan knife and killed the headman, besides wounding a few others. The evidence ran without flaw, as smoothly as well-arranged cases should, and the Pathan was condemned to death for wilful murder. He appealed and, by some arrangement or other, got leave to state his case personally to the Court of Revision. 'Said, I believe, that he did not much trust lawyers, but that if the sahibs would give him a hearing, as man to man, he might have a run for his money.

Out of the jail, then, he came, and, Pathan-like, not content with his own good facts, must needs begin by some fairy-tale that he was a secret agent of the government sent down to spy on that village. Then he warmed to it. Yes, he *was* that money-lender's agent—a persuader of the reluctant, if you like—working for a Hindu employer. Naturally, many men owed him grudges. A lot of the evidence against him was quite true, but the prosecution had twisted it abominably. About that knife, for instance. True, he had a knife in his hand exactly as they had alleged. But why? Because with that very knife he was cutting up and distributing a roast sheep which he had given as a feast to the villagers. At that feast, he sitting in amity with all his world, the village rose up at the word of command, laid hands on him, and dragged him off to the headman's house. How could he have broken *any* man's caste when they were all eating his sheep? And in the courtyard of the headman's house they surrounded him with heavy sticks and worked themselves into anger against him, each man exciting his neighbour. He was a Pathan. He knew what that sort of talk meant. A man cannot collect debts without making enemies. So he warned them. Again and again he warned them, saying: 'Leave me alone. Do not lay hands on me.' But the trouble grew worse, and he saw it was intended that he should be clubbed to death like a jackal in a drain. Then he said, 'If blows are struck, I strike, and *I* strike to kill, because I am a Pathan,' But the blows were struck, heavy ones. Therefore, with the very Afghan knife that had cut up the mutton, he struck the headman. 'Had you meant to kill the headman?' 'Assuredly! I am a Pathan. When I strike, I strike to kill. I had warned them again and again. I think I got him in the liver. He died. And that is all there is to it, sahibs. It was my life or theirs. They would have taken mine over my freely given meats. *Now* , what'll you do with me?'

In the long run, he got several years for culpable homicide.

'But,' said I, when the tale had been told, 'whatever made the lower court accept all that village evidence? It was too good on the face of it,'

'The lower court said it could not believe it possible that so many respectable native gentle could have banded themselves together to tell a lie.'

'Oh! Had the lower court been long in the country?'

'It was a native judge,' was the reply.

If you think this over in all its bearings, you will see that the lower court was absolutely sincere. Was not the lower court itself a product of Western civilisation, and, as such, bound to play up—to pretend to think along Western lines—translating each grade of Indian village society into its English equivalent, and ruling as an English judge would have ruled? Pathans and, incidentally, English officials must look after themselves.

There is a fell disease of this century called 'snobbery of the soul.' Its germ has been virulently developed in modern cultures from the uncomplex bacillus isolated sixty years ago by the late William Makepeace Thackeray. Precisely as Major Ponto, with his plated dishes and stable-boy masquerading as footman, lied to himself and his guests so—but the *Book of Snobs* can only be brought up to date by him who wrote it.

Then, a man struck in from the Sudan—far and far to the south—with a story of a discomposed judge and a much too collected prisoner.

To the great bazaars of Omdurman, where all things are sold, came a young man from the uttermost deserts of somewhere or other and heard a gramophone. Life was of no value to him till he had bought the creature. He took it back to his village, and at twilight set it going among his ravished friends. His father, sheik of the village, came also, listened to the loud shoutings without breath, the strong music lacking musicians, and said, justly enough: 'This thing is a devil. You must not bring devils into my village. Lock it up.'

They waited until he had gone away and then began another tune. A second time the sheik came, repeated the command, and added that if the singing box was heard again, he would slay the buyer. But their curiosity and joy defied even this, and for the third time (late at night) they slipped in pin and record and let the djinn rave. So the sheik, with his rifle, shot his son as he had promised, and the English judge before whom he eventually came had all the trouble in the world to save that earnest gray head from the gallows. Thus:

'Now, old man, you must say guilty or not guilty.'

'But I shot him. That is why I am here. I——'

'Hush! It is a form of words which the law asks. *(Sotte voce* . Write down that the old idiot doesn't understand.) Be still now.'

'But I shot him. What else could I have done? He bought a devil in a box, and——'

'Quiet! That comes later. Leave talking.'

'But I am sheik of the village. One must not bring devils into a village. I *said* I would shoot him.'

'This matter is in the hands of the law. *I* judge.'

'What need? I shot him. Suppose that *your* son had brought a devil in a box to *your* village——'

They explained to him, at last, that under British rule fathers must hand over devil-dealing children to be shot by the white men (the first step, you see, on the downward path of State aid), and that he must go to prison for several months for interfering with a government shoot.

We are a great race. There was a pious young judge in Nigeria once, who kept a condemned prisoner waiting very many minutes while he hunted through the Hausa dictionary, word by word, for, 'May—God—have—mercy—on—your—soul.'

And I heard another tale—about the Suez Canal this time—a hint of what may happen some day at Panama. There was a tramp steamer, loaded with high explosives, on her way to the East, and at the far end of the Canal one of the sailors very naturally upset a lamp in the fo'c'sle. After a heated interval the crew took to the desert alongside, while the captain and the mate opened all cocks and sank her, not in the fairway but up against a bank, just leaving room for a steamer to squeeze past. Then the Canal authorities wired to her charterers to know exactly what there might be in her; and it is said that the reply kept them awake of nights, for it was their business to blow her up.

Meantime, traffic had to go through, and a P. & O. steamer came along. There was the Canal; there was the sunken wreck, marked by one elderly Arab in a little boat with a red flag, and there was about five foot clearance on each side for the P. & O. She went through a-tiptoe, because even fifty tons of dynamite will jar a boat, perceptibly, and the tramp held more—very much more, not to mention detonators. By some absurd chance, almost the only passenger who knew about the thing at the time was an old lady rather proud of the secret.

'Ah,' she said, in the middle of that agonised glide, 'you may depend upon it that if everybody knew what, I know, they'd all be on the other side of the ship.'

Later on, the authorities blew up the tramp with infinite precautions from some two miles off, for which reason she neither destroyed the Suez Canal nor dislocated the Sweet Water Canal alongside, but merely dug out a hole a hundred feet or a hundred yards deep, and so vanished from Lloyd's register.

But no stories could divert one long from the peculiarities of that amazing line which exists strictly for itself. There was a bathroom (occupied) at the windy end of an open alleyway. In due time the bather came out.

Said the steward, as he swabbed out the tub for his successor: 'That was the Chief Engineer. 'E's been some time. Must 'ave 'ad a mucky job below, this mornin'.'

I have a great admiration for Chief Engineers. They are men in authority, needing all the comforts and aids that can possibly be given them—such as bathrooms of their own close to their own cabins, where they can clean off at leisure.

It is not fair to mix them up with the ruck of passengers, nor is it done on real ships. Nor, when a passenger wants a bath in the evening, do the stewards of real ships roll their eyes like vergers in a cathedral and say, 'We'll see if it can be managed.' They double down the alleyway and shout, 'Matcham' or 'Ponting' or 'Guttman,' and in fifteen seconds one of those swift three has the taps going and the towels out. Real ships are not annexes of Westminster Abbey or Borstal Reformatory. They supply decent accommodation in return for good money, and I imagine that their directors instruct their staffs to look pleased while at work.

Some generations back there must have been an idea that the P. & O. was vastly superior to all lines afloat—a sort of semipontifical show not to be criticised. How much of the notion was due to its own excellence and how much to its passenger-traffic monopoly does not matter. To-day, it neither feeds nor tends its passengers, nor keeps its ships well enough to put on any airs at all.

For which reason, human nature being what it is, it surrounds itself with an ungracious atmosphere of absurd ritual to cover grudged and inadequate performance.

What it really needs is to be dropped into a March North Atlantic, without any lascars, and made to swim for its life between a C.P.R. boat and a North German Lloyd—till it learns to smile.

II

A RETURN TO THE EAST

The East is a much larger slice of the world than Europeans care to admit. Some say it begins at St. Gothard, where the smells of two continents meet and fight all through that terrible restaurant-car dinner in the tunnel. Others have found it at Venice on warm April mornings. But the East is wherever one sees the lateen sail—that shark's fin of a rig which for hundreds of years has dogged all white bathers round the Mediterranean. There is still a suggestion of menace, a hint of piracy, in the blood whenever the lateen goes by, fishing or fruiting or coasting.

'This is *not* my ancestral trade,' she whispers to the accomplice sea. 'If everybody had their rights I should be doing something quite different; for my father, he was the Junk, and my mother, she was the Dhow, and between the two of 'em they made Asia.' Then she tacks, disorderly but deadly quick, and shuffles past the unimaginative steam-packet with her hat over one eye and a knife, as it were, up her baggy sleeves.

Even the stone-boats at Port Said, busied on jetty extensions, show their untamed descent beneath their loaded clumsiness. They are all children of the camel-nosed dhow, who is the mother of mischief; but it was very good to meet them again in raw sunshine, unchanged in any rope and patch.

Old Port Said had disappeared beneath acres of new buildings where one could walk at leisure without being turned back by soldiers.

Two or three landmarks remained; two or three were reported as still in existence, and one Face showed itself after many years—ravaged but respectable—rigidly respectable.

'Yes,' said the Face, 'I have been here all the time. But I have made money, and when I die I am going home to be buried.'

'Why not go home before you are buried, O Face?'

'Because I have lived here *so* long. Home is only good to be buried in.'

'And what do you do, nowadays?'

'Nothing now. I live on my *rentes* —my income.'

Think of it! To live icily in a perpetual cinematograph show of excited, uneasy travellers; to watch huge steamers, sliding in and out all day and all night like railway trucks, unknowing and unsought by a single soul aboard; to talk five or six tongues indifferently, but to have no country—no interest in any earth except one reservation in a Continental cemetery.

It was a cold evening after heavy rain and the half-flooded streets reeked. But we undefeated tourists ran about in droves and saw all that could be seen before train-time. We missed, most of us, the Canal Company's garden, which happens to mark a certain dreadful and exact division between East and West.

Up to that point—it is a fringe of palms, stiff against the sky—the impetus of home memories and the echo of home interests carry the young man along very comfortably on his first journey. But at Suez one must face things. People, generally the most sympathetic, leave the boat there; the older men who are going on have discovered each other and begun to talk shop; no newspapers come aboard, only clipped Reuter telegrams; the world seems cruelly large and self-absorbed. One goes for a walk and finds this little bit of kept ground, with comfortable garden-gated houses on either side of the path. Then one begins to wonder—in the twilight, for choice—when one will see those palms again from the other side. Then the black hour of homesickness, vain regrets, foolish promises, and weak despair shuts down with the smell of strange earth and the cadence of strange tongues.

Cross-roads and halting-places in the desert are always favoured by djinns and afrits. The young man will find them waiting for him in the Canal Company's garden at Port Said.

On the other hand, if he is fortunate enough to have won the East by inheritance, as there are families who served her for five or six generations, he will meet no ghouls in that garden, but a free and a friendly and an ample welcome from good spirits of the East that awaits him. The voices of the gardeners and the watchmen will be as the greetings of his father's servants in his father's house; the evening smells and the sight of the hibiscus and poinsettia will unlock his tongue in words and sentences that he thought he had clean forgotten, and he will go back to the ship (I have seen) as a prince entering on his kingdom.

There was a man in our company—a young Englishman—who had just been granted his heart's desire in the shape of some raw district south of everything southerly in the Sudan, where, on two-thirds of a member of Parliament's wage, under conditions of life that would horrify a self-respecting operative, he will see perhaps some dozen white men in a year, and will certainly pick up two sorts of fever. He had been moved to work very hard for this billet by the representations of a friend in the same service, who said that it was a 'rather decent sort of service,' and he was all of a heat to reach Khartum, report for duty, and fall to. If he is lucky, he may get a district where the people are so virtuous that they do not know how to wear any clothes at all, and so ignorant that they have never yet come across strong drink.

The train that took us to Cairo was own sister in looks and fittings to any South African train—for which I loved her—but she was a trial to some citizens of the United States, who, being used to the Pullman, did not understand the side-corridored, solid-compartment idea. The trouble with a standardised democracy seems to be that, once they break loose from their standards, they have no props. People are *not* left behind and luggage is rarely mislaid on the railroads of the older world. There is an ordained ritual for the handling of all things, to which if a man will only conform and keep quiet, he and his will be attended to with the rest. The people that I watched would not believe this. They charged about futilely and wasted themselves in trying to get ahead of their neighbours.

Here is a fragment from the restaurant-car: 'Look at here! Me and some friends of mine are going to dine at this table. We don't want to be separated and—'

'You 'ave your number for the service, sar?' 'Number? What number? We want to dine *here* , I tell you.'

'You shall get your number, sar, for the first service?'

'Haow's that? Where in thunder do we *get* the numbers, anyway?'

'I will give you the number, sar, at the time—for places at the first service.'

'Yes, but we want to dine together here—right *now.* '

'The service is not yet ready, sar.'

And so on—and so on; with marchings and counter-marchings, and every word nervously italicised. In the end they dined precisely where there was room for them in that new world which they had strayed into.

On one side our windows looked out on darkness of the waste; on the other at the black Canal, all spaced with monstrous headlights of the night-running steamers. Then came towns, lighted with electricity, governed by mixed commissions, and dealing in cotton. Such a town, for instance, as Zagazig, last seen by a very small boy who was lifted out of a railway-carriage and set down beneath a whitewashed wall under naked stars in an illimitable emptiness because, they told him, the train was on fire. Childlike, this did not worry him. What stuck in his sleepy mind was the absurd name of the place and his father's prophecy that when he grew up he would 'come that way in a big steamer.'

So all his life, the word 'Zagazig' carried memories of a brick shed, the flicker of an oil-lamp's floating wick, a sky full of eyes, and an engine coughing in a desert at the world's end; which memories returned in a restaurant-car jolting through what seemed to be miles of brilliantly lighted streets and factories. No one at the table had even turned his head for the battlefields of Kassassin and Tel-el-Kebir. After all, why should they? That work is done, and children are getting ready to be born who will say: '*I* can remember Gondokoro (or El-Obeid or some undreamed of Clapham Junction, Abyssinia-way) before a single factory was started—before the overhead traffic began. Yes, when there was a fever—actually fever—in the city itself!'

The gap is no greater than that between to-day's and t'other day's Zagazig—between the horsed vans of the Overland Route in Lieutenant Waghorn's time and the shining motor that flashed us to our Cairo hotel through what looked like the suburbs of Marseilles or Rome.

Always keep a new city till morning, 'In the daytime,' as it is written in the Perspicuous Book,[5] 'thou hast long occupation,' Our window gave on to the river, but before one moved toward it one heard the thrilling squeal of the kites—those same thievish Companions of the Road who, at that hour, were watching every Englishman's breakfast in every compound and camp from Cairo to Calcutta.

Voices rose from below—unintelligible words in maddeningly familiar accents. A black boy in one blue garment climbed, using his toes as fingers, the tipped mainyard of a Nile boat and framed himself in the window. Then, because he felt happy, he sang, all among the wheeling kites. And beneath our balcony rolled very Nile Himself, golden in sunshine, wrinkled under strong breezes, with a crowd of creaking cargo-boats waiting for a bridge to be opened.

On the cut-stone quay above, a line of cab drivers—a *ticca-gharri* stand, nothing less—lolled and chaffed and tinkered with their harnesses in every beautiful attitude of the ungirt East. All the ground about was spotted with chewed sugarcane—first sign of the hot weather all the world over.

Troops with startlingly pink faces (one would not have noticed this yesterday) rolled over the girder bridge between churning motors and bubbling camels, and the whole long-coated loose-sleeved Moslem world

---

[5] The Koran.

was awake and about its business, as befits sensible people who pray at dawn.

I made haste to cross the bridge and to hear the palms in the wind on the far side. They sang as nobly as though they had been true coconuts, and the thrust of the north wind behind them was almost as open-handed as the thrust of the Trades. Then came a funeral—the sheeted corpse on the shallow cot, the brisk-pacing bearers (if he was good, the sooner he is buried the sooner in heaven; if bad, bury him swiftly for the sake of the household—either way, as the Prophet says, do not let the mourners go too long weeping and hungry)—the women behind, tossing their arms and lamenting, and men and boys chanting low and high.

They might have come forth from the Taksali Gate in the city of Lahore on just such a cold weather morning as this, on their way to the Mohammedan burial-grounds by the river. And the veiled countrywomen, shuffling side by side, elbow pressed to hip, and eloquent right hand pivoting round, palm uppermost, to give value to each shrill phrase, might have been the wives of so many Punjabi cultivators but that they wore another type of bangle and slipper. A knotty-kneed youth sitting high on a donkey, both amuleted against the evil eye, chewed three purplish-feet of sugar-cane, which made one envious as well as voluptuously homesick, though the sugar-cane of Egypt is not to be compared with that of Bombay.

Hans Breitmann writes somewhere:

Oh, if you live in Leyden town You'll meet, if troot be told, Der forms of all der freunds dot tied When du werst six years old.

And they were all there under the chanting palms—saices, orderlies, pedlars, water-carriers, street-cleaners, chicken-sellers and the slate-coloured buffalo with the china-blue eyes being talked to by a little girl with the big stick. Behind the hedges of well-kept gardens squatted the brown gardener, making trenches indifferently with a hoe or a toe, and under the municipal lamp-post lounged the bronze policeman—a touch of Arab about mouth and lean nostril—quite unconcerned with a ferocious row between two donkey-men. They were fighting across the body of a Nubian who had chosen to sleep in that place. Presently, one of them stepped back on the sleeper's stomach. The Nubian grunted, elbowed himself up, rolled his eyes, and pronounced a few utterly dispassionate words. The warriors stopped, settled their headgear, and went away as quickly as the Nubian went to sleep again. This was life, the real, unpolluted stuff—worth a desert-full of mummies. And right through the middle of it—hooting and kicking up the Nile—passed a Cook's steamer all ready to take tourists to Assuan. From the Nubian's point of view she, and not himself, was the wonder—as great as the Swiss-controlled, Swiss-staffed hotel behind her, whose lift, maybe, the Nubian helped to run. Marids, and afrits, guardians of hidden gold, who choke or crush the rash seeker; encounters with the long-buried dead in a Cairo back-alley; undreamed-of promotions, and suddenly lit loves are the stuff of any respectable person's daily life; but the white man from across the water, arriving in hundreds with his unveiled womenfolk, who builds himself flying-rooms and talks along wires, who flees up and down the river, mad to sit upon camels and asses, constrained to throw down silver from both hands—at once a child and a warlock—this thing must come to the Nubian sheer out of the *Thousand and One Nights* . At any rate, the Nubian was perfectly sane. Having eaten, he slept in God's own sunlight, and I left him, to visit the fortunate and guarded and desirable city of Cairo, to whose people, male and female, Allah has given subtlety in abundance. Their jesters are known to have surpassed in refinement the jesters of Damascus, as did their twelve police captains the hardiest and most corrupt of Bagdad in the tolerant days of Harun-al-Raschid; while their old women, not to mention their young wives, could deceive the Father of Lies himself. Delhi is a great place—most bazaar storytellers in India make their villain hail from there; but when the agony and intrigue are piled highest and the tale halts till the very last breathless sprinkle of cowries has ceased to fall on his mat, why then, with wagging head and hooked forefinger, the storyteller goes on:

'*But* there was a man from Cairo, an Egyptian of the Egyptians, who'—and all the crowd knows that a bit of real metropolitan devilry is coming.

III

A SERPENT OF OLD NILE

Modern Cairo is an unkempt place. The streets are dirty and ill-constructed, the pavements unswept and often broken, the tramways thrown, rather than laid, down, the gutters neglected. One expects better than this in a city where the tourist spends so much every season. Granted that the tourist is a dog, he comes at least with a bone in his mouth, and a bone that many people pick. He should have a cleaner kennel. The official answer is that the tourist-traffic is a flea-bite compared with the cotton industry. Even so, land in Cairo city must be too valuable to be used for cotton growing. It might just as well be paved or swept. There is some sort of authority supposed to be in charge of municipal matters, but its work is crippled by what is called 'The Capitulations.' It was told to me that every one in Cairo except the English, who appear to be the mean whites of these parts, has the privilege of appealing to his consul on every conceivable subject from the disposal of a garbage-can to that of a corpse. As almost every one with claims to respectability, and certainly every one without any, keeps a consul, it follows that there is one consul per superficial meter, arshin, or cubit of Ezekiel within the city. And since every consul is zealous for the honour of his country and not at all above annoying the English on general principles, municipal progress is slow.

Cairo strikes one as unventilated and unsterilised, even when the sun and wind are scouring it together. The tourist talks a good deal, as you may see here, but the permanent European resident does not open his mouth more than is necessary—sound travels so far across flat water. Besides, the whole position of things, politically and administratively, is essentially false.

Here is a country which is not a country but a longish strip of market-garden, nominally in charge of a government which is not a government but the disconnected satrapy of a half-dead empire, controlled pecksniffingly by a Power which is not a Power but an Agency, which Agency has been tied up by years, custom, and blackmail into all sorts of intimate relations with six or seven European Powers, all with rights and perquisites, none of whose subjects seem directly amenable to any Power which at first, second, or third hand is supposed to be responsible. That is the barest outline. To fill in the details (if any living man knows them) would be as easy as to explain baseball to an Englishman or the Eton Wall game to a citizen of the United States. But it is a fascinating play. There are Frenchmen in it, whose logical mind it offends, and they revenge themselves by printing the finance-reports and the catalogue of the Bulak Museum in pure French. There are Germans in it, whose demands must be carefully weighed—not that they can by any means be satisfied, but they serve to block other people's. There are Russians in it, who do not very much matter at present but will be heard from later. There are Italians and Greeks in it (both rather pleased with themselves just now), full of the higher finance and the finer emotions. There are Egyptian pashas in it, who come back from Paris at intervals and ask plaintively to whom they are supposed to belong. There is His Highness, the Khedive, in it, and *he* must be considered not a little, and there are women in it, up to their eyes. And there are great English cotton and sugar interests, and angry English importers clamouring to know why they cannot do business on rational lines or get into the Sudan, which they hold is ripe for development if the administration there would only see reason. Among these conflicting interests and amusements sits and perspires the English official, whose job is irrigating or draining or reclaiming land on behalf of a trifle of ten million people, and he finds himself tripped up by skeins of intrigue and bafflement which may ramify through half a dozen harems and four consulates. All this makes for suavity, toleration, and the blessed habit of not being surprised at anything whatever.

Or, so it seemed to me, watching a big dance at one of the hotels. Every European race and breed, and half of the United States were represented, but I fancied I could make out three distinct groupings. The tourists with the steamer-trunk creases still across their dear, excited backs; the military and the officials sure of their partners beforehand, and saying clearly what ought to be said; and a third contingent, lower-voiced, softer-footed, and keener-eyed than the other two, at ease, as gipsies are on their own ground, flinging half-words in local *argot* over shoulders at their friends, understanding on the nod and moved by springs common to their clan only. For example, a woman was talking flawless English to her partner, an English officer. Just before the next dance began, another woman beckoned to her, Eastern fashion, all four fingers flicking downward. The first woman crossed to a potted palm; the second moved toward it also, till the two drew, up, not looking at each other, the plant between them. Then she who had beckoned spoke in a strange tongue *at* the palm. The first woman, still looking away, answered in the same fashion with a rush of words that rattled like buckshot through the stiff fronds. Her tone had nothing to do with that in which she greeted her new partner, who came up as the music began. The one was a delicious drawl; the other had been the guttural rasp and click of the kitchen and the bazaar. So she moved off, and, in a little, the second woman disappeared into the crowd. Most likely it was no more than some question of the programme or dress, but the prompt, feline stealth and coolness of it, the lightning-quick return to and from world-apart civilisations stuck in my memory.

So did the bloodless face of a very old Turk, fresh from some horror of assassination in Constantinople in which he, too, had been nearly pistolled, but, they said, he had argued quietly over the body of a late colleague, as one to whom death was of no moment, until the hysterical Young Turks were abashed and let him get away—to the lights and music of this elegantly appointed hotel.

These modern 'Arabian Nights' are too hectic for quiet folk. I declined upon a more rational Cairo—the Arab city where everything is as it was when Maruf the Cobbler fled from Fatima-el-Orra and met the djinn in the Adelia Musjid. The craftsmen and merchants sat on their shop-boards, a rich mystery of darkness behind them, and the narrow gullies were polished to shoulder-height by the mere flux of people. Shod white men, unless they are agriculturists, touch lightly, with their hands at most, in passing. Easterns lean and loll and squat and sidle against things as they daunder along. When the feet are bare, the whole body thinks. Moreover, it is unseemly to buy or to do aught and be done with it. Only people with tight-fitting clothes that need no attention have time for that. So we of the loose skirt and flowing trousers and slack slipper make full and ample salutations to our friends, and redouble them toward our ill-wishers, and if it be a question of purchase, the stuff must be fingered and appraised with a proverb or so, and if it be a fool-tourist who thinks that he cannot be cheated, O true believers! draw near and witness how we shall loot him.

But I bought nothing. The city thrust more treasure upon me than I could carry away. It came out of dark alleyways on tawny camels loaded with pots; on pattering asses half buried under nets of cut clover; in the exquisitely modelled hands of little children scurrying home from the cookshop with the evening meal, chin pressed against the platter's edge and eyes round with responsibility above the pile; in the broken lights from jutting rooms overhead, where the women lie, chin between palms, looking out of windows not a foot from the floor; in every glimpse into every courtyard, where the men smoke by the tank; in the heaps of rubbish and rotten bricks that flanked newly painted houses, waiting to be built, some day, into houses once more; in the slap and slide or the heelless red-and-yellow slippers all around, and, above all, in the mixed delicious smells of frying butter, Mohammedan bread, kababs, leather, cooking-smoke, assafetida, peppers, and turmeric. Devils cannot abide the smell of burning turmeric, but the right-minded man loves it. It stands for evening that brings all home, the evening meal, the dipping of friendly hands in the dish, the one face, the dropped veil, and the big, guttering pipe afterward.

Praised be Allah for the diversity of His creatures and for the Five Advantages of Travel and for the glories of the Cities of the Earth! Harun-al-Raschid, in roaring Bagdad of old, never delighted himself to the limits of such a delight as was mine, that afternoon. It is true that the call to prayer, the cadence of some of the street-cries, and the cut of some of the garments differed a little from what I had been brought up to; but for the rest, the shadow on the dial had turned back twenty degrees for me, and I found myself saying, as perhaps the dead say when they have recovered their wits, 'This is my real world again,'

Some men are Mohammedan by birth, some by training, and some by fate, but I have never met an Englishman yet who hated Islam and its people as I have met Englishmen who hated some other faiths. *Musalmani awadani*, as the saying goes—where there are Mohammedans, there is a comprehensible civilisation.

Then we came upon a deserted mosque of pitted brick colonnades round a vast courtyard open to the pale sky. It was utterly empty except for its own proper spirit, and that caught one by the throat as one entered. Christian churches may compromise with images and side-chapels where the unworthy or abashed can traffic with accessible saints. Islam has but one pulpit and one stark affirmation—living or dying, one only—and where men have repeated that in red-hot belief through centuries, the air still shakes to it.

Some say now that Islam is dying and that nobody cares; others that, if she withers in Europe and Asia, she will renew herself in Africa and will return—terrible—after certain years, at the head of all the nine sons of Ham; others dream that the English understand Islam as no one else does, and, in years to be, Islam will admit this and the world will be changed. If you go to the mosque Al Azhar—the thousand-year-old University of Cairo—you will be able to decide for yourself. There is nothing to see except many courts, cool in hot weather, surrounded by cliff-like brick walls. Men come and go through dark doorways, giving on to yet darker cloisters, as freely as though the place was a bazaar. There are no aggressive educational appliances. The students sit on the ground, and their teachers instruct them, mostly by word of mouth, in grammar, syntax, logic; *al-hisab*, which is arithmetic; *al-jab'r w'al muqabalah*, which is algebra; *at-tafsir,* commentaries on the Koran, and last and most troublesome, *al-ahadis,* traditions, and yet more commentaries on the law of Islam, which leads back, like everything, to the Koran once again. (For it is written, 'Truly the Quran is none other than a revelation.') It is a very comprehensive curriculum. No man can master it entirely, but any can stay there as long as he pleases. The university provides commons—twenty-five thousand loaves a day, I believe,—and there is always a place to lie down in for such as do not desire a shut room and a bed. Nothing could be more simple or, given certain conditions, more effective. Close upon six hundred professors, who represent officially or unofficially every school or thought, teach ten or twelve thousand students, who draw from every Mohammedan community, west and east between Manila and Morocco, north and south between Kamchatka and the Malay mosque at Cape Town. These drift off to become teachers of little schools, preachers at mosques, students of the Law known to millions (but rarely to Europeans), dreamers, devotees, or miracle-workers in all the ends of the earth. The man who interested me most was a red-bearded, sunk-eyed mullah from the Indian frontier, not likely to be last at any distribution of food, who stood up like a lean wolfhound among collies in a little assembly at a doorway.

And there was another mosque, sumptuously carpeted and lighted (which the Prophet does not approve of), where men prayed in the dull mutter that, at times, mounts and increases under the domes like the boom of drums or the surge of a hot hive before the swarm flings out. And round the corner of it, one almost ran into Our inconspicuous and wholly detached Private of Infantry, his tunic open, his cigarette alight, leaning against some railings and considering the city below. Men in forts and citadels and garrisons all the world over go up at twilight as automatically as sheep at sundown, to have a last look round. They say little and return as silently across the crunching gravel, detested by bare feet, to their whitewashed rooms and regulated lives. One of the men told me he thought well of Cairo. It was interesting. 'Take it from me,' he said, 'there's a lot in seeing places, because you can remember 'em afterward.'

He was very right. The purple and lemon-coloured hazes of dusk and reflected day spread over the throbbing, twinkling streets, masked the great outline of the citadel and the desert hills, and conspired to confuse and suggest and evoke memories, till Cairo the Sorceress cast her proper shape and danced before me in the heartbreaking likeness of every city I had known and loved, a little farther up the road.

It was a cruel double-magic. For in the very hour that my homesick soul had surrendered itself to the dream of the shadow that had turned back on the dial, I realised all the desolate days and homesickness of all the men penned in far-off places among strange sounds and smells.

IV

UP THE RIVER

Once upon a time there was a murderer who got off with a life-sentence. What impressed him most, when he had time to think, was the frank boredom of all who took part in the ritual.

'It was just like going to a doctor or a dentist,' he explained. '*You* come to 'em very full of your affairs, and then you discover that it's only part of their daily work to *them* . I expect,' he added, 'I should have found it the same if—er—I'd gone on to the finish.'

He would have. Break into any new Hell or Heaven and you will be met at its well-worn threshold by the bored experts in attendance.

For three weeks we sat on copiously chaired and carpeted decks, carefully isolated from everything that had anything to do with Egypt, under chaperonage of a properly orientalised dragoman. Twice or thrice daily, our steamer drew up at a mud-bank covered with donkeys. Saddles were hauled out of a hatch in our bows; the donkeys were dressed, dealt round like cards: we rode off through crops or desert, as the case might be, were introduced in ringing tones to a temple, and were then duly returned to our bridge and our Baedekers. For sheer comfort, not to say padded sloth, the life was unequalled, and since the bulk of our passengers were citizens of the United States—Egypt in winter ought to be admitted into the Union as a temporary territory—there was no lack of interest. They were overwhelmingly women, with here and there a placid nose-led husband or father, visibly suffering from congestion of information about his native city. I had the joy of seeing two such men meet. They turned their backs resolutely on the River, bit and lit cigars, and for one hour and a quarter ceased not to emit statistics of the industries, commerce, manufacture, transport, and journalism of their towns;—Los Angeles, let us say, and Rochester, N.Y. It sounded like a duel between two cash-registers.

One forgot, of course, that all the dreary figures were alive to them, and as Los Angeles spoke Rochester visualised. Next day I met an Englishman from the Soudan end of things, very full of a little-known railway which had been laid down in what had looked like raw desert, and therefore had turned out to be full of paying freight. He was in the full-tide of it when Los Angeles ranged alongside and cast anchor, fascinated by the mere roll of numbers.

'Haow's that?' he cut in sharply at a pause.

He was told how, and went on to drain my friend dry concerning that railroad, out of sheer fraternal interest, as he explained, in 'any darn' thing that's being made anywheres,'

'So you see,' my friend went on, 'we shall be bringing Abyssinian cattle into Cairo.'

'On the hoof?' One quick glance at the Desert ranges.

'No, no! By rail and River. And after *that* we're going to grow cotton between the Blue and the White Nile and knock spots out of the States.'

'Ha-ow's that?'

'This way.' The speaker spread his first and second fingers fanwise under the big, interested beak. 'That's the Blue Nile. And that's the White. There's a difference of so many feet between 'em, an' in that fork here, 'tween my fingers, we shall—'

'*I* see. Irrigate on the strength of the little difference in the levels. How many acres?'

Again Los Angeles was told. He expanded like a frog in a shower. 'An' I thought,' he murmured, 'Egypt was all mummies and the Bible! *I* used to know something about cotton. Now we'll talk.'

All that day the two paced the deck with the absorbed insolente of lovers; and, lover-like, each would steal away and tell me what a splendid soul was his companion.

That was one type; but there were others—professional men who did not make or sell things—and these the hand of an all-exacting Democracy seemed to have run into one mould. They 'were not reticent, but no matter whence they hailed, their talk was as standardised as the fittings of a Pullman.

I hinted something of this to a woman aboard who was learned in their sermons of either language.

'I think,' she began, 'that the staleness you complain of—'

'I never said "staleness,"' I protested.

'But you thought it. The staleness you noticed is due to our men being so largely educated by old women—old maids. Practically till he goes to College, and not always then, a boy can't get away from them.'

'Then what happens?'

'The natural result. A man's instinct is to teach a boy to think for himself. If a woman can't make a boy think *as* she thinks, she sits down and cries. A man hasn't any standards. He makes 'em. A woman's the most standardised being in the world. She has to be. *Now* d'you see?'

'Not yet.'

'Well, our trouble in America is that we're being school-marmed to death. You can see it in any paper you pick up. What were those men talking about just now?'

'Food adulteration, police-reform, and beautifying waste-lots in towns,' I replied promptly.

She threw up her hands. 'I knew it!' she cried. 'Our great National Policy of co-educational housekeeping! Ham-frills and pillow-shams. Did you ever know a man get a woman's respect by parading around creation with a dish-clout pinned to his coat-tails?'

'But if his woman ord——told him to do it?' I suggested.

'Then she'd despise him the more for doing it. *You* needn't laugh. 'You're coming to the same sort of thing in England.'

I returned to the little gathering. A woman was talking to them as one accustomed to talk from birth. They listened with the rigid attention of men early trained to listen to, but not to talk with, women. She was, to put it mildly, the mother of all she-bores, but when she moved on, no man ventured to say as much.

'That's what I mean by being school-manned to death,' said my acquaintance wickedly. 'Why, she bored 'em stiff; but they are so well brought up, they didn't even know they were bored. Some day the American Man is going to revolt.'

'And what'll the American Woman do?'

'She'll sit and cry—and it'll do her good.'

Later on, I met a woman from a certain Western State seeing God's great, happy, inattentive world for the first time, and rather distressed that it was not like hers. She had always understood that the English were brutal to their wives—the papers of her State said so. (If you only knew the papers of her State I) But she had not noticed any scandalous treatment so far, and Englishwomen, whom she admitted she would never understand, seemed to enjoy a certain specious liberty and equality; while Englishmen were distinctly kind to girls in difficulties over their baggage and tickets on strange railways. Quite a nice people, she concluded, but without much sense of humour. One day, she showed me what looked like a fashion-paper print of a dress-stuff—a pretty oval medallion of stars on a striped grenadine background that somehow seemed familiar.

'How nice! What is it?' I asked.

'Our National Flag,' she replied.

'Indeed. But it doesn't look quite——'

'No. This is a new design for arranging the stars so that they shall be easier to count and more decorative in effect. We're going to take a vote on it in our State, where *we* have the franchise. I shall cast my vote when I get home.'

'Really! And how will you vote?'

'I'm just thinking that out.' She spread the picture on her knee and considered it, head to one side, as though it were indeed dress material.

All this while the land of Egypt marched solemnly beside us on either hand. The river being low, we saw it from the boat as one long plinth, twelve to twenty feet high of brownish, purplish mud, visibly upheld every hundred yards or so by glistening copper caryatides in the shape of naked men baling water up to the crops above. Behind that bright emerald line ran the fawn-or tiger-coloured background of desert, and a pale blue sky closed all. There was Egypt even as the Pharaohs, their engineers and architects, had seen it—land to cultivate, folk and cattle for the work, and outside that work no distraction nor allurement of any kind whatever, save when the dead were taken to their place beyond the limits of cultivation. When the banks grew lower, one looked across as much as two miles of green-stuff packed like a toy Noah's-ark with people, camels, sheep, goats, oxen, buffaloes, and an occasional horse. The beasts stood as still, too, as the toys, because they were tethered or hobbled each to his own half-circle of clover, and moved forward when that was eaten. Only the very little kids were loose, and these played on the flat mud roofs like kittens.

No wonder 'every shepherd is an abomination to the Egyptians.' The dusty, naked-footed field-tracks are cut down to the last centimetre of grudged width; the main roads are lifted high on the flanks of the canals, unless the permanent-way of some light railroad can be pressed to do duty for them. The wheat, the pale ripened tufted sugar-cane, the millet, the barley, the onions, the fringed castor-oil bushes jostle each other for foothold, since the Desert will not give them room; and men chase the falling Nile inch by inch, each dawn, with new furrowed melon-beds on the still dripping mud-banks.

Administratively, such a land ought to be a joy. The people do not emigrate; all their resources are in plain sight; they are as accustomed as their cattle to being led about. All they desire, and it has been given them, is freedom from murder and mutilation, rape and robbery. The rest they can attend to in their silent palm-shaded villages where the pigeons coo and the little children play in the dust.

But Western civilisation is a devastating and a selfish game. Like the young woman from 'our State,' it says in effect: 'I am rich. I've nothing to do. I *must* do something. I shall take up social reform.'

Just now there is a little social reform in Egypt which is rather amusing. The Egyptian cultivator borrows money; as all farmers must. This land without hedge or wild-flower is his passion by age-long inheritance and suffering, by, in and for which he lives. He borrows to develop it and to buy more at from £30 to £200 per acre, the profit on which, when all is paid, works out at between £5 to £10 per acre. Formerly, he borrowed from the local money-lenders, mostly Greeks, at 30 per cent per annum and over. This rate is not excessive, so long as public opinion allows the borrower from time to time to slay the lender; but modern administration calls that riot and murder. Some years ago, therefore, there was established a State-guaranteed Bank which lent to the cultivators at eight per cent, and the cultivator zealously availed himself of that privilege. He did not default more than in reason, but being a farmer, he naturally did not pay up till threatened with being sold up. So he prospered and bought more land, which was his heart's desire. This year—1913—the administration issued sudden orders that no man owning less than five acres could borrow on security of his land. The matter interested me directly, because I held five hundred pounds worth of shares in that State-guaranteed Bank, and more than half our clients were small men of less than five acres. So I made inquiries in quarters that seemed to possess information, and was told that the new law was precisely on all-fours with the Homestead Act or the United States and France, and the intentions of Divine Providence—or words to that effect.

'But,' I asked, 'won't this limitation of credit prevent the men with less than five acres from borrowing more to buy more land and getting on in the world?'

'Yes,' was the answer, 'of course it will. That's just what we want to prevent. Half these fellows ruin themselves trying to buy more land. We've got to protect them against themselves.'

That, alas! is the one enemy against which no law can protect any son of Adam; since the real reasons that make or break a man are too absurd or too obscene to be reached from outside. Then I cast about in other quarters to discover what the cultivator was going to do about it.

'Oh, him?' said one of my many informants. '*He's* all right. There are about six ways of evading the Act that, *I* know of. The fellah probably knows another six. He has been trained to look after himself since the days of Rameses. He can forge land-transfers for one thing; borrow land enough to make his holding more than five acres for as long as it takes to register a loan; get money from his own women (yes, that's one result of modern progress in this land!) or go back to his old friend the Greek at 30 per cent.'

'Then the Greek will sell him up, and that will be against the law, won't it?' I said.

'Don't you worry about the Greek. He can get through any law ever made if there's five piastres on the other side of it.'

'Maybe; but *was* the Agricultural Bank selling the cultivators up too much?'

'Not in the least. The number of small holdings is on the increase, if anything. Most cultivators won't pay a loan until you point a judgment-summons at their head. They think that shows they're men of consequence. This swells the number of judgment-summonses issued, but it doesn't mean a land-sale for each summons. Another fact is that in real life some men don't get on as well as others. Either they don't farm well enough, or they take to hashish, or go crazy about a girl and borrow money for her, or—er—something of that kind, and they are sold up. You may have noticed that.'

'I have. And meantime, what is the fellah doing?'

'Meantime, the fellah has misread the Act—as usual. He thinks it's retrospective, and that he needn't pay past debts. They may make trouble, but I fancy your Bank will keep quiet.'

'Keep quiet! With the bottom knocked out of two-thirds of its business and—and my five hundred pounds involved!'

'Is that your trouble? I don't think your shares will rise in a hurry; but if you want some fun, go and talk to the French about it,'

This seemed as good a way as any of getting a little interest. The Frenchman that I went to spoke with a certain knowledge of finance and politics and the natural malice of a logical race against an illogical horde.

'Yes,' he said. 'The idea of limiting credit under these circumstances is absurd. But that is not all. People are not frightened, business is not upset by one absurd idea, but by the possibilities of more,'

'Are there any more ideas, then, that are going to be tried on this country?'

'Two or three,' he replied placidly. 'They are all generous; but they are all ridiculous. Egypt is not a place where one should promulgate ridiculous ideas.'

'But my shares—my shares!' I cried. 'They have already dropped several points.'

'It is possible. They will drop more. Then they will rise.'

'Thank you. But why?'

'Because the idea is fundamentally absurd. That will never be admitted by your people, but there will be arrangements, accommodations, adjustments, till it is all the same as it used to be. It will be the concern of the Permanent Official—poor devil!—to pull it straight. It is always his concern. Meantime, prices will rise for all things.'

'Why?'

'Because the land is the chief security in Egypt. If a man cannot borrow on that security, the rates of interest will increase on whatever other security he offers. That will affect all work and wages and Government contracts.'

He put it so convincingly and with so many historical illustrations that I saw whole perspectives of the old energetic Pharaohs, masters of life and death along the River, checked in mid-career by cold-blooded accountants chanting that not even the Gods themselves can make two plus two more than four. And the vision ran down through the ages to one little earnest head on a Cook's steamer, bent sideways over the vital problem of rearranging 'our National Flag' so that it should be 'easier to count the stars.'

For the thousandth time: Praised be Allah for the diversity of His creatures!

V

DEAD KINGS

The Swiss are the only people who have taken the trouble to master the art of hotel-keeping. Consequently, in the things that really matter—beds, baths, and victuals—they control Egypt; and since every land always throws back to its aboriginal life (which is why the United States delight in telling aged stories), any ancient Egyptian would at once understand and join in with the life that roars through the nickel-plumbed tourist-barracks on the river, where all the world frolics in the sunshine. At first sight, the show lends itself to cheap moralising, till one recalls that one only sees busy folk when they are idle, and rich folk when they have made their money. A citizen of the United States—his first trip abroad—pointed out a middle-aged Anglo-Saxon who was relaxing after the manner of several school-boys.

'There's a sample!' said the Son of Hustle scornfully. 'Tell me, *he* ever did anything in his life?' Unluckily he had pitched upon one who, when he is in collar, reckons thirteen and a half hours a fairish day's work.

Among this assembly were men and women burned to an even blue-black tint—civilised people with bleached hair and sparkling eyes. They explained themselves as 'diggers'—just diggers—and opened me a new world. Granted that all Egypt is one big undertaker's emporium, what could be more fascinating than to get Government leave to rummage in a corner of it, to form a little company and spend the cold weather trying to pay dividends in the shape of amethyst necklaces, lapis-lazuli scarabs, pots of pure gold, and priceless bits of statuary? Or, if one is rich, what better fun than to grub-stake an expedition on the supposed site of a dead city and see what turns up? There was a big-game hunter who had used most of the Continent, quite carried away by this sport.

'I'm going to take shares in a city next year, and watch the digging myself,' he said. 'It beats elephants to pieces. In *this* game you're digging up dead things and making them alive. Aren't you going to have a flutter?'

He showed me a seductive little prospectus. Myself, I would sooner not lay hands on a dead man's kit or equipment, especially when he has gone to his grave in the belief that the trinkets guarantee salvation. Of course, there is the other argument, put forward by sceptics, that the Egyptian was a blatant self-advertiser, and that nothing would please him more than the thought that he was being looked at and admired after all these years. Still, one might rob some shrinking soul who didn't see it in that light.

At the end of spring the diggers flock back out of the Desert and exchange chaff and flews in the gorgeous verandahs. For example, A's company has made a find of priceless stuff, Heaven knows how old, and is—not too meek about it. Company B, less fortunate, hints that if only A knew to what extent their native diggers had been stealing and disposing of the thefts, under their very archaeological noses, they would not be so happy.

'Nonsense,' says Company A. 'Our diggers are above suspicion. Besides, we watched 'em.'

'*Are* they?' is the reply. 'Well, next time you are in Berlin, go to the Museum and you'll see what the Germans have got hold of. It must have come out of your ground. The Dynasty proves it.' So A's cup is poisoned—till next year.

No collector or curator of a museum should have any moral scruples whatever; and I have never met one who had; though I have been informed by deeply-shocked informants of four nationalities that the Germans are the most flagrant pirates of all.

The business of exploration is about as romantic as earth-work on Indian railways. There are the same narrow-gauge trams and donkeys, the same shining gangs in the borrow-pits and the same skirling dark-blue crowds of women and children with the little earth-baskets. But the hoes are not driven in, nor the clods jerked aside at random, and when the work fringes along the base of some mighty wall, men use their hands carefully. A white man—or he was white at breakfast-time—patrols through the continually renewed dust-haze. Weeks may pass without a single bead, but anything may turn up at any moment, and it is his to answer the shout of discovery.

We had the good fortune to stay a while at the Headquarters of the Metropolitan Museum (New York) in a valley riddled like a rabbit-warren with tombs. Their stables, store-houses, and servants' quarters are old tombs; their talk is of tombs, and their dream (the diggers' dream always) is to discover a virgin tomb where the untouched dead lie with their jewels upon them. Four miles away are the wide-winged, rampant hotels. Here is nothing whatever but the rubbish of death that died thousands of years ago, on whose grave no green thing has ever grown. Villages, expert in two hundred generations of grave-robbing, cower among the mounds of wastage, and whoop at the daily tourist. Paths made by bare feet run from one half-tomb, half-mud-heap to the next, not much more distinct than snail smears, but they have been used since....

Time is a dangerous thing to play with. That morning the concierge had toiled for us among steamer-sailings to see if we could save three days. That evening we sat with folk for whom Time had stood still since the Ptolemies. I wondered, at first, how it concerned them or any man if such and such a Pharaoh had used to his own glory the plinths and columns of such another Pharaoh before or after Melchizedek. Their whole background was too inconceivably remote for the mind to work on. But the next morning we were taken to the painted tomb of a noble—a Minister of Agriculture—who died four or five thousand years ago. He said to me, in so many words: 'Observe I was very like your friend, the late Mr. Samuel Pepys, of your Admiralty. I took an enormous interest in life, which I most thoroughly enjoyed, on its human and on its spiritual side. I do not think you will find many departments of State better managed than mine, or a better-kept house, or a nicer set of young people ... My daughters! The eldest, as you can see, takes after her mother. The youngest, my favourite, is supposed to favour me. Now I will show you all the things that I did, and delighted in, till it was time for me to present my accounts elsewhere.' And he showed me, detail by detail, in colour and in drawing, his cattle, his horses, his crops, his tours in the district, his accountants presenting the revenue returns, and he himself, busiest of the busy, in the good day.

But when we left that broad, gay ante-room and came to the narrower passage where once his body had lain and where all his doom was portrayed, I could not follow him so well. I did not see how he, so experienced in life, could be cowed by friezes of brute-headed apparitions or satisfied by files of repeated figures. He explained, something to this effect:

'We live on the River—a line without breadth or thickness. Behind us is the Desert, which nothing can affect; wither no man goes till he is dead, (One does not use good agricultural ground for cemeteries.) Practically, then, we only move in two dimensions—up stream or down. Take away the Desert, which we don't consider any more than a healthy man considers death, and you will see that we have no background whatever. Our world is all one straight bar of brown or green earth, and, for some months, mere sky-reflecting water that wipes out everything You have only to look at the Colossi to realise how enormously and extravagantly man and his works must scale in such a country. Remember too, that our crops are sure, and our life is very, very easy. Above all, we have no neighbours That is to say, we must give out, for we cannot take in. Now, I put it to you, what is left for a priest with imagination, except to develop ritual and multiply gods on friezes? Unlimited leisure, limited space of two dimensions, divided by the hypnotising line of the River, and bounded by visible, unalterable death—must, *ipso facto* ——'

'Even so,' I interrupted. 'I do not comprehend your Gods—your direct worship of beasts, for instance?'

'You prefer the indirect? The worship of Humanity with a capital H? My Gods, or what I saw in them, contented me.'

'What did you see in your Gods as affecting belief and conduct?'

'You know the answer to the riddle of the Sphinx?'

'No,' I murmured. 'What is it?'

'"All sensible men are of the same religion, but no sensible man ever tells,"' he replied. With that I had to be content, for the passage ended in solid rock.

There were other tombs in the valley, but the owners were dumb, except one Pharaoh, who from the highest motives had broken with the creeds and instincts of his country, and so had all but wrecked it. One of his discoveries was an artist, who saw men not on one plane but modelled full or three-quarter face, with limbs suited to their loads and postures. His vividly realised stuff leaped to the eye out of the acreage of low-relief in the old convention, and I applauded as a properly brought-up tourist should.

'Mine was a fatal mistake,' Pharaoh Ahkenaton sighed in my ear,' I mistook the conventions of life for the realities.'

'Ah, those soul-crippling conventions!' I cried.

'You mistake *me* ,' he answered more stiffly. 'I was so sure of their reality that I thought that they were really lies, whereas they were only invented to cover the raw facts of life.'

'Ah, those raw facts of life!' I cried, still louder; for it is not often that one has a chance of impressing a Pharaoh.' We must face them with open eyes and an open mind! Did *you* ?'

'I had no opportunity of avoiding them,' he replied. 'I broke every convention in my land.'

'Oh, noble! And what happened?'

'What happens when you strip the cover off a hornet's nest? The raw fact of life is that mankind is just a little lower than the angels, and the conventions are based on that fact in order that men may become angels. But if you begin, as I did, by the convention that men are angels they will assuredly become bigger beasts than ever.'

'That,' I said firmly, 'is altogether out-of-date. You should have brought a larger mentality, a more vital uplift, and—er—all that sort of thing, to bear on—all that sort of thing, you know.'

'I did,' said Ahkenaton gloomily. 'It broke me!' And he, too, went dumb among the ruins.

There is a valley of rocks and stones in every shade of red and brown, called the Valley of the Kings, where a little oil-engine coughs behind its hand all day long, grinding electricity to light the faces of dead Pharaohs a hundred feet underground. All down the valley, during the tourist season, stand char-a-bancs and donkeys and sand-carts, with here and there exhausted couples who have dropped out of the processions and glisten and fan themselves in some scrap of shade. Along the sides of the valley are the tombs of the kings neatly numbered, as it might be mining adits with concrete steps leading up to them, and iron grilles that lock of nights, and doorkeepers of the Department of Antiquities demanding the proper tickets. One enters, and from deeps below deeps hears the voices of dragomans booming through the names and titles of the illustrious and thrice-puissant dead. Rock-cut steps go down into hot, still darkness, passages-twist and are led over blind pits which, men say, the wise builders childishly hoped would be taken for the real tombs by thieves to come. Up and down these alley-ways clatter all the races of Europe with a solid backing of the United States. Their footsteps are suddenly blunted on the floor of a hall paved with immemorial dust that will never dance in any wind. They peer up at the blazoned ceilings, stoop down to the minutely decorated walls, crane and follow the sombre splendours of a cornice, draw in their breaths and climb up again to the fierce sunshine to re-dive into the next adit on their programme. What they think proper to say, they say aloud—and some of it is very interesting. What they feel you can guess from a certain haste in their movements—something between the shrinking modesty of a man under fire and the Hadn't-we-better-be-getting-on attitude of visitors to a mine. After all, it is not natural for man to go underground except for business or for the last time. He is conscious of the weight of mother-earth overhead, and when to her expectant bulk is added the whole beaked, horned, winged, and crowned hierarchy of a lost faith flaming at every turn of his eye, he naturally wishes to move away. Even the sight of a very great king indeed, sarcophagused under electric light in a hall full of most fortifying pictures, does not hold him too long.

Some men assert that the crypt of St. Peter's, with only nineteen centuries bearing down on the groining, and the tombs of early popes and kings all about, is more impressive than the Valley of the Kings because it explains how and out of what an existing creed grew. But the Valley of the Kings explains nothing except that most terrible line in *Macbeth* :

To the last syllable of recorded time.

Earth opens her dry lips and says it.

In one of the tombs there is a little chamber whose ceiling, probably because of a fault in the rock, could not be smoothed off like the others. So the decorator, very cunningly, covered it with a closely designed cloth-pattern—just such a chintz-like piece of stuff as, in real life, one would use to underhang a rough roof with. He did it perfectly, down there in the dark, and went his way. Thousands of years later, there was born a man of my acquaintance who, for good and sufficient reason, had an almost insane horror of anything in the nature of a ceiling-cloth. He used to make excuses for not going into the dry goods shops at Christmas, when hastily enlarged annexes are hidden, roof and sides, with embroideries. Perhaps a snake or a lizard had dropped on his mother from the roof before he was born; perhaps it was the memory of some hideous fever-bout in a tent. At any rate, that man's idea of The Torment was a hot, crowded underground room, underhung with patterned cloths. Once in his life at a city in the far north, where he had to make a speech, he met that perfect combination. They led him up and down narrow, crowded, steam-heated passages, till they planted him at last in a room without visible windows (by which he knew he was, underground), and directly beneath a warm-patterned ceiling-cloth—rather like a tent-lining. And there he had to say his say, while panic terror sat in his throat. The second time was in the Valley of the Kings, where very similar passages, crowded with people, led him into a room cut of rock, fathoms underground, with what looked like a sagging chintz cloth not three feet above his head. The man I'd like to catch,' he said when he came outside again, 'is that decorator-man. D'you suppose he meant to produce that effect?'

Every man has his private terrors, other than those of his own conscience. From what I saw in the Valley of the Kings, the Egyptians seem to have known this some time ago. They certainly have impressed it on most unexpected people. I heard two voices down a passage talking together as follows:

She . I guess we weren't ever meant to see these old tombs from inside, anyway.

He . How so?

She . For one thing, they believe so hard in being dead. Of course, their outlook on spiritual things wasn't as broad as ours.

He . Well, there's no danger of *our* being led away by it. Did you buy that alleged scarab off the dragoman this morning?

VI

THE FACE OF THE DESERT

Going up the Nile is like running the gauntlet before Eternity. Till one has seen it, one does not realise the amazing thinness of that little damp trickle of life that steals along undefeated through the jaws of established death. A rifle-shot would cover the widest limits of cultivation, a bow-shot would reach the narrower. Once beyond them a man may carry his next drink with him till he reaches Cape Blanco on the west (where he may signal for one from a passing Union Castle boat) or the Karachi Club on the east. Say four thousand dry miles to the left hand and three thousand to the right.

The weight of the Desert is on one, every day and every hour. At morning, when the cavalcade tramps along in the rear of the tulip-like dragoman, She says: 'I am here——just beyond that ridge of pink sand that you are admiring. Come along, pretty gentleman, and I'll tell you your fortune.' But the dragoman says very clearly: 'Please, sar, do not separate yourself at *all* from the main body,' which, the Desert knows well, you had no thought of doing. At noon, when the stewards rummage out lunch-drinks from the dewy ice-chest, the Desert whines louder than the well-wheels on the bank: 'I am here, only a quarter of a mile away. For mercy's sake, pretty gentleman, spare a mouthful of that prickly whisky-and-soda you are lifting to your lips. There's a white man a few hundred miles off, dying on my lap of thirst—thirst that you cure with a rag dipped in lukewarm water while you hold him down with the one hand, and he thinks he is cursing you aloud, but he isn't, because his tongue is outside his mouth and he can't get it back. Thank *you* , my noble captain!' For naturally one tips half the drink over the rail with the ancient prayer: 'May it reach him who needs it,' and turns one's back on the pulsing ridges and fluid horizons that are beginning their mid-day mirage-dance.

At evening the Desert obtrudes again—tricked out as a Nautch girl in veils of purple, saffron, gold-tinsel, and grass-green. She postures shamelessly before the delighted tourists with woven skeins of homeward-flying pelicans, fringes of wild duck, black spotted on crimson, and cheap jewellery of opal clouds. 'Notice Me!' She cries, like any other worthless woman. 'Admire the play of My mobile features— the revelations of My multi-coloured soul! Observe My allurements and potentialities. Thrill while I stir you!' So She floats through all Her changes and retires upstage into the arms of the dusk. But at midnight She drops all pretence and bears down in Her natural shape, which depends upon the conscience of the beholder and his distance from the next white man.

You will observe in the *Benedicite Omnia Opera* that the Desert is the sole thing not enjoined to 'bless the Lord, praise Him and magnify Him for ever.' This is because when our illustrious father, the Lord Adam, and his august consort, the Lady Eve, were expelled from Eden, Eblis the Accursed, fearful lest mankind should return ultimately to the favour of Allah, set himself to burn and lay waste all the lands east and west of Eden.

Oddly enough, the Garden of Eden is almost the exact centre of all the world's deserts, counting from Gobi to Timbuctoo; and all that land *qua* land is 'dismissed from the mercy of God.' Those who use it do so at their own risk. Consequently the Desert produces her own type of man exactly as the sea does. I was fortunate enough to meet one sample, aged perhaps twenty-five. His work took him along the edge of the Red Sea, where men on swift camels come to smuggle hashish, and sometimes guns, from dhows that put in to any convenient beach. These smugglers must be chased on still swifter camels, and since the wells are few and known, the game is to get ahead of them and occupy their drinking-places.

But they may skip a well or so, and do several days' march in one. Then their pursuer must take e'en greater risks and make crueller marches that the Law may be upheld. The one thing in the Law's favour is that *hashish* smells abominably—worse than a heated camel—so, when they range alongside, no time is lost in listening to lies. It was not told to me how they navigate themselves across the broken wastes, or by what arts they keep alive in the dust-storms and heat. That was taken for granted, and the man who took it so considered himself the most commonplace of mortals. He was deeply moved by the account of a new aerial route which the French are laying out somewhere in the Sahara over a waterless stretch of four hundred miles, where if the aeroplane is disabled between stations the pilot will most likely die and dry up beside it. To do the Desert justice, she rarely bothers to wipe out evidence of a kill. There are places in the Desert, men say, where even now you come across the dead of old battles, all as light as last year's wasps' nests, laid down in swaths or strung out in flight, with, here and there, the little sparkling lines of the emptied cartridge-cases that dropped them.

There are valleys and ravines that the craziest smugglers do not care to refuge in at certain times of the year; as there are rest-houses where one's native servants will not stay because they are challenged on their way to the kitchen by sentries of old Soudanese regiments which have long gone over to Paradise. And of voices and warnings and outcries behind rocks there is no end. These last arise from the fact that men very rarely live in a spot so utterly still that they can hear the murmuring race of the blood over their own ear-drums. Neither ship, prairie, nor forest gives that silence. I went out to find it once, when our steamer tied up and the rest of them had gone to see a sight, but I never dared venture more than a mile from our funnel-smoke. At that point I came upon a hill honey-combed with graves that held a multitude of paper-white skulls, all grinning cheerfully like ambassadors of the Desert. But I did not accept their invitation. They had told me that all the little devils learn to draw in the Desert, which explains the elaborate and purposeless detail that fills it. None but devils could think of etching every rock outcrop with wind-lines, or skinning it down to its glistening nerves with sand-blasts; of arranging hills in the likeness of pyramids and sphinxes and wrecked town-suburbs; of covering the space of half an English county with sepia studies of interlacing and recrossing ravines, dongas, and nullahs, each an exposition of much too clever perspective; and of wiping out the half-finished work with a wash of sand in three tints, only to pick it up again in silver-point on the horizon's edge. This they do in order to make lost travellers think they can recognise landmarks and run about identifying them till the madness comes. The Desert is all devil-device—as you might say 'blasted cleverness'—crammed with futile works, always promising something fresh round the next corner, always leading out through heaped decoration and over-insistent design into equal barrenness.

There was a morning of mornings when we lay opposite the rock-hewn Temple of Abu Simbel, where four great figures, each sixty feet high, sit with their hands on their knees waiting for Judgment Day. At their feet is a little breadth of blue-green crop; they seem to hold back all the weight of the Desert behind them, which, none the less, lips over at one side in a cataract of vividest orange sand. The tourist is recommended to see the sunrise here, either from within the temple where it falls on a certain altar erected by Rameses in his own honour, or from without where another Power takes charge.

The stars had paled when we began our watch; the river birds were just whispering over their toilettes in the uncertain purplish light. Then the river dimmered up like pewter; the line of the ridge behind the Temple showed itself against a milkiness in the sky; one felt rather than saw that there were four figures in the pit of gloom below it. These blocked themselves out, huge enough, but without any special terror, while the glorious ritual of the Eastern dawn went forward. Some reed of the bank revealed itself by reflection, black on silver; arched wings flapped and jarred the still water to splintered glass; the desert ridge turned to topaz, and the four figures stood clear, yet without shadowing, from their background. The stronger light flooded them red from head to foot, and they became alive—as horridly and tensely yet blindly alive as pinioned men in the death-chair before the current is switched on. One felt that if by any miracle the dawn could be delayed a second longer, they would tear themselves free, and leap forth to heaven knows what sort of vengeance. But that instant the full sun pinned them in their places—nothing more than statues slashed with light and shadow—and another day got to work.

A few yards to the left of the great images, close to the statue of an Egyptian princess, whose face was the very face of 'She,' there was a marble slab over the grave of an English officer killed in a fight against dervishes nearly a generation ago.

From Abu Simbel to Wady Halfa the river, escaped from the domination of the Pharaohs, begins to talk about dead white men. Thirty years ago, young English officers in India lied and intrigued furiously that they might be attached to expeditions whose bases were sometimes at Suakim, sometimes quite in the desert air, but all of whose deeds are now quite forgotten. Occasionally the dragoman, waving a smooth hand east or south-easterly, will speak of some fight. Then every one murmurs: 'Oh yes. That was Gordon, of course,' or 'Was that before or after Omdurman?' But the river is much more precise. As the boat quarters the falling stream like a puzzled hound, all the old names spurt up again under the paddle-wheels—'Hicks' army—Val Baker—El Teb—Tokar—Tamai—Tamanieb and Osman Digna!' Her head swings round for another slant: *'We cannot land English or Indian troops: if consulted, recommend abandonment of the Soudan within certain limits.* ' That was my Lord Granville chirruping to the advisers of His Highness the Khedive, and the sentence comes back as crisp as when it first shocked one in '84. Next—here is a long reach between flooded palm trees—next, of course, comes Gordon—and a delightfully mad Irish war correspondent who was locked up with him in Khartoum. Gordon—Eighty-four—Eighty-five—the Suakim-Berber Railway really begun and quite as really abandoned. Korti—Abu Klea—the Desert Column—a steamer called the *Safieh* > not the *Condor* , which rescued two other steamers wrecked on their way back from a Khartoum in the red hands of the Mahdi of those days. Then—the smooth glide over deep water continues—another Suakim expedition with a great deal of Osman Digna and renewed attempts to build the Suakim-Berber Railway. 'Hashin,' say the paddle-wheels, slowing all of a sudden—'MacNeill's Zareba—the 15th Sikhs and another native regiment—Osman Digna in great pride and power, and Wady Halfa a frontier town. Tamai, once more; another siege of Suakim: Gemaiza; Handub; Trinkitat, and Tokar—1887.'

The river recalls the names; the mind at once brings up the face and every trick of speech of some youth met for a few hours, maybe, in a train on the way to Egypt of the old days. Both name and face had utterly vanished from one's memory till then.

It was another generation that picked up the ball ten years later and touched down in Khartoum. Several people aboard the Cook boat had been to that city. They all agreed that the hotel charges were very high, but that you could buy the most delightful curiosities in the native bazaar. But I do not like bazaars of the Egyptian kind, since a discovery I made at Assouan. There was an old man—a Mussulman—who pressed me to buy some truck or other, but not with the villainous camaraderie that generations of low-caste tourists have taught the people, nor yet with the cosmopolitan light-handedness of appeal which the town-bred Egyptian picks up much too quickly; but with a certain desperate zeal, foreign to his whole creed and nature. He fingered, he implored, he fawned with an unsteady eye, and while I wondered I saw behind him the puffy pink face of a fezzed Jew, watching him as a stoat watches a rabbit. When he moved the Jew followed and took position at a commanding angle. The old man glanced from me to him and renewed his solicitations. So one could imagine an elderly hare thumping wildly on a tambourine with the stoat behind him. They told me afterwards that Jews own most of the stalls in Assouan bazaar, the Mussulmans working for them, since tourists need Oriental colour. Never having seen or imagined a Jew coercing a Mussulman, this colour was new and displeasing to me.

VII

THE RIDDLE OF EMPIRE

At Halfa one feels the first breath of a frontier. Here the Egyptian Government retires into the background, and even the Cook steamer does not draw up in the exact centre of the postcard. At the telegraph-office, too, there are traces, diluted but quite recognisable, of military administration. Nor does the town, in any way or place whatever, smell—which is proof that it is not looked after on popular lines. There is nothing to see in it any more than there is in Hulk C. 60, late of her Majesty's troopship *Himalaya* , now a coal-hulk in the Hamoaze at Plymouth. A river front, a narrow terraced river-walk of semi-oriental houses, barracks, a mosque, and half-a-dozen streets at right angles, the Desert racing up to the end of each, make all the town. A mile or so up stream under palm trees are bungalows of what must have been cantonments, some machinery repair-shops, and odds and ends of railway track. It is all as paltry a collection of whitewashed houses, pitiful gardens, dead walls, and trodden waste spaces as one would wish to find anywhere; and every bit of it quivers with the remembered life of armies and river-fleets, as the finger-bowl rings when the rubbing finger is lifted. The most unlikely men have done time there; stores by the thousand ton have been rolled and pushed and hauled up the banks by tens of thousands of scattered hands; hospitals have pitched themselves there, expanded enormously, shrivelled up and drifted away with the drifting regiments; railway sidings by the mile have been laid down and ripped up again, as need changed, and utterly wiped out by the sands.

Halfa has been the rail-head, Army Headquarters, and hub of the universe—the one place where a man could make sure of buying tobacco and sardines, or could hope for letters for himself and medical attendance for his friend. Now she is a little shrunken shell of a town without a proper hotel, where tourists hurry up from the river to buy complete sets of Soudan stamps at the Post Office.

I went for a purposeless walk from one end of the place to the other, and found a crowd of native boys playing football on what might have been a parade-ground of old days.

'And what school is that?' I asked in English of a small, eager youth.

'Madrissah,' said he most intelligently, which being translated means just 'school.'

'Yes, but *what* school?'

'Yes, Madrissah, school, sir,' and he tagged after to see what else the imbecile wanted.

A line of railway track, that must have fed big workshops in its time, led me between big-roomed houses and offices labelled departmentally, with here and there a clerk at work. I was directed and re-directed by polite Egyptian officials (I wished to get at a white officer if possible, but there wasn't one about); was turned out of a garden which belonged to an Authority; hung round the gate of a bungalow with an old-established compound and two white men sitting in chairs on a verandah; wandered down towards the river under the palm trees, where the last red light came through; lost myself among rusty boilers and balks of timber; and at last loafed back in the twilight escorted by the small boy and an entire brigade of ghosts, not one of whom I had ever met before, but all of whom I knew most intimately. They said it was the evenings that used to depress *them* most, too; so they all came back after dinner and bore me company, while I went to meet a friend arriving by the night train from Khartoum.

She was an hour late, and we spent it, the ghosts and I, in a brick-walled, tin-roofed shed, warm with the day's heat; a crowd of natives laughing and talking somewhere behind in the darkness. We knew each other so well by that time, that we had finished discussing every conceivable topic of conversation—the whereabouts of the Mahdi's head, for instance—work, reward, despair, acknowledgment, flat failure, all the real motives that had driven us to do anything, and all our other longings. So we sat still and let the stars move, as men must do when they meet this kind of train.

Presently I asked: 'What is the name of the next station out from here?'

'Station Number One,' said a ghost.

'And the next?'

'Station Number Two, and so on to Eight, I think.'

'And wasn't it worth while to name even *one* of these stations from some man, living or dead, who had something to do with making the line?'

'Well, they didn't, anyhow,' said another ghost. 'I suppose they didn't think it worth while. Why? What do *you* think?'

'I think, I replied, 'it is the sort of snobbery that nations go to Hades for.'

Her headlight showed at last, an immense distance off; the economic electrics were turned up, the ghosts vanished, the dragomans of the various steamers flowed forward in beautiful garments to meet their passengers who had booked passages in the Cook boats, and the Khartoum train decanted a joyous collection of folk, all decorated with horns, hoofs, skins, hides, knives, and assegais, which they had been buying at Omdurman. And when the porters laid hold upon their bristling bundles, it was like MacNeill's Zareba without the camels.

Two young men in tarboushes were the only people who had no part in the riot. Said one of them to the other:

'Hullo?'

Said the other: 'Hullo!'

They grunted together for a while. Then one pleasantly:

'Oh, I'm sorry for *that* ! I thought I was going to have you under me for a bit. Then you'll use the rest-house there?'

'I suppose so,' said the other. 'Do you happen to know if the roof's on?'

Here a woman wailed aloud for her dervish spear which had gone adrift, and I shall never know, except from the back pages of the Soudan Almanack, what state that rest-house there is in.

The Soudan Administration, by the little I heard, is a queer service. It extends itself in silence from the edges of Abyssinia to the swamps of the Equator at an average pressure of one white man to several thousand square miles. It legislates according to the custom of the tribe where possible, and on the common sense of the moment when there is no precedent. It is recruited almost wholly from the army, armed chiefly with binoculars, and enjoys a death-rate a little lower than its own reputation. It is said to be the only service in which a man taking leave is explicitly recommended to get out of the country and rest himself that he may return the more fit to his job. A high standard of intelligence is required, and lapses are not overlooked. For instance, one man on leave in London took the wrong train from Boulogne, and instead of going to Paris, which, of course, he had intended, found himself at a station called Kirk Kilissie or Adrianople West, where he stayed for some weeks. It was a mistake that might have happened to any one on a dark night after a stormy passage, but the authorities would not believe it, and when I left Egypt were busily engaged in boiling him in hot oil. They are grossly respectable in the Soudan now.

Long and long ago, before even the Philippines were taken, a friend of mine was reprimanded by a British Member of Parliament, first for the sin of blood-guiltiness because he was by trade a soldier, next for murder because he had fought in great battles, and lastly, and most important, because he and his fellow-braves had saddled the British taxpayer with the expense of the Soudan. My friend explained that all the Soudan had ever cost the British taxpayer was the price of about one dozen of regulation Union Jacks—one for each province. 'That,' said the M.P. triumphantly, 'is all it will ever be worth.' He went on to justify himself, and the Soudan went on also. To-day it has taken its place as one of those accepted miracles which are worked without heat or headlines by men who do the job nearest their hand and seldom fuss about their reputations.

But less than sixteen years ago the length and breadth of it was one crazy hell of murder, torture, and lust, where every man who had a sword used it till he met a stronger and became a slave. It was—men say who remember it—a hysteria of blood and fanaticism; and precisely as an hysterical woman is called to her senses by a dash of cold water, so at the battle of Omdurman the land was reduced to sanity by applied death on such a scale as the murderers and the torturers at their most unbridled could scarcely have dreamed. In a day and a night all who had power and authority were wiped out and put under till, as the old song says, no chief remained to ask after any follower. They had all charged into Paradise. The people who were left looked for renewed massacres of the sort they had been accustomed to, and when these did not come, they said helplessly: 'We have nothing. We are nothing. Will you sell us into slavery among the Egyptians?' The men who remember the old days of the Reconstruction—which deserves an epic of its own—say that there was nothing left to build on, not even wreckage. Knowledge, decency, kinship, property, tide, sense of possession had all gone. The people were told they were to sit still and obey orders; and they stared and fumbled like dazed crowds after an explosion. Bit by bit, however, they were fed and watered and marshalled into some sort of order; set to tasks they never dreamed to see the end of; and, almost by physical force, pushed and hauled along the ways of mere life. They came to understand presently that they might reap what they had sown, and that man, even a woman, might walk for a day's journey with two goats and a native bedstead and live undespoiled. But they had to be taught kindergarten-fashion.

And little by little, as they realised that the new order was sure and that their ancient oppressors were quite dead, there returned not only cultivators, craftsmen, and artisans, but outlandish men of war, scarred with old wounds and the generous dimples that the Martini-Henry bullet used to deal—fighting men on the lookout for new employ. They would hang about, first on one leg, then on the other, proud or uneasily friendly, till some white officer circulated near by. And at his fourth or fifth passing, brown and white having approved each other by eye, the talk—so men say—would run something like this:

OFFICER (*with air of sudden discovery*). Oh, you by the hut, there, what is your business?

WARRIOR (*at 'attention' complicated by attempt to salute*). I am So-and-So, son of So-and-So, from such and such a place.

OFFICER. I hear. And ...?

WARRIOR (*repeating salute*). And a fighting man also.

OFFICER (*impersonally to horizon*). But they *all* say that nowadays.

WARRIOR (*very loudly*). But there is a man in one of your battalions who can testify to it. He is the grandson of my father's uncle.

OFFICER (*confidentially to his boots*). Hell is *quite* full of such grandsons of just such father's uncles; and how do I know if Private So-and-So speaks the truth about his family? (*Makes to go.*)

WARRIOR (*swiftly removing necessary garments*). Perhaps. But *these* don't lie. Look! I got this ten, twelve years ago when I was quite a lad, close to the old Border, Yes, Halfa. It was a true Snider bullet. Feel it! This little one on the leg I got at the big fight that finished it all last year. But I am not lame (*violent leg-exercise*), not in the least lame. See! I run. I jump. I kick. Praised be Allah!

OFFICER. Praised be Allah! And then?

WARRIOR (*coquettishly*). Then, I shoot. I am not a common spear-man. (*Lapse into English.*) Yeh, dam goo' shot! (*pumps lever of imaginary Martini*).

OFFICER (*unmoved*). I see. And then?

WARRIOR (*indignantly*). *I* am come here—after many days' marching. (*Change to childlike wheedle* .) Are *all* the regiments full?

At this point the relative, in uniform, generally discovered himself, and if the officer liked the cut of his jib, another 'old Mahdi's man' would be added to the machine that made itself as it rolled along. They dealt with situations in those days by the unclouded light of reason and a certain high and holy audacity.

There is a tale of two Sheikhs shortly after the Reconstruction began. One of them, Abdullah of the River, prudent and the son of a slave-woman, professed loyalty to the English very early in the day, and used that loyalty as a cloak to lift camels from another Sheikh, Farid of the Desert, still at war with the English, but a perfect gentleman, which Abdullah was not. Naturally, Farid raided back on Abdullah's kine,

Abdullah complained to the authorities, and the Border fermented. To Farid in his desert camp with a clutch of Abdullah's cattle round him, entered, alone and unarmed, the officer responsible for the peace of those parts. After compliments, for they had had dealings with each other before: 'You've been driving Abdullah's stock again,' said the Englishman.

'I should think I had!' was the hot answer. 'He lifts my camels and scuttles back into your territory, where he knows I can't follow him for the life; and when I try to get a bit of my own back, he whines to you. He's a cad—an utter cad.'

'At any rate, he is loyal. If you'd only come in and be loyal too, you'd both be on the same footing, and then if he stole from you, he'd catch it!'

'He'd never dare to steal except under your protection. Give him what he'd have got in the Mahdi's time—a first-class flogging. *You* know he deserves it!'

'I'm afraid that isn't allowed. You have to let me shift all those bullocks of his back again.'

'And if I don't?'

'Then, I shall have to ride back and collect all my men and begin war against you.'

'But what prevents my cutting your throat where you sit?'

'For one thing, you aren't Abdullah, and——'

'There! You confess he's a cad!'

'And for another, the Government would only send another officer who didn't understand your ways, and then there *would* be war, and no one would score except Abdullah. He'd steal your camels and get credit for it.'

'So he would, the scoundrel! This is a hard world for honest men. Now, you admit Abdullah is a cad. Listen to me, and I'll tell you a few more things about him. He was, etc., etc. He is, etc., etc.'

'You're perfectly right, Sheikh, but don't you see I can't tell him what I think of him so long as he's loyal and you're out against us? Now, if *you* come in I promise you that I'll give Abdullah a telling-off—yes, in your presence—that will do you good to listen to.'

'No! I won't come in! But—I tell you what I will do. I'll accompany you to-morrow as your guest, understand, to your camp. Then you send for

Abdullah, and *if* I judge that his fat face has been sufficiently blackened in my presence, I'll think about coming in later.'

So it was arranged, and they slept out the rest of the night, side by side, and in the morning they gathered up and returned all Abdullah's cattle, and in the evening, in Farid's presence, Abdullah got the tongue-lashing of his wicked old life, and Farid of the Desert laughed and came in; and they all lived happy ever afterwards.

Somewhere or other in the nearer provinces the old heady game must be going on still, but the Soudan proper has settled to civilisation of the brick-bungalow and bougainvillea sort, and there is a huge technical college where the young men are trained to become fitters, surveyors, draftsmen, and telegraph employees at fabulous wages. In due time, they will forget how warily their fathers had to walk in the Mahdi's time to secure even half a bellyful; then, as has happened elsewhere. They will honestly believe that they themselves originally created and since then have upheld the easy life into which they were bought at so heavy a price. Then the demand will go up for 'extension of local government,' 'Soudan for the Soudanese,' and so on till the whole cycle has to be retrodden. It is a hard law but an old one—Rome died learning it, as our western civilisation may die—that if you give any man anything that he has not painfully earned for himself, you infallibly make him or his descendants your devoted enemies.

THE END

Infinite Gives
Expanding universe
This is our Path
We have the technology
We may Descide.
WHAT IS THE NORM.
CHANGE-CHANGE-CHANGE
We will move off
This planet our
Evolution of Mind
Is out there
WHERE body goes
MIND ALSO
TRAVELS with
HOPE COURAGE
DIGNITY RESPECT.

MY PATH
MAN